QUEEN AND I

Also by Laura Jackson

Golden Stone: The Untold Life
and Mysterious Death of
Brian Jones

LAURA JACKSON

QUEEN & I

THE BRIAN MAY STORY

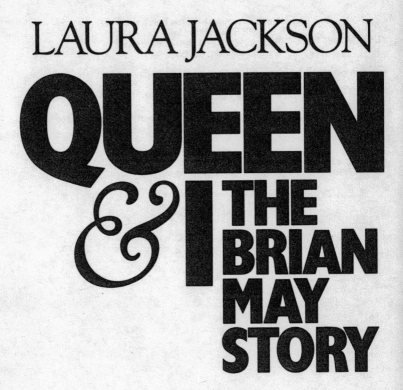

SMITH GRYPHON
PUBLISHERS

First published in paperback in Great Britain in 1995 by
SMITH GRYPHON LIMITED
Swallow House, 11–21 Northdown Street
London N1 9BN

First published in hardback by Smith Gryphon in 1994

A CIP catalogue record for this book is available from the British Library

ISBN 1 85685 099 4

Typeset by Computerset, Harmondsworth, Middlesex
Printed in Great Britain by Cox & Wyman Ltd, Reading

CONTENTS

ACKNOWLEDGEMENTS

My gratitude for their time and trouble goes to all those whom I interviewed: Mike Bersin; Tony Blackman; Tony Brainsby; Richard Branson; Pete Brown; Derek Dean; Simon Denbigh; Dave Dilloway; Wayne Eagling; Spike Edney; Joe Elliott; David Essex; Kent P. Falb; Eric Faulkner; Fish; Trevor Francis; Gordon Giltrap; Gary Glitter; Scott Gorham; Mike Grose; Tony Hale; Bob Harris; Dr Tom Hicks; Geoff Higgins; Tony Iommi; Andy Jones; Mandla Langa; Gary Langhan; Jane L'Epine Smith; Prof. Sir Bernard Lovell OBE; Ian Maclay; Hank B. Marvin; Helen McConnell; Barry Mitchell; Chris O'Donnell; Norman Pace; John Peel; Nigel Planer; Andy Powell; Dr N. K. Reay; Zandra Rhodes; Prof. Jim Ring CBE; Paul Rodgers; Richie Sambora; Joe Satriani; Tim Staffell; Jackie Stewart OBE; Michael Stimpson; Ken Testi; Malcolm Thomas; Bert Weedon; Brian White; Mike Winsor; Terry Yeadon; Paul Young.

Also for their help: Ann Barrett/Imperial College of Science, Technology and Medicine; Andrew Booker/Imperial College Jazz & Rock; BBC TV; British Film Institute; Channel 4 TV; Mary Chibnall/Royal Astronomical Society; Chrysalis Records; Jackie de Costa; Elgin Library staff; Epic Records; Elaine McIntosh; Stuart McIntosh; National Sound Archive; Nene Valley Railway Ltd; Phonogram Records; Phonographic Performance Ltd; Riverside Studio Theatre; Ray Staff/the Exchange, London; E. J. Staffell; Janet Street-Porter; the Detroit Lions, Michigan; the Royal Ballet Company.

Grateful thanks to my publisher Robert Smith for his much-appreciated support and continuing faith in me; also my editors Esther Jagger and Helen Armitage.

I especially want to thank Brian May for the personal contributions his time allowed him to be able to make and for time and again granting the necessary clearance to interviewees to cooperate with me. Also, much appreciation to Jim Beach and Julie Glover/Queen Productions Ltd for all their kind help.

Finally, I owe a huge debt of gratitude to my husband David for his love, enormous support, encouragement and invaluable help as my chief researcher, head listener and all-round linchpin of my life.

WHICH WAY'S THE STAGE, MAN?

Brian May is an intensely private person. Yet for twenty years, as one dynamic quarter of Queen, he strode the world's stage with relentless professionalism, firmly establishing his place as one of rock's finest lead guitarists. Reassuringly dependable, scarcely changing his unique style either physically or musically, he has provided an anchor of continuity through two decades of chaotic, sometimes confusing, musical directions. To Queen's worldwide legions of fans he played his public part to perfection, yet for the last five of those twenty years he battled in private with intense personal turmoil. His depth of depression was once so acute that he contemplated driving off a bridge, yet he emerged strong – to launch his solo career in the autumn of 1992 with an album appropriately entitled *Back to the Light*.

He was born on 19 July 1947 in the Gloucester House Nursing Home at Hampton in Middlesex, the only child of Ruth and Harold May, a senior draughtsman with the Ministry of Aviation. Even as a child Brian was lean and lanky, with an angular bone structure, but his ever-ready winning smile made him popular in the comfortable middle-class neighbourhood. Home, shared with a tortoiseshell cat named Squeaky, was a neat three-bedroomed thirties semi in Feltham, not far from London Airport. Only many years later would Brian realize that the family of a certain Frederick Bulsara had lived only a few hundred yards away.

By nature Brian was inquisitive, and it quickly became apparent that he had inherited his father's dexterity with his hands: he spent many happy hours making model toys. He also displayed an early liking for music, and would sing and dance to the radio. By the time Brian was five and was starting at primary school his parents had enrolled him for piano lessons at a local music school. Their intention was to encourage his aptitude, but Brian loathed the discipline of lessons; playing with his friends on a Saturday was much more fun than sitting indoors practising boring scales.

At this time he started indulging a foible which would remain a part of his make-up throughout his life – collecting things. It could be anything from matchboxes to little packets of sugar from restaurants. Perhaps it signalled an unrecognized need for security or was simply a highly fastidious streak in his developing nature; but whatever the reason he became an avid hoarder. Probably his favourite pastime was collecting *Eagle* comics. He adored the boys' hero Dan Dare – in particular it was the illustrations by Frank Hampson that captured his imagination; it was this interest which would later provide an initial link with Tim Staffell, one of the two musicians with whom he would form the pre-Queen band, Smile. Such a vivid imagination, however, was not always a good thing. Sometimes in the stillness of the night it would run riot in his bedroom, and he often imagined that a wooden chair in the corner had a face. Frightened rigid, he would tell his mother that he was convinced it was watching him.

When Brian was six, Harold decided to teach him to play the ukulele, on which he himself was proficient. The boy took to it immediately, but then quickly turned his sights on to a guitar. On his seventh birthday he was thrilled to be presented with a six-steel-stringed Egmond. The chords he had learned on the ukulele gave him a head start, but there was one obstacle – the size of the instrument. It was too big for a boy to handle comfortably, and its strings were too high off the fret board. So father and son set about altering it – carving down its wooden bridge, which in turn brought the strings closer to the fret board and made it easier to play. At the same time they decided to give it the electric sound for which Brian had been craving. Brian figured that a coil wrapped around three eclipse magnets should do the job, and Harold, being by trade an electronics engineer, showed his son how to do it. Copper wire wound around three little button magnets provided him with crude but effective pick-ups which he then fixed on to the instrument, making the acoustic sound electric once it was plugged into Dad's home-made wireless, which had to double as a makeshift amplifier.

Electrifying that guitar was by no means the only project on which father and son worked closely. They also built a four-inch telescope so that Brian could indulge in yet another early passion – astronomy. The stars fascinated him and he would spend hours gazing at the infinite mysteries of the universe, even carting the contraption with him on family holidays to Sidmouth in Devon in order to take advantage of the clearer skies in that area. Yet for all that, what he gravitated to most was undoubtedly music.

Having persevered at his piano lessons long enough to pass Grade IV by the age of nine Brian decided he had had enough and gave up. With the logic typical of children, once he was no longer compelled to practise he actually enjoyed tinkling the ivories on the family upright at home. Sometimes he even composed the odd song, but nothing serious; at this point he was much happier to listen.

Artists such as Lonnie Donegan, Tommy Steele and Buddy Holly provided inspiration to the budding musician and he would play their records over and over again. Gradually he grew confident enough to play along with them on his guitar, progressing in time from chords to picking out single notes. From an early age he had a very analytical mind and in a remarkably short space of time he had broken down and dissected each song – finding the key to how it worked and why – and the perfectionist in him ensured that he kept at it until he had exhausted all its secrets. From that moment on, music would anchor his entire life.

In 1958, when he had turned eleven, Brian passed the scholarship exam which qualified him for a place at the highly sought after Hampton Grammar School. The headmaster, George Whitfield – later ordained as a clergyman – was a strong disciplinarian who ran a tough regime with an iron fist. Full uniform had to be worn at all times – caps could only be removed at home. Frequent surveillance operations were mounted to identify any pupils who flouted these rules. And all the staff wore academic gowns, in pursuit of establishing a reputation for austere excellence.

Hampton Grammar was also gaining another reputation at this

time – as a nursery for rock musicians. Two of the Yardbirds, who were two years older than Brian, Jim McCarty and Paul Samwell-Smith, were already making names for themselves while still at school, and it was here that Brian's appetite for music really began to flourish. Not, however, to the detriment of his studies – academically he was an excellent pupil and astronomy continued to fascinate him. But every spare moment was spent with his guitar slung around his neck.

Guitar playing was frowned upon as an activity at school, so all practice was secret. Several boys fancied themselves as guitarists and, keen to learn from each other, would congregate at lunchtime to jam together. Brian was recognized as having special aptitude and by the time he was in his second year he had attracted a sort of early fan club, as one of his classmates in 2LA, Dave Dilloway, remembers. 'Someone in the corridor one day told me that there was a guy playing a guitar in the geography room, so out of interest I went to see. When I got there and looked in, Brian was sitting on a stool in the middle of a circle of schoolkids playing and singing Guy Mitchell's hit "I Never Felt More Like Singing the Blues" and I was really impressed. These were early days and it was just a simple three-chord song, but I'm sure Brian knew more even then.'

Brian and Dave became good friends; both had tape recorders and so would meet up at each other's houses to make recordings, just for their own amusement. 'It was all very basic, as was most equipment available in those days,' explains Dave. 'We mainly played instrumental material from the likes of Les Paul, Chet Atkins, the Ventures and the Spotniks. Brian had his original Spanish acoustic with its home-made pick-up and I had a home-made six-string electric guitar as well as a home-made bass. At this point I was still learning all the chords, so I used to tackle the lead guitar and Brian would play the more awkward rhythm lines.' He goes on, 'We would record these two parts together on to one tape recorder, and then while this prerecorded track was played back we would record on it again. This time Brian would be playing my home-made bass while I played drums – by which I mean anything percussive we could find at home, including my mother's hat boxes! Meccano strips doubled for cymbals.'

Despite the crude methods, the results were surprisingly good; at any rate it gave them useful early experience. Unlike many parents, Brian's were eager to encourage their son and actively indulged these sessions. When at his house the pair would commandeer one of the downstairs rooms – the back one when using the amplifier, the front when they needed the piano – and from time to time Ruth would bring them in a welcome tea tray. Harold for his part happily assisted on a technical level, sorting out yards of jumbled guitar and microphone leads and thinking nothing of letting the boys use the family hi-fi as a makeshift amplifier.

Dave's first guitar was a traditional large Spanish acoustic given to him by his grandfather. He had started learning to play it before he met Brian, but had often found it too hard to handle. 'Arguably it was a better-sounding and superior instrument to Brian's Egmond,' he says, 'but one day somehow the idea of swapping guitars came up in conversation. So that's what we did. Brian promptly stripped it down to the wood and did a very nice restoration job on it. I was quite envious, and wondered whether I'd done the right thing – but I could hardly ask for it back.'

To a great extent Brian was reacting to the changes taking place on the music scene as the fifties ended. There had been a definite shift towards a guitar-based sound – a crucial development which would prove to be a hotbed for a new generation of talent bursting on to the scene. A new addition to his growing list of heroes and influences was the British group the Shadows, who in July 1960 had hit the number one spot in the British singles chart with the instrumental 'Apache'. What captured Brian's attention in particular was the style and skill of their lead guitarist, Brian Marvin – better known by his nickname of Hank.

Thirty years later Hank Marvin reflects on the reasons for this new popular trend. 'To put it simply, it was a more accessible form of music. The music of the forties and fifties involved a lot of big bands and wasn't the sort that you could recreate with your mates. Then skiffle came along – it was really a development of the folk music which had always been around, but it was much more commercial now. Suddenly there were these catchy songs which appealed to young and old – and, more important, you could actually perform those guitar pieces yourself.' He goes on, 'With the advent of rock and roll, electric guitars came into their own. All you needed was a bass, drums, two guitars and a singer like Cliff Richard or Marty Wilde, and you had a band. Plus people were attracted to participate now, instead of just being onlookers.' The fact that the guitar was so portable meant that with the addition of a small amplifier you could perform anywhere, any time.

'Not to be forgotten, either,' adds Hank, 'was the image! The guitar's a cool instrument – and very synonymous with white rock and roll –

think of Elvis. You didn't even need to be able to play the thing – it could just be a cool prop. There's no instrument like it. Just imagine trying to look cool blowing a trumpet with your cheeks all bulging and bloated!'

Brian's burning ambition in 1963 was to leave behind the acoustic guitar and branch out on to an electric. Some of his friends already had the new and wildly expensive Gibsons and Stratocasters: one school-mate, John Garnham, had a Colorama which Brian would have given his eye teeth for. But while Ruth and Harold would have given their only child anything, they simply could not afford to buy him a luxury instrument of this class. Yet all was not lost. Brian and his father decided that if they couldn't buy one, they would build their own.

In August 1963 work began in a spare bedroom. It would take some eighteen months to complete, and to keep an exact record of its construction Brian conscientiously photographed and logged every stage. The guitar they would produce was to become world-famous in the years ahead.

First, he painstakingly carved the neck of the guitar from an antique solid mahogany fireplace which a family friend was throwing out, shaping it to perfection with a penknife. The body into which the neck would later be fitted was made from a piece of oak, some blockboard and odds and ends. It was a long, laborious task but both father and son possessed the necessary patience and determination. A great deal of thought and imagination went into not just the construction but also the design: Harold and Brian believed that they had identified three common faults in conventional guitar-making methods.

Firstly, the necks of many modern electric guitars tended to bend because of the enormous stress placed on the strings – by their calculations, a pressure of nearly 500 lb. So they decided to incorporate a steel truss rod into the neck, setting it at an angle to the tension through the neck and holding it in place with a steel bolt.

Next their attention focused on the bridge. When the strings were tightened over it, increasing use of the tremolo arm sawed away at them and increased the risk of their snapping. Equally importantly, the strings failed to return to pitch after the tremolo arm had been used. Instead of the conventional bridge, therefore, they designed a set of small rollers over which the strings could tighten without inviting the same wear and tear. 'We tried various methods,' says Brian, 'including one with ball-races at each end of a cylinder. But the one which worked best was a mild steel plate rocking on a knife-edge.'　　•

The tension of the strings was balanced by two valve springs which Harold found on a 1928 Panther motorcycle. The rocking mechanism was hand-carved by Brian from a piece of mild steel, and the arm itself was improvised from a cycle saddle-bag support finished off with a piece of large, fat knitting needle.

And their ingenuity had not dried up yet. For fret markers Brian raided Ruth's button box, making off with the shiny mother-of-pearl ones which he then cut down to size. He was forced, however, to buy the fret wire because he could not find anything else suitable. But this was re-profiled using special jigs that Brian and Harold made up specially. When it came to the pick-ups he once again tried to make his own, to a similar design to that which had worked on the Spanish guitar. But he had to concede that they were less than satisfactory and so paid out £9.45 for a set of three Burns pick-ups which he promptly modified by filling with epoxy resin to stop them being microphonic.

The pick-ups themselves were important. In an interview Harold once said, 'The secret of these pick-ups is in the position that each one is set, because this alters the tonal harmonic effect and by some really clever switching you can have any combination of twenty-four tones – and that's something that no other guitar manufacturer has ever done commercially at all. When he plays that solo on 'Brighton Rock' Brian is accompanying himself, using echoes. . . .'

Together they had built a guitar which, quite apart from going on to become the mainstay of his career, had tonal range and depth far exceeding those of most commercially available instruments at that time – and at a total cost of a mere £17.45. The deep reddish-brown of the mahogany made Brian christen this treasured and remarkable instrument the Red Special. Not surprisingly, he has built up a special bond with it. 'It's quite an emotional thing, playing the guitar,' he admits. 'You need to be in contact with your strings, because that's all you've got.' Hank Marvin explains, 'It's like another person you're embracing – an extension of your body, altering your shape. Some people abuse the instrument and act out a lot of violence. I don't know that it's erotic love, because you'd have to be pretty perverted to feel like that about a bit of wood, but there's certainly a relationship between you and your guitar.'

This emotional tie is echoed by Andy Powell, lead guitarist with Wishbone Ash, who also built his own instrument. 'I remember when the music shop near me got in their first Fender Stratocaster. It was like

Wayne's World. I went to town every day just to press my face up against the glass to look at it. I didn't even have the guts like some to go in and take measurements. I was that intimidated by the thing. So I estimated everything. It's a really intense thing, you know – making your own guitar. You get right into what makes it tick. There's undoubtedly a unique bond there – I was besotted with the thing.' Andy Powell with Wishbone Ash would become probably the best example of the British progressive rock movement – music which would prove attractive to the fledgling Queen.

In the early sixties Brian may not yet have decided that music was where his destiny lay – astronomy still fascinated him – but he felt its attraction strongly. At school he continued to jam anywhere he and his friends could slink into with their guitars: classrooms, above the library or even in the lost property office – though keeping the volume down in case it carried through the airvent which came out near the headmaster's study. Outside school hours there was a strong local music scene. All coffee bars boasted juke boxes, there was an abundance of school dances, and on top of this live bands played weekends at church and other halls and at small clubs.

Probably Brian's best known and most popular local 'hall' was at Eel Pie Island in the Thames at Twickenham. The only access was by a narrow footbridge from the bank. It was just possible to drive over it: bands had to off-load their gear on to a mini-van at the foot of the bridge and then transport the stuff over, one vanload at a time.

Audiences were spoiled for choice in the quality of the bands gigging there at this time. The raw and raunchy rhythm and blues had grabbed the British music world by the throat and its best exponents by far were the Rolling Stones. Their lead guitarist was founder member Brian Jones, a phenomenally gifted musician who understood this true brand of underground music perhaps better than any of his contemporaries. Even then he was relentlessly carving his band's way into rock mythology. 'The Stones were certainly regulars at Eel Pie Island,' recalls Dave Dilloway, 'and I also remember seeing Fleetwood Mac and Cream, among others.'

To the teenage May all this talent only increased his own urge to form a band. To date his experience had been limited to jamming with Dave, although recently he had had his first taste of being inside an actual recording studio. Another Hampton Grammar pupil, would-be songwriter Bill Richards, had landed a music publishing deal. When he had to record a demo tape of 'The Left Handed Marriage' at Abbey Road studios in north London, Bill invited Brian and Dave along to provide instrumental backing. Says Dave, 'Brian played lead and sang and I played bass. Goodness knows what else we recorded, but it was good experience for us.'

Brian's first band was a four-piece with no name. He played lead guitar, Dave bass, a friend called Malcolm provided the rhythm guitar, while yet another classmate, John Sanger, at one point drifted in on piano. Since no one knew a drummer, at first they made do without. Malcolm was soon replaced by John Garnham, whose Colorama Brian had once coveted so much. Garnham's other attractions were practical ones. He owned a proper amplifier, as well as microphone stands with mikes; and, unlike any of the others, he had that all-important advantage – previous experience of performing live.

The line-up was not yet complete, though, because they had no singer. Then one night Brian and the embryonic band went to a dance to watch another local group perform. During the evening Brian noticed at the back of the hall a guy from school, who was softly playing harmonica and singing along. His name was Tim Staffell. The two soon found that they shared a love of music, though for different reasons. For Tim it represented a much-needed release from the drudgery. 'School was a total drag as far as I was concerned,' he admits. 'That was partly because I lost a lot of ground after I was involved in a serious road accident which kept me off school. Being in a group was a way to escape all that for me.'

For a while they haunted the the clubs together, studying the bands still using the Others as their yardstick. 'They were really very good,' reflects Tim, 'and very much like the Rolling Stones, who were appearing every other week at the Station Hotel in Richmond. At the time, in fact, we used to think they were more polished than the Stones, although on hindsight I don't know if that was really true. There was a lot of music going on and we used to tour the different pubs and clubs to take stock of who was doing what. We saw quite a lot of the Yardbirds and also a band called the Muleskinners, whose lead guitarist at that time was Eric Clapton. It all made a deep impression on us.'

Such was the impression that soon they knuckled down to some serious rehearsing. This took place at Chase Bridge Primary School in Whitton next to the Twickenham rugby ground. The venue was made available by the local authority, which wanted to give the local young people somewhere to go to expend their energies.

The discipline of regular rehearsals was exactly what the band had all needed, and progress over the next several months was rapid. Brian thoroughly enjoyed these evenings. He thrived on the way they bounced ideas off each other, experimenting to their hearts' content. In addition they got to know one another better as people and strong friendships developed.

But it soon became apparent that they could not go on indefinitely without a drummer, and so they traipsed down to Albert's, Twickenham's music shop, to place an advert in the window. There was only one applicant, Richard Thompson from Hounslow; he was hired on the spot.

Now that the six-piece line-up was complete, another loose end had to be tied up – finding a name for themselves. Two or three were suggested before they finally settled on 1984, after George Orwell's novel – science fiction was very much in vogue then. The band agreed that it had an appealingly futuristic sound. Now all they needed was a gig for which they would get paid.

That event came about through a friend of a friend and took place at St Mary's church hall in Twickenham on 28 October 1964. They were paid the then going rate of £10, which worked out at less than two quid apiece. Out of this sum each band member was responsible for buying his own equipment and organizing and paying for his own transport. The following month 1984 played their second gig, at Richmond Girls' School. After this one John Sanger left the band and went to Manchester University, though he would rejoin many years later, long after Brian had left. The band's members were at the age when soon they would go their separate ways for higher education, though for a while they would still play together.

In those days they played mostly weekend gigs. Sometimes they played three times a week, then they would hit leaner spells and be lucky to secure three bookings in one month. 'We had a regularish gig at the Thames Boat Club on the riverfront at Putney,' recalls Tim. 'In the same building, in fact, in which Michael Winner's remake of Raymond Chandler's *The Big Sleep* was shot. We used to play mainly on a Saturday night for no more than a few pounds, and for considerably longer than was average for bands, too – often as long as three hours. The set was peppered with schoolboy humour when I look back on it now, but it seemed to please the crowd at the time.'

Brian was certainly pleased to have his first band off the ground and earning cash, although there was little glamour attached to it. According to Tim, 'Equipment was always a problem – home-made speaker cabinets and PA systems that were no more than rudimentary lash-ups, usually underpowered into the bargain.' Transport, too, was a very much hit-and-miss affair for some time. For the moment John Garnham came to the rescue as much as he could with his tiny two-seater Heinkel bubble car – this strange-looking vehicle crammed with a hotchpotch of gear, and with its roof removed so that chrome microphone stands could stick periscope-like out of the top, became a common sight in the neighbourhood. In order to get to gigs Tim occasionally had to squeeze himself into the already overladen vehicle, and even Brian managed to concertina his lanky body, already in excess of six feet, into that confined space.

By this time Brian was dating a local girl called Pat. 'I certainly remember her,' says Dave. 'Quiet girl. One Christmas I went to see Cliff Richard and the Shadows at the London Palladium. Brian and I were sitting in the front row. I'd taken Pat's place that night because she'd gone down with the flu.' He goes on, 'It's funny to think of Brian down there watching a guitar hero of his then, and now Brian is quoted in the press as being a guitar hero of Hank Marvin's!' Unlike many of his mates who preferred to play the field, Brian was steady in his relationships; he and Pat dated for quite some time.

Back in school he was still managing to keep pace with his studies. Canny by nature, he knew that nothing would be gained by recklessly neglecting them in favour of his music. He and his parents were delighted when in February 1965 he was awarded an open scholarship in physics at Imperial College of Science and Technology in London. By the time he left Hampton Grammar that summer, aged eighteen, his ten O-Levels had been supplemented by A-Levels in physics, pure maths, applied maths and additional maths. He was to study physics and infra-red astronomy, with the intention of becoming an astro-physicist. Music as a career was not a decision he had yet made.

Brian and Tim were now both in London – the latter about to study graphics at Ealing College of Art. So, despite the absence of the other members of the band – Dave, for instance, was now away reading electronics at Southampton University – Brian was determined that 1984 would continue to play gigs. 'Believe it or not, we used to rehearse by post!' reveals Dave. 'Southampton was only an hour or so away and I had a motorbike then, so I came home at weekends. We'd listen to material, decide what to learn, and go away and learn it. But if new ideas came to us while we were apart, we'd write.' Brian and Tim for obvious reasons found it easier to keep in touch. It was now that they began to write songs together, although sometimes this tended to be conducted in an atmosphere of semi-hostility as Tim's parents did not approve of 'this band nonsense'.

It was an intolerance which was mirrored in homes throughout Britain at this time. The freedom of expression so characteristic of the mid-sixties was visibly evident in clothes and hairstyles. Many parents' stomachs curdled on seeing their sons resplendent in floral-print bell-sleeved shirts, lurid trousers and a billowy curtain of hair flying behind them. 'My mother used to hope I'd only go out at night so that the neighbours wouldn't see me,' confesses Dave. Brian was just as fashion-conscious as the rest of his age group, and faithfully followed all the latest trends. At the end of 1965 Dave failed his exams and parted company with Southampton University; instead he found a place on an HND electronics course at Twickenham College of Technology. This meant that Tim, Brian and Dave were once again within easy reach of each other and so could rehearse more often and to better effect. They could also now chase more regular bookings. Their experience was mounting and their repertoire widening all the time. Brian, ever eager to experiment, used to spend hours working out variations and trying out arrangements of their own. As well as Stones, Yardbirds and Spencer Davis material, Beatles songs featured well, with Brian coming in on the three-part harmony sections of numbers such as 'Help!'. 'Sometimes Brian would sing lead on "Yesterday",' recalls Tim, 'and the audience loved it – they'd scream and bring the house down with their applause!' He goes on jokingly, 'It made me dead jealous, the rat! But he sang them far better than I ever could.' Brian's singing voice has a highish register, and often he and Tim would duel to see who could hit the highest note. Brian says, 'No competition! Tim always won.'

Never an extrovert, Brian had no wish to be the showman in the band and was more than happy to stand left of centre playing his guitar at his considerable best, leaving audiences breathless with a display of speed and dexterity rarely seen in amateur bands. Dave agrees, 'His skill enabled us to play virtually anything. Audiences recognized his unique talent even then. I don't know how many other bands ever tried to poach him away from us, but I imagine he had quite a few offers.'

Visually, too, by now Brian had begun to carve a unique image which would remain with him for years. Being far above average height and as thin as a beanpole set him apart anyway. In addition his hair, which had gone through a Beatlesque stage in 1965, was now dramatically evolving into a thick mop of frizzy curls not unlike the bushy Afro associated with the brilliant American blues guitarist Jimi Hendrix. Brian by now had acquired a nickname – Brimi!

The gigs themselves were stimulating and fun, although on occasions fights would break out in the audience for no obvious reason. One such night was at Twickenham. 'I don't know why,' says Dave, 'but I remember looking out into the audience and thinking, fancy dancing with chairs like that – that's a bit unusual. Then I realized a couple of guys seemed to be beating each other over the head with steel fold-up seats! I guess they were ejected by the bouncers, but anyway we carried on playing through it all.' It happened again at the White Hart in Southall, a regular trouble spot even though it was next door to the police station. That night the rumpus resembled a Wild West saloon brawl.

But it was a gig in Addington, near Croydon, which would stand out most to Brian – for a very different reason. For some reason he had rushed away before the rest that night and had gone quite a distance before it suddenly dawned on him that he had left his Red Special behind. In a blind panic he belted back, only to find the others still packing away their gear – and his precious, irreplaceable guitar still where he had left it.

Managing to climb the ladder of success, however, was a slow process and Brian felt very frustrated that they did not seem to be getting anywhere. So he jumped at the opportunity of entering a prestigious annual competition held at the Top Rank Club in Croydon: it was a national talent search, whose outright winner would secure a recording contract. Initial heats were by selection from prerecorded material; so, with the help of a college friend who owned a high-quality tape recorder, 1984 put down three tracks in stereo. On the strength of this tape they secured a place in one of the heats.

That night they would perform not just as 1984 but – minus Tim – were persuaded also to back the singer Liza Perez. The look they adopted was stunning. Tim wore a bold blue shirt with pink polka dots, while Richard shone resplendent in a silver silk shirt; but Brian's style was the most eye-catching. Old military uniforms were all the rage at the beginning of 1967, and he had dressed up to look like a 1920s' policeman in a blue serge Royal Marine jacket which he had picked up at the Chelsea antique market.

1984 performed four numbers: 'So Sad', Jimi Hendrix's 'Stone Free', Buddy Knox's 'She's Gone' and 'Knock on Wood' by Eddie Floyd. They played and sang well and, much to their delight, deservedly won their heat. The prize was a reel of Scotch tape and a CBS album each. They weren't given a choice – just five LPs to fight amongst themselves for. Tim made off with what everyone considered to be the cream of the crop, Simon and Garfunkel's *Sounds of Silence*, whilst Brian had to make do with a Barbra Streisand album.

Their success featured the following month in the local newspaper, the *Middlesex Chronicle*, when reporter Ray Hammond wrote a favourable piece on them. At that point, buoyed up with having won their heat, they were eagerly anticipating news of the national winners and big success was obviously on their minds. However, Brimi was quoted as modestly confessing his personal ambition 'to be able to play well enough to respect ourselves'. The article concluded that '1984 are one of the most forward-looking groups of today' – something which remained true even though they did not win the final and so never got the coveted recording contract.

None of that mattered, however, just three months later, when on 13 May 1967 they played one of their most memorable support gigs ever at Imperial College. Topping the bill was Jimi Hendrix, on the brink of his big breakthrough but already surrounded by an electrifying aura.

'We were booked to play first for dancing downstairs on that occasion,' recalls Dave, 'and stopped when we knew Hendrix was due on in the main hall.'

Being regulars at IC they knew their way around backstairs and were able to work their way up to the front row of the audience. As they passed the dressing room doors in the corridor suddenly Hendrix himself came out and uttered to a dumbstruck Tim what privately became five famous words: 'Which way's the stage, man?'

With Jimi Hendrix that night was his close friend and mentor, Rolling Stone Brian Jones. At this point Jones was struggling with all kinds of pressures and problems, physical, mental and emotional – a condition all too apparent to anyone who saw him in the flesh. Says Dave, 'Brian Jones came out of the dressing room behind Hendrix and went with him to the stage, where he stood quietly watching Jimi perform from the wings. I don't think I'd ever seen anyone look so skeletal and ill as Jones did that night.'

Because they had all seen Hendrix perform before, the experience itself was not unique; but they had never been this close and so were able to study him, trying to glean some tricks of the trade from watching this consummate showman at work. Brian was very impressed and left IC that night fired with renewed enthusiasm. From then on, whenever Hendrix material featured in their repertoire Brian performed with even greater authenticity. 'That night we played Jimi's "Purple Haze", and rumour has it that Jimi looked in, smiled and moved on!'

1984 definitely seemed to be on a roll, for they were to complete their hat-trick of significant gigs with a support slot at a star-studded event planned for the end of the year. It came about entirely by accident. Whilst playing at the London School of Medicine they were approached by two pop promoters who had actually come along to see the other band on the double bill. The pair were on the look-out for someone to fill a single support slot left at a forthcoming all-night event at Olympia. As it turned out, after watching both groups perform they decided they preferred 1984. 'They chatted away to us for a while, then suggested we might like to do this gig,' recalls Dave. 'Naturally we jumped at it.'

Quickly they knuckled down to rehearsals, as Brian worked out which cover versions they would do and also boldly decided to incorporate a song called 'Step On Me' which he had co-written with Tim. Occasionally the promoters turned up at their rehearsals with suggestions about how they should look, dress, behave and so on; while accepted with some appreciation, this advice also aroused an element of suspicion in Brian. In his heart he knew that 1984 did not feel like a band going places, and hardly qualified for this 'I'll groom you for stardom' routine. Scepticism was happily shelved, however, when they were invited to come to the promoters' Soho office and be taken on a shopping spree in London's trendy Carnaby Street. They had a whale of a time being kitted out with new stage clothes for their half-hour set.

At last the big night, 23 December 1967, arrived. It was billed as *Christmas on Earth*, and the line-up featured Jimi Hendrix, the Herd, Pink Floyd, Traffic and Tyrannosaurus Rex. Although 1984, fifteenth on the bill, had been told they would not be announced on stage until near midnight, they arrived keen as mustard at 3 p.m. and parked outside.

They spent the next few hours being made up and changing into their new stage gear, which they had been told they could keep, as well as watching the other acts. But it proved to be a long, frustrating wait, and in the end they did not get to play their set until about 5.30 a.m. on Christmas Eve. 'By this time we were quite tired,' remembers Dave. 'We didn't get a sound check or anything fancy like that – just pushed straight on and expected to play.' But they had never before played on such an illustrious bill to quite such a large audience, and never through anything like the bank of expensive Marshall equipment as was provided that night. All in all it was an amazing experience.

But their exhilaration was punctured the second they came off stage. Whilst they had been performing, thieves had ransacked their dressing room and made off with their wallets and anything else worth taking. Then on top of this, when they went outside to start loading up their gear they discovered that all their cars had been towed away to the Hammersmith pound.

'We all had to walk, still in our stage gear, to the pound to pay whatever it cost then to get our cars back,' recalls Dave. It was a long, dreary walk at that time of the morning – not to mention an embarrassing one as they attracted quite a few startled stares from passers-by. They could have changed back into their ordinary clothes, but they were too depressed to bother. 'I wouldn't have minded,' moans Dave, 'but my hair was piled up in a backcombed style and my eyes had been heavily made up to give me a mean and moody look. At 7 a.m. in the police pound it didn't go down very well!'

Quite early in 1968 Brian decided to leave the band. For a while now he had been feeling the need to spend more time on his work, and with finals coming up at the end of his three-year course he could afford few distractions. Brian had been very happy at Imperial College. He was extremely able and popular, and many a tutor had marked his card as someone who would go places. Professor Jim Ring remembers, 'Brian was very likeable and friendly and an excellent student. At that time, at least in my mind, there was no suggestion of him becoming a rock star. To me he was first and foremost a very bright physicist, although I was aware that he played in a band.'

Strictly speaking, Brian was no longer in a band; it was the first time it had happened in about four years, and it felt strange. He still kept in touch with Tim, who stayed on for a while and took over lead guitar as well as handling the vocals. But then he too left, and the more time Tim and Brian spent together talking about music, the more they realized just how much they both missed being in a band. Soon they were talking of forming a new group. The pair decided to post an advertisement on the Imperial College noticeboard asking for a 'Mitch Mitchell/Ginger Baker-type drummer' to form a new band with them. They were swamped with replies, and auditions began immediately.

Among the students attracted to that notice was a young man called Les Brown, who shared a flat in Shepherd's Bush with a dental student at the London Hospital Medical School by the name of Roger Meddows Taylor. Roger was a drummer, and mad keen on joining the band. Born on 26 July 1949 at King's Lynn in Norfolk, when he was eight he had moved with his family to Truro in Cornwall. Like Brian, Roger started out on the ukulele before progressing to the guitar. In 1961, however, he was given the beginnings of his first drum set and realized that percussion was where his talent lay. In his teens he had played drums in local West Country bands such as the Cousin Jacks and Johnny Quale and the Reaction – later known simply as Reaction – and had cultivated a large local following, but London was where it was at and he couldn't wait to get there in October 1967. Slim, blond, good-looking and bursting with energy, he had been turned on to Jimi Hendrix and had gone instantly psychedelic. Les knew how avidly Roger had been scanning the music press, dying for an opening with a band, and felt he was an ideal candidate.

Soon Brian and Tim were on their way to Shepherd's Bush to see Roger. Unfortunately his drums were still at home in Cornwall and he only had a set of bongos with which to impress the pair. Brian and Tim had brought their acoustic guitars and, after rattling through a few tunes together, were knocked out by Roger's evident skill and style. Tim says, 'I wouldn't actually say we auditioned Roger as such. It wasn't like that. It just became obvious that Roger was dead right for us.'

Brian felt the same, but he still wanted to see how the sound would knit together when everything was properly plugged in. He made arrangements to use the College Jazz Club room so that the three of them could have a chance to play for real. That session was a resounding success. Tim reveals, 'The chemistry was spot on. It was clear right away that we would effortlessly evolve into a unit as equal partners. We had the same musical tastes, same sense of humour and fundamentally the same aspirations.' Individually their knowledge of the music business may have been flimsy, but collectively their ideas were strong and their determination that they would make a go of it gave them all the impetus they needed. They decided to call their band Smile.

The name had no profound origins. It was short, it had an optimistic ring to it – and it was the only one they could all agree on. Tim immediately designed a logo for them, which was a rather unusual thing to do – in those days there weren't many rock bands who would have wanted a corporate image. In fact Tim's design of a grinning mouth, pillar-box red lips and gleaming white teeth bore an interesting resemblance to the famous slavering tongue logo that was to be adopted by the Rolling Stones in the early seventies.

Brian was in his element now. Although he was approaching his finals he still found time to rehearse hard, perfecting their music and style and writing more songs with Tim. 'For me,' Tim admits, 'this was the beginning of really taking myself seriously with music. I wrote my first songs with Smile, some in collaboration with Brian, some alone.' Things seemed to be falling neatly into place all around. They had even acquired a van now, courtesy of Pete Edmunds, an old school friend of Brian's; and so a bottle green Thames van became their transport and with it came Pete, their first official roadie.

Brian was highly impressionable at this time. Immersed in rehearsals with his own bands, he gazed with eager eyes at the established groups, particularly those playing what was then called progressive rock – bands such as Free, Pink Floyd, Deep Purple and Wishbone Ash. Progressive music had a feel all of its own which communicated itself vividly to true musicians. Andy Powell, lead guitarist with Wishbone Ash explains, 'The feeling was that post-1967 – which is classed as a watershed year with the *Sgt Pepper* album – the floodgates had opened and everything was up for grabs. There was no corporate rock. There was a great innocence and ignorance in us. We'd draw on fifties' jazz, folk music, Celtic music, R&B – anything that got the juices flowing. We'd no embarrassment, either, about delving down alleys in search of inspiration and it got very eclectic, never mainstream.'

Brian fed avidly on this very rich and individual feast of musical influences. It had a strength and independence all of its own which appealed to him greatly. He vividly remembers attending a huge open-air concert in June in Hyde Park and being mesmerized by Jethro Tull, another progressive rock band. 'I was knocked out by Mick Abraham's guitar playing – wonderful tone!'

In the other major strand of Brian's life, too, things were moving onward at great speed. On 24 October 1968 at the Royal Albert Hall, he received his BSc (Hons) degree certificate from the Chancellor of London University, the Queen Mother. Naturally his parents were very proud of his academic achievements, although they realized how important his music was to him too. They quietly hoped he would continue with his studies, but in the end they were happy to settle for whatever he chose, confident he'd do it well.

Something that Brian was determined to do well right then was launch his new band into life. The rehearsing was done, and Smile's first public appearance, in support of Pink Floyd, was due to take place in just two days' time at Imperial College.

2

SOME DAY
ONE DAY

n 1968 Smile described themselves as a progressive rock band; many of their songs lasted as long as twenty minutes. Their first gig went down surprisingly well, considering how nervous and unknown they all were. They mostly played cover versions of recent hits in a wild and rather undisciplined fashion, but it was exciting. At last, Brian felt, one day his music might get him somewhere.

With a degree to his name, and a band with potential, his personal life too was about to take a significant turn. Christine Mullen, known as Chrissy, was a student at the Maria Assumpta Teacher Training College in Kensington. Her flat mate, Jo, was dating Roger Taylor, and when Jo took Chrissy along to one of Smile's gigs at Imperial College she was introduced to Roger's mate.

From his staggering height Brian gazed down at Chrissy's long, dark hair and pretty elfin face. Her head hardly came up to his shoulder, and perhaps an instinctive male protectiveness stirred in Brian. There was an instant rapport. At first, they settled for being just good friends: Chrissy was more than content to join the ever-expanding circle of mates who formed the band's back-up at gigs.

Bookings were healthy, although they often had to travel to Cornwall as Roger was using his West Country music connections to secure work in and around Truro. Recently the band had acquired an assistant, John Harris, for their roadie, Pete Edmunds. Besides being music-mad, Harris also had valuable electronics expertise and so he was quickly drafted in as their first sound engineer. 'The Tremendous London Band Smile', as they unashamedly billed themselves, began to attract a considerable following at venues such as PJ's in Truro and the Flamingo Ballroom in Redruth. Brian's dazzling guitar skills struck audiences dumb with admiration, but he scarcely noticed the effect he was having – he was too busy concentrating on perfecting his technique. To him gigs were an opportunity not just to play, but to experiment with the sounds he could create.

Jaunting about the countryside was a necessary evil, and the band much preferred the college circuit. In the early sixties bands had had to tough it out in the pubs and clubs, earning their stripes the hard way for meagre fees. By the mid- to late sixties the college circuit had taken over as the main stomping-ground. Playing in universities and colleges paid better: many student unions were able and willing to stump up decent fees to attract the latest and best in entertainment.

The London college circuit also made more sense because the band were London-based, particularly in the Kensington area. Since the mid-sixties Kensington had become very important: it was the home of the famous Biba boutique and of Kensington Market – a very arty, in-place to hang out. There was a feeling of being in the right place at the right time. By January 1969 Brian and his friends were spending much of their spare time at a popular pub called the Kensington. It was a great place to enjoy a beer, have a laugh with your mates and plot out where the elusive big break would come from.

Things were going well for Brian in his personal life, too. His relationship with Chrissy had deepened to the point where they had fallen very much in love. This romantic commitment went further than Brian had ever experienced before, but no matter how much he analysed it, he already knew it would be hard to envisage life without her. The warmth of her love provided him with a strong sense of stability which in turn fed his other ambitions.

One of those ambitions was for Smile to land another major gig. It had been almost three months since their debut with Pink Floyd and, although they had recently had a taster supporting Tyrannosaurus Rex and Family, nothing else seemed to be happening. But then February turned up trumps. Not only did they land an important gig supporting the popular band Yes at the Richmond Athletic Club, but they were also invited to take part in a concert in aid of the National Council for the Unmarried Mother and Her Child, which Imperial College had organized to take place at the Albert Hall on 27 February. The prestigious line-up included Free, Joe Cocker and the Bonzo Dog Doo Dah Band. Brian was amazed to discover that Smile – far from being stapled on to the bottom of the bill, as they expected – was actually placed above Free, featuring lead guitarist Paul Kossoff and vocalist Paul Rodgers. The event was compered by the influential DJ John Peel who, through his late-night radio shows, had championed many a British or American underground band to which no one else would give airplay.

A bit of cheek on Tim's part got them some good-quality equipment to use on the night. 'Down the Ealing Road,' he recalls, 'a new music shop had opened up. We would drift in and out from time to time plinking on the guitars and pestering the owner with naive questions about amplification we couldn't possibly afford. A few days before the Albert Hall gig I said to the guy, half-jokingly: wouldn't it be a good idea if he lent us some of his gear so that it could be displayed prominently at a prestigious venue? To my immense surprise, he agreed! So we were able to use a quality Simms-Watts PA system at the gig, which I was delighted about.'

However, despite this unexpected bonus something lurked at the backs of their minds to mar the anticipation. Recently they had toyed with the notion of adding a keyboard player to their line-up, mainly because guitar, bass and drum are the absolute minimum required to produce a full sound and didn't allow any leeway. For a short while they had been rehearsing with Chris Smith, a fellow student of Tim's at Ealing. But the gig was imminent and they had not yet rehearsed enough to produce a tight-knit, cohesive sound. They also discovered that they were using the wrong kind of keyboard. The band had had no time to gain their strength, and that meant ditching their newest recruit. No one relished having to tell Chris that he was sacked, especially the day before a glamour gig. But they were unanimous in their decision, and it was Tim who drew the short straw. 'I think Chris understood,' he asserts, 'although of course it smarted at the time.'

Tim could have been forgiven for the fleeting suspicion that Chris had put a curse on him. After Smile was announced at the Albert Hall he and Brian ran out on to the huge stage. But, unknown to him, Tim was short of some twenty feet of guitar lead, and he didn't realize until he hit the first vital chord that his jack plug had been wrenched from its socket. An embarrassing silence ensued. On top of that he had decided to play this gig without shoes, and as a result his feet ended up full of splinters from the stage. Nevertheless Smile were well pleased with themselves, and even had the excitement of receiving their very first review when one journalist referred to them as 'the loudest group in the western world'. Pity he didn't give them a name check while he was at it.

Elated by the whole affair, they lived on its memory for some time, reminiscing with friends. And into that circle of friends at this time Tim brought a young man called Freddie Bulsara. Farookh Bulsara, to give him his proper name, was born of Persian parents, Bomi and Jer Bulsara, on 5 September 1946 on the island of Zanzibar in the Indian Ocean. It has been said that Freddie was born a star; certainly his origins were exotic. After attending a missionary school run by British nuns he was whisked away to India where he attended St Peter's English boarding school in Panchgani, some fifty miles outside Bombay. It was here that Farookh became Freddie. Here, too, he studied the piano, loved to sing and formed his first band, called the Hectics – an appropriate name since the ebony-eyed, dark-haired, skinny boy could not stand still for a second. He was full of restless, inquisitive energy and oozed originality.

In 1964, when he was seventeen, Zanzibar achieved independence, and in the ensuing upheaval the Bulsara family decided to emigrate to Britain. They moved into a house in Feltham not far from Brian's family. It was at Ealing College of Art, where he studied graphic illustration, that Freddie fell in with Tim Staffell.

Tim, Freddie and another student, Nigel Foster, spent a lot of time at college making music. Freddie's party piece was an over-the-top impersonation of Jimi Hendrix, miming wildly to his records whilst cavorting about pretending his wooden ruler was a guitar. Tim reflects, 'Freddie was intuitively a performer. His persona was developing rapidly even in those days, linking his natural flamboyance with the confidence he acquired from his singing, and of course it would later crystallize around his marvellous songs. Personally I think as far as being a star was concerned, Freddie was already in the ascendant. People responded to him.'

He certainly made an impact on Brian when Tim introduced the pair. 'He was outrageous,' states Brian. 'He was always a star, even when he hadn't a penny to his name. Very flamboyant. On the face of it very confident, but everyone has a soft bit inside – a little insecure bit.' However, this intuitive understanding would not come until much later in their acquaintance. Right then all Brian could see was a very vibrant and irrepressibly colourful young man who, having once had a band of his own, was showing a distressing eagerness to muscle in on Smile.

Both Brian and Roger, however, took to Freddie instantly, even when he became the bane of their lives at rehearsals – ceaselessly bombarding them with his views on how they should look, act and play, rapidly followed by lengthy, detailed and usually fantastically imaginative suggestions as to just how much he could jazz them all up. Brian patiently tolerated these ideas at the same time ignoring Freddie's pleas to be allowed to join the band. If Bulsara had his way he would up-end them all – he was as volatile as a stick of dynamite looking for a match. But that's not to say that Brian didn't respond to Freddie's enthusiasm – he did. Freddie became Smile's unofficial fourth member; whenever they went to gigs, he squeezed into the overcrowded van with the gear.

On 19 April Smile played at the Revolution Club in London. It was after this performance that they were introduced to Lou Reizner, who was involved with Mercury Records – an American label which was just starting up a British arm. Reizner had been watching them all night and liked what he saw. When he asked Smile if they would consider signing with Mercury they couldn't believe their ears. It seemed to be the big break they had all been dreaming of and Brian, Roger and Tim didn't have to think twice about their answer.

A few weeks later, in May 1969, they signed a contract. Mercury wasted no time and quickly booked some sessions at Trident Studios in Soho with producer John Anthony. The whole experience overwhelmed the band and they truly felt they were on their way now. When Mercury Records set the release date for Smile's first single as August that year they were ecstatic. 'I had written a number called "Earth",' says Tim, 'and Mercury had us record this for our single, with the B-side "Step on Me" which Brian and I had written back in the days of 1964.'

In the hot summer of 1969 the ranks of the Kensington crowd were swelled with the invasion of a Liverpool band called Ibex and their manager, Ken Testi. His girlfriend was Helen McConnell, whose sister, Pat, was a fellow student of Chrissy's. Ibex were a three-piece band comprising lead guitarist Mike Bersin, bass player John 'Tupp' Taylor and drummer Mick 'Miffer' Smith. They had decided to pile into their old red van, leave Merseyside and head to London to seek their fortune.

'My girlfriend was staying in a flat in Earls Court with her sister, so at least we had somewhere to doss,' explains Ken. 'Not long after we arrived it was Pat's birthday and we decided to take her out for a drink. She was quite insistent that we went to the Kensington down the road. There was nothing casual in her choice. She'd been going regularly to see a band called Smile, and she knew that the guys supped in that pub. Pat fancied Roger Taylor like crazy so she dragged us down there.' He goes on, 'The idea was that as we were a band and so were they, she'd get Ibex introduced to Smile. None of us were fooled, though – she was just looking for a way of ingratiating herself with Roger! Anyway, that's what happened and Pat introduced us all.'

To Ibex, Brian, Roger and Tim seemed very trendy indeed. 'They were all good-lookin' dudes for a start,' says Ken, 'and we felt like real northern hicks beside them. They actually had a record contract too and had just cut their first single. This seemed absolutely fabulous to us!' He adds, 'They had a chap with them who wasn't in the band, called Fred. He was quiet and reserved.'

Of that first meeting Mike Bersin recalls, 'We had a few beers together and a laugh. Brian made an instant impression on me. He's a gentle giant of a man, soft-spoken and kind and the most considering person I've ever known. What I mean is, if you asked Brian something like "How ya doin'?" he'd actually take time to think about it, then give you a detailed answer!' Being a guitarist himself, Mike was dead keen to see and hear Brian play and was delighted when later that evening they all decided to go back to the McConnells' flat.

Probably Mike's first surprise was when he saw Brian use a six-pence coin instead of the traditional plectrum. Brian had been doing so for some time because, he says, 'I could never find a plectrum which was stiff and rigid enough for me. The coin is totally rigid so you feel the movement from the strings in your fingers.' It is an idiosyncrasy which continues to intrigue guitarists more than twenty years on.

The evening also made a particular mark on Ken Testi. He recalls, 'Suddenly Brian, Roger and Tim began to play us their songs and talk about what they were looking for. I knew immediately that I was in the presence of something extraordinary. They were playing remarkable stuff and Brian's technique was outstanding. It was a seminal Queen. They were special, and everyone watching them in the flat that night knew it.' The two bands met up quite often after that and spent many a balmy summer evening at the Kensington. It was a time of sharing – sharing bands, sharing flats, sharing ideas and above all sharing a great hope of making it in the glitzy ritz of the music business.

But all was not glitz in the world of rock in that hazy hot summer of 1969. On the morning of 3 July came the news that Brian Jones, who had quit the Rolling Stones just weeks before, had died some time before midnight at his country home in Sussex. He was just twenty-seven. His sudden death sent shockwaves ricocheting around the music world. It was made all the worse when it later transpired that there was something suspicious about his death.

This was also the year of the Apollo moon walk. Just after Brian celebrated his twenty-second birthday, he and an estimated five hundred million other people sat glued to their television sets as Neil Armstrong stepped on to the surface of the moon and uttered those immortal words: 'That's one small step for a man, but a giant leap for mankind.' For ambitious young men like Brian, Roger, Tim and Freddie it showed how such dreams could indeed be realized.

Roger had already made a conscious decision in that direction. After achieving the first part of his dental degree in August 1968 he had decided to take a year off and concentrate full-time on becoming a rock star. This meant that in the summer of 1969 he was ripe for Freddie's suggestion that, in order to earn some much-needed cash, they should take a stall at Kensington Market.

The stall they got was in an avenue known somewhat dishearteningly amongst the traders as 'Death Row'. 'Years later I had to laugh,' says Ken, 'when I saw it referred to in Queen's publicity blurb as "a gentlemen's outfitters". Their stall wasn't much bigger than a telephone box!' At first they stocked it with paintings and drawings courtesy of their Ealing art student friends, but sales were disappointing and so Roger and Freddie turned to selling clothes. 'They recycled bits of Victoriana, really,' explains Ken, 'silk scarves, some of which were of very fine quality, lace, stoles – that sort of thing.' This was better, and relatively quickly their endeavours began to show a small profit.

Freddie too had come to a decision. It was quite clear he wasn't going to be allowed to join Smile no matter how much he pestered them, so he had focused instead on Ibex. Mike Bersin was currently vocalist as well as guitarist, but found it difficult at times to combine the two roles satisfactorily. He was therefore just as keen as the others to audition Freddie to become their singer. Within minutes of hearing that remarkable voice the verdict was unanimous; Bulsara was in. Freddie appeared delighted , but Mike wasn't fooled. 'We all knew Freddie was desperate to join Smile,' he says, 'but they weren't having it at that point. That's the only reason he joined Ibex.'

With Freddie off his back, Brian could look forward in peace to the public release of Smile's first single. Mercury Records, as promised, released 'Earth/Step on Me' in August 1969. But it was only released in America. It was certainly not what they had hoped for, but they tried not to be too downhearted. After all, Mercury Records still wanted them to record some more tracks with a view to producing an album, indeed, later that year more studio time was booked and they were set to work with producer Fritz Freyer. By now Brian and Tim had written a few songs and they were eager for the chance to record them properly, using the latest equipment. 'We cut several tracks for that album,' recalls Tim, 'including "April Lady" on which Brian did the vocals, "Polar Bear", "Blag", as well as "Earth" and "Step on Me".' Brian was happy with the results, but Mercury decided not to release the material. 'Although, funnily enough, the album did surface in Japan many years later,' reflects Tim. 'More for archive purposes than anything else, I guess.'

To offset their disappointment at the way things were turning out in this quarter, Smile threw themselves as much as possible into playing gigs. By now they had enlisted the help of the Rondo booking agency in Kensington High Street, which already represented the band Genesis, and for whom Tim had done some graphic work. Smile were still very much in demand at Imperial College, and Ibex manager Ken Testi, with whom they had kept in touch, was proving to have very useful contacts in the north of England. He frequently got work for his own band in the Liverpool area and quite often Brian and the others would tag along for the experience and the fun.

Getting to these gigs constituted the biggest problem but usually they managed to rustle up a beat-up van from someone. On one memorable occasion in August 1969 Ken arranged for Ibex to play a gig at the Bolton Octagon Theatre one day, and then play the following day at an open-air festival in Bolton's Queens Park. Brian was to join them for the open-air gig, travelling up separately by train.

Ken recalls, 'By this time when Ibex went to gigs, more often than not Brian, Roger and Tim would come too, along with assorted girl-friends and whoever else could squeeze into the vans. I did all the driving. I'll never forget that Bolton gig. There was this guy nicknamed

"Big Shit Richard" [Richard Thompson, ex-drummer with Brian's school band 1984] who worked as a driver at Heathrow Airport. Quite illegally we borrowed his Transit van and started to pick up everybody who was coming to Bolton. Tupp Taylor wanted us to pick him up in Piccadilly, and by the time we got there the van was crammed with people up front while in the back they were playing guitars and singing – making a right racket. I stopped the van just long enough for them to roll up the shutter and let Tupp jump in. As soon as the shutter shot up everyone in the street was gaping at all these hippies banging hell out of their guitars!'

They were to spring upon an unsuspecting public at their journey's end, too. 'We arrived in Bolton very early in the morning,' remembers Ken, 'and I pulled up outside the Octagon Theatre. As I switched off the engine, I slowly became aware of a strange rhythmic echo. It took a moment, then I realized what it was. Up ahead of us a works bus had stopped and a load of miners coming off shift were walking home through the streets, their heavy steel-capped boots clattering on the cobbles. It was deafening. Some were coming in our direction. I thought everyone in the back was still sound asleep, but watching in my wing mirror I saw Freddie hit the pavement. Amazingly, in that press of bodies, he was looking as immaculate as ever. He had on his white trousers, white T-shirt and a short fur jacket, and he was just stretching and yawning when suddenly he was engulfed by these tired, hard-working miners in their dirty overalls and big boots. It was such an incongruous sight! Freddie kind of glanced at them and they at him, then the moment passed. But just for those few seconds I thought, what a beautiful juxtaposition!'

It was indeed to be a day of imagery. Mike remembers getting ready for that Saturday lunchtime gig. 'We had decided to dress up a bit more than usual that day. My mum had gone and made me a gold lamé cloak which I felt obliged to wear, although when the time came I felt a bit of a twit. Freddie stood out a mile, although in those days he had only one outfit. All he had to his name was one pair of boots, one pair of trousers (admittedly white satin), one granny vest, one belt and one furry jacket. At the theatre Freddie stood for ages twitching at himself in the mirror. Eventually I yelled at him, "For God's sake, Freddie, stop messin' with your hair!" To which he happily tossed back, "But I'm a star, dear boy!" He meant it, too!'

That Saturday evening Brian was due to arrive. Says Ken, 'I was meeting Brian off the train at Lime Street Station, so again we all piled into the Transit van. In the back was Pat McConnell and a few of her friends. Freddie had his girlfriend Mary Austin on board, Roger was there, and of course all of Ibex.'

He goes on, 'In those days you could reverse a truck right through the front entrance of the station. I reversed up the ramp and told everyone to be quiet. I mean we had no insurance, the van was in effect stolen and we didn't want to draw attention to ourselves. So I was looking in the rear view mirror watching what I was doing, and what did I see? Not only a police constable but a high-ranking officer with braid everywhere on his uniform and a stick under his arm, and they were approaching the van. I was trying to look cool by this time, hissing at everyone to keep absolutely silent. There was a knock on the window and I rolled it down, saying, "Yes, officer, what can I do for you?"

'"Are you waiting for the London train, sir?" one of them asked. I was trying to stop my knees from knocking, convinced everyone was breathing too hard in the back, but I managed to squeak that I was. Well, next thing, the braided officer told me that I had his permission to reverse right on to the platform. Two railway porters hurried off to pull back the corrugated gates, and I backed this hot Heathrow Airport van along the platform flagged all the way by these two coppers.'

'By this time,' he continues, 'I was sweating, and I was scared stiff that when Brian arrived his reaction would give us all away. Everyone in the back kind of knew what was going on, and you could have cut the atmosphere with a knife. Well, the train pulled in and all the passengers emptied on to the platform. Brian stepped off the train – and God, he was good! He sussed the situation in a second. As bold as brass he strode, guitar case in hand, right up to van, passed the policemen without blinking an eye, and got in beside me at the front as if he was a VIP being picked up. Then we drove off, but it was a very long time before any of us let our breath out!'

Those visits to Liverpool tended to be memorable for various reasons. Helen McConnell recalls, 'Once Brian was staying at my family's house in St Helen's. He wasn't used to the strength of northern beer and he'd had a few, so we left him to sleep it off. He was sitting in front of the hearth with those long legs of his stretched up above the coal fire, and after a while my mum went dashing into the room because there was this awful stench of burning rubber. Brian's boots were on fire, the thick soles melting, and the dozy soul hadn't even noticed!'

For a while Ibex decided to put an end to the endless trips up and down the motorway. Nothing was happening for them in London, so they thought they would stay in Liverpool – an arrangement not very appealing to Freddie. Brian, Roger and Tim would travel up when they were free to join Freddie at his digs, which consisted of a big bedroom above the Dovedale Towers Banqueting Halls in Penny Lane. The mother of one of their friends, Geoff Higgins, was catering manageress at the Dovedale and would often put up Geoff's friends.

Ken was still managing to get Ibex bookings in Liverpool, often running himself ragged in the process. 'The worst was when we'd all been down in London for a spell and I had hitched up to St Helen's because I'd recently decided to go to college there. I'd just arrived when Bersin rang up to say that the band had a booking for the following day and to ask if I could come back to get them and bring them up in Pete Edmunds' van. I grabbed a sandwich and hitched straight back to London, arriving late. Then very early the next morning I went round to Imperial College for the gear. There was a music room there on the third floor which had a tower at one end with a spiral staircase – the equipment was stored at the top. Freddie was the one designated to help me, which was unfortunate because while I humped all the heavy stuff time after time down this spiral staircase to the van, I think Freddie only managed one music stand, a tambourine and few drumsticks. But never mind. One never expected too much manual from Freddie.' He adds, 'Brian and Roger were coming up just to groove, because this was Freddie's band and they wanted to support him.'

That gig was at the Sink in Hardman Street, a basement club below the Rumbling Tum. The Sink wasn't licensed to sell alcohol, and so before they went on they decided to nip along to a nearby pub. En route they suddenly came face to face with a gang of skinheads. This was a new breed of thug whose policy was to hit anything they didn't like the look of, or anyone who didn't look like them with their shaven heads, braces and bovver boots. Hippies in particular made excellent Saturday night punching material.

Geoff Higgins recalls the incident vividly. 'It was outside the Liverpool Art College. Round the corner came this gang of skinheads and I thought "Aw Naw!" There was six or seven of us, and a whole lot more of them. We were dressed in our London gear – velvet trousers and frilly shirts – and you didn't dress like that in Liverpool then. We looked a right bunch of poofs, I can tell you! All skinny, frail and cowards. I was just wondering what would happen next when Roger, quick as a flash, bluffs that he's a black belt in judo and the law said he must warn them of this first because if they ignored his warnings and got hurt, it was their own look-out. My head was in my hands by this time. I thought, Bastard Taylor! He'll get us all bloody massacred. I hissed at him, "You don't try it on with scouse skins, you idiot!" But it worked. I don't know whether they believed Roger or whether they were just amused at his hard neck, but they left us alone and walked away. We were all shivering with fear by this time.'

About the performance itself that night Ken says, 'I don't remember all that much about it because I napped on and off – I'd done that trip three times. But I do know that Brian and Roger got up and did a couple of guest spots with Freddie joining in. Freddie already knew all of Smile's stuff, you see.' Watching Freddie perform, Brian could see just how well he was developing. Just as Freddie had had instant respect for Brian's musicianship, so Brian admired Freddie's inimitable panache and the attention to detail which he brought to every performance. But however much he enjoyed the gigs, having his home base in Liverpool wasn't suiting Freddie. By September he had headed back to London with Mike Bersin in time to graduate from Ealing Art college with a diploma in graphic art and design.

For Brian, September also marked a change. Now passed in his second year as a postgraduate student, he was able to pursue an avenue in astro-physics on which he had set his heart for some time. Earlier in the year he had seriously considered joining Professor Sir Bernard Lovell's research laboratory at Jodrell Bank in Cheshire. It was an honour even to have been invited. According to Sir Bernard, 'We would normally interview about forty students every year for postgraduate studies at Jodrell. About 10 per cent are invited to come here for a one-year MSc or three-year PhD course.' Lovell felt that, with Brian's existing astronomical work and musical ability, he was a prime candidate for their select list. 'I was sorry when he rejected our offer,' he admits.

In fact, Brian had turned Jodrell Bank down in favour of an invitation from Imperial College's Prof. Jim Ring to do a PhD as part of his research team studying zodiacal light – a subject which already fascinated Brian. Prof. Ring explains, 'I started research into zodiacal light when I was at Manchester University. Ken Reay was a student of mine, just as in turn Brian became a student of Ken's. I recruited from the top 10 per cent of the cream of the brightest graduates. I'd joined Imperial in 1967 and Brian in fact was one of the first research students I selected. Jodrell Bank was, I suppose, a rival to us, but Brian chose to join my team.'

Brian's involvement in astronomy was a source of admiration among his friends. Mike confesses, 'You couldn't help but be impressed by the guy. I mean on top of being a great guitarist, he was well up with this astronomy lark.' While Ken adds, 'Later on we used to think it awfully grand whenever Brian was gone for long spells to his observatory in Tenerife.'

There was nothing grand, however, about the state of their accommodation in London by late 1969. Suffering *en masse* from a perennial shortage of cash, Smile, Ibex and a ragbag of friends decided to throw their lot in together in a flat in Ferry Road, Barnes. 'It was only supposed to house three people,' laughs Mike, 'so when the landlady came for the rent we'd all hide in the bedroom. At one point we ended up pushing the three beds together to make one great big bed and we all slept in that – girls as well. At times we tried all sleeping sideways to see if that was any more comfortable – it wasn't!' He goes on, 'The flat itself was pretty hideous. Besides the odd chair there was just one red plastic sofa which had holes in it with the stuffing sprouting out all over the place. One of my most vivid memories of that flat is playing Led Zeppelin's first album all day, every day on the old Dansette record player until the needle wore out.'

Despite the chaos, it was a time of enormous friendship. A former resident had left behind a tatty old acoustic guitar on which Brian would strum away in a corner. It was in such a state that no one else could get it to sound right, but with a little nurturing Brian managed to coax some pretty impressive numbers out of it. Geoff Higgins recalls, 'I was asleep one morning on the grubby chaise longue and woke up to find him sitting looking out of the big stained glass windows at one end of the room, softly playing the Beatles number "Martha My Dear" complete with bass line and everything. This was on that battered gut-strung guitar which no one else could possibly play. I thought, I don't believe this.'

Mike Bersin also reveals, 'Brian quite often used to show me bits on the guitar. Once he taught me a special way of playing the G-chord which gave a wonderful sound. That chord was perfect for checking your tuning too, which at that time was a huge thing to me. Brian favoured the VOX AC30 amp – that's a 30-watt valve amp with speakers. It looked like a black suitcase with control knobs on top but it gave out a lovely rich, warm tone. In the late sixties everyone went for Marshall stacks, but Brian was very distinctive and swore by his two VOX AC30s. I think his very distinctive sound comes 70 per cent from his brilliantly unique Red Special and 30 per cent from the VOX amps.' He goes on, 'In style at this time there was a very classical influence in Brian's approach to rock. Yet he had the blues feel of a five-note scale as opposed to the full thirteen notes in a run which you get in classical playing.'

Brian, Freddie and Roger would regularly rehearse harmonies in what was grandly called the breakfast room. Mike also used to watch Brian quietly compose songs at the kitchen table. 'I thought then that he was a special songwriter. In fact years later, when Queen were famous and Freddie had established himself so firmly as a frontman, I always felt that Brian was perhaps one step back from the limelight – but he always had a lot of nice things to say.'

Not to be outdone, Freddie too would play the guitar – at least he would strum the few chords he had forced himself to learn in order to help him write songs. With a white Fender Telecaster dangling impressively around his neck he would make a pest of himself at the crack of dawn as a wandering minstrel, roaming around the flat and stepping over sleeping bodies whilst singing and playing the only song he knew all the way through, which was the Who's latest hit 'Pinball Wizard'.

Mad times were had by all as the year drew to a close. Geoff reveals, 'At Kensington Market we'd get marijuana mixed with jasmine tea, and then take it in turns to separate the grass from the tea. One day Tupp took it home and hadn't got time to separate it. Now in those days Freddie wouldn't go near dope, but he didn't know that it was still all mixed up and made himself what he thought was a pot of jasmine tea. When we got home he was smashed out of his head! He had a Frank Zappa album, *Only in It for the Money*, and on one track there's a noise like a stylus scraping across a record – but it's meant to sound like that. Well, Freddie was busy wheeling around the room, arms flapping, and he'd put on his Zappa LP. When it came to this bit he thought somebody had scratched his precious album and went flying across to the turntable, throwing himself on the LP to check it. He was clean out of his box that day!'

Freddie couldn't wait to try the trick out on someone else as unsuspecting as he had been. He got his chance not long afterwards when the police, summoned by angry neighbours, arrived late one night to break up a particularly noisy party. Freddie placated the officers with tea and cakes – marijuana-laced. Off went the cops feeling they had handled the disturbance well, not realizing what lay in store for them once the effects took hold.

Life might have seemed a barrel of laughs, but musically it was very different. At the end of 1969 Mercury Records had arranged a showcase gig for Smile at the famous Marquee Club in Wardour Street, playing support to the group Kippington Lodge. The thirty-minute slot, however, felt like an eternity. The crowd didn't like them and the band came off stage dejected, feeling it had been a resounding flop all round – just like their association with Mercury Records full stop. Brian had begun the year so full of hope; now, as it drew to a close, that optimism had splintered in disillusionment. His ultimate belief that they would make it in the rock world had not soured, but now he harboured serious doubts that they would make it as Smile. If they were going to succeed, big changes would have to be made.

THE LOUDEST BAND ON THE PLANET

At the start of the seventies Brian could clearly see that Smile was entering its death throes. For one thing he found he had to give more of his time to his work at Imperial College than to his music. As well as having to do research for his PhD he gave tutorials on two half-days a week, and on top of that there were plans for him to join his supervisor, Ken Reay, on a trip to build an observatory in Tenerife in the Canary Islands.

Smile's bookings were also definitely drying up. More often than not, if Brian went to a gig it was not to perform but rather to lend moral support to Freddie, who was now fronting a band called Wreckage. 'It wasn't really a new band,' explains Mike Bersin. 'One night I got a phone call from Freddie saying that nobody in the band was terribly happy with name the Ibex and would I object if it were changed to Wreckage. I said that if everyone else had said OK, then it was OK with me. A couple of days later I turned up for rehearsal and discovered that all our gear had already been stencilled with the new name. Turns out we all got the same call that night. Mind you,' Mike adds, 'that was Freddie. If he wanted something, he got it.'

By late February 1970 no one in Smile felt that they were getting what they wanted out of the arrangement. Tim reflects, 'It understandably suffered from a lack of finance, just as most student bands did at that time. But we'd played some notable gigs and supported some very big names. We'd also had a good time doing it. I think I'd say that at our worst we may have been a little shaky, but at our best I'm sure we were quite worth the admission price.'

He decided that, for him, now was the time to move on. 'To be honest, I was growing a little tired of rock played loud,' he admits. 'I went to audition for Colin Petersen's band. Colin had been drummer with the Bee Gees and, whilst I wasn't 100 per cent convinced that I was doing the right thing, I did like the quieter style that the new band offered. Probably it also had something to do with what I was writing at the time. My songs seemed as if they might fit into that context more successfully.' He adds, 'Whereas I left Smile for my own reasons, in one sense I was moving out of the way and the birth and evolution of Queen were a natural and inevitable outcome.' Tim later went on to play guitar with several bands, including Morgan and Jonathan Kelly's Outside, before leaving the music business altogether.

Not long after Tim's departure, Mercury Records dropped Smile – a move not entirely unexpected by Brian and Roger. Relations with the company had been stale for some time and anyway their original contract had only been for one single, which had been fulfilled.

After these changes Brian and Roger talked incessantly about their musical future – and they were still convinced that they did have a future. Freddie, feeling that Wreckage was not going to make him famous, had disbanded the group after only a couple of months and so he too was at a loose end. The three debated the issue intensely. It was, as Tim said, inevitable that Brian, Freddie and Roger would team up at last in one band. Individually they were all highly talented, they were friends, and they shared the same burning ambition to become a major force in rock music. It was just going to take planning and a lot of hard work.

For Brian, however, other activities were shortly to take precedence over any new band. Prof. Ring, Ken Reay and he were off to Tenerife to set up their observatory on the slopes near the 12,000ft Mount Teide – the dormant volcano which dominates the island and resembles a lunar landscape. Brian was thrilled at the prospect.

'We built a prefab hut of aluminium which we lived in as well as using it as a lab,' explains Jim Ring. 'I was the project group leader, so I used to apply for all the grants I possibly could to finance their work.

Brian was responsible for maintaining all the equipment and was there for much longer spells at a stretch than I was, or even Ken Reay.'

Ken himself says, 'I vividly remember the first time we flew to Tenerife, which involved a one-night stopover in Casablanca. We'd arrived in the Canaries, and were walking through the shopping centre in the capital, Santa Cruz. At this time Brian always wore the same thing – blue jeans, very flared, with tiny bells sewn all around the bottom of each leg, a black velvet jacket, which was all the rage then, and his hair much as it is now, long and curly. Don't get me wrong, he didn't look weird – remember, this was the fashion in the early seventies. But over there I guess he looked a bit of a bizarre character.'

He goes on, 'We were walking along, talking of Casablanca – which, combined with the way Brian looked, must have sparked off the incident which followed. Suddenly this American guy, who'd obviously been listening to us, leaped in front of Brian, grabbed him tight by the lapels and gasped into his face, 'Where d'you get your stuff, man? I *must* have it!' We got the shock of our lives. The best of it is, in all the time I knew Brian he never touched drugs. But that American clearly thought different and wasn't about to let go!'

It was on Brian's return in April 1970 from his first scientific trip that he, Roger and Freddie would set themselves up as Queen. First on the agenda was to find themselves a bass player; a problem which Roger solved by roping in an ex-member of Reaction, Mike Grose, a good musician who was also co-owner of PJ's in Truro. Says Mike, 'Smile used to play at PJ's now and then. Sometimes there was a lot of friction between Roger and Tim – but nothing serious, just squabbles really. Anyway, one night they turned up for their gig and Tim had quit so I stepped in and played. That was the first time I met Brian. That guitar of his has a fingerboard on it like silk. Lightly touch it, and you're there. He was a tremendous player even then – far ahead of anyone I'd ever seen or heard. Since then, of course, lots of guitarists have copied him, but in those days he was so damned original.'

'A few weeks later Roger rang and asked me to join the band. They didn't yet have a name for it, but it was going to consist of Roger, Brian and Freddie.' He continues, 'The timing was just right for me. PJ's was under a demolition order, so I took up the offer and went to London to stay with them in a flat in Earls Court.' Mike brought with him not only a huge Marshall amplifier but also a Volkswagen van – both invaluable assets.

From the point of view of rehearsing, Brian's connections at Imperial College were crucial. Ken Reay explains, 'I used to book lecture theatres in the physics block for Brian and the band to practise in free. As a tutor there I could do that, so Brian would bring along a constant flow of forms for me to sign.'

'As well as practising live once or twice a week at Imperial,' Mike picks up, 'Brian, Roger, Freddie and I often used to sit out in the garden at the flat tossing ideas about. Quite a bit of songwriting went on there too, especially by Brian and Freddie. Songs like "Keep Yourself Alive" and "Seven Seas of Rhye" were emerging even then. In fact almost all the songs which later turned up on Queen's debut album got their first airing in that garden.'

Mike also maintains that the name Queen came up for the very first time one day as they were jamming in the garden. 'I remember that clearly,' he claims, 'and at the same time there was also an idea for them to adopt a very rude logo. Freddie's influence, of course!' According to Mike the two live wires, Roger and Freddie, used to squabble about anything and everything. The more reserved Brian just took it all in and kept well out of it. 'When Brian did speak, though, it was always worth listening,' Mike adds.

Naming the band Queen, however, gave rise to some hefty debating among the four. They were naturally aware of its camp overtones, yet the word had a regal quality which appealed to them. It was also universal and immediate. Brian chewed the name over in his mind, then asked Ken for his view one day when he was handing him yet another request for permission to rehearse in one of the lecture theatres. 'I told him it sounded extremely camp to me,' says Reay. 'I didn't need to be told that it was Freddie's idea, but I wouldn't say Brian had too much trouble with it. He seemed more amused, than anything, at the risqué connotations. Above all else, he obviously saw it as a good move to call themselves that.' Occasionally Ken would drop by Queen's practice sessions, each time coming away temporarily deafened. He could tell they were itching for a live gig.

That first gig took place on 27 June 1970 at the City Hall in Truro – but they were still billed as Smile, not as Queen. 'The reason for that,' explains Mike, 'is that Roger's mother was in the Red Cross in Cornwall and Roger had promised a while back that Smile would play at a charity event they were organizing. Although Smile was now defunct he wasn't about to let his mum down, and so Queen went in its place.'

He goes on, 'The hall held about eight hundred people, but only a quarter of that number turned up. Nobody knew who we were, obviously, which was perhaps just as well since we were awfully loose that night. More like rough, to be brutally frank. We'd practised hard, but the real thing isn't the same as rehearsing in some lecture theatre. We also had quite complicated arrangements worked into our repertoire, and when you write your own music you tend to change those arrangements a lot. One of us remembered a song one way and someone else remembered it another way. I'm not saying we were bad as such, but there were a lot of gaffes made that night.'

Gaffes or not, Queen as a group had played their first gig and had already left a lasting impression. Freddie would pick holes in his own unpolished performance for a long time afterwards, but they had been paid the handsome fee of £50 for their efforts. Also, instead of wearing the stage uniform of faded denim jeans and T-shirts, adopted by bands such as Black Sabbath, Deep Purple and Free, Queen had decked themselves out in silky smooth black and white costumes guaranteed to set them apart straightaway. With the addition of junk jewellery hung liberally around their necks and wrists, they had achieved a raw visual impact which no one was likely to forget.

It was about now that Freddie decided he needed to change his name. He was proud of his family name, but Bulsara didn't trip off the tongue and certainly wasn't part of the satin and silk image of Queen. He chose to call himself after the Roman messenger of the gods, and from then on he became known as Freddie Mercury.

Brian, meanwhile, was still balancing his music with his academic studies and still giving his tutorials. At these classes he would demonstrate in the lab and wander amongst the students, helping with problems and answering questions. 'He was a very good teacher,' says Prof. Ring, 'very sympathetic and popular with the students.'

This was all well and good, but Brian had begun to get itchy feet about Queen's lack of progress. He felt it was high time that they tried to get record companies interested in them. After their relationship with Mercury Records he and Roger were wary of the music business, but at the same time they felt they had profited by that experience: as long as they never again lost control of the band's career, things should be all right. Freddie felt the same and, although to the uninitiated the sight of him mincing up and down Kensington High Street every Saturday swathed in feather boas looked nothing more than Freddie just being

Freddie, behind this apparently facile ritual lay a calculated intent to bump into 'by accident' certain influential people in the record business who could help them.

Unwilling, however, to cradle all their hopes in the hands of Providence, Brian pressed on with his plans until he managed to arrange a gig to take place in Lecture Theatre A at Imperial College on 18 July. The audience would be made up of personally invited record company executives, with close friends of the band in attendance to provide moral support and to help impress the businessmen with their enthusiasm. The exercise demonstrated how much the band had improved; but unfortunately nothing else seemed to come of it.

One week later they again played PJ's in Truro, only this night billed for the very first time as Queen. That gig turned out to be the last for Mike Grose. 'I left Queen because I'd had enough of playing, basically. I had just got to that point. We weren't earning anything to speak of, and we were living in squalor. I just didn't want to be a part of it anymore. Brian had another year of studies to go, and so did Roger – and I thought, to hell with it.' He adds frankly, 'I knew I'd regret leaving, because I knew in my bones that they were going to make it.'

The parting in August was amicable, but the vacancy had to be filled with some urgency since Queen had a gig booked for near the end of the month. Mike's replacement turned out to be a guy called Barry Mitchell. Says Barry, 'That summer in Cornwall a friend of mine met Roger, who told him that his band was in need of a bass player. My friend gave me a number to ring, and as a result Roger asked me to an audition at Imperial College.' He continues, 'The audition was very friendly – a blues jam, really. We did a couple of their numbers and I got the job straightaway.'

With his long blond hair and trendy style Barry also looked the part, although personally he never felt that he quite fitted in. 'No, to a certain degree I always felt an outsider. It wasn't them. It was me. I guess it was because they were all so very well educated that I felt out of it, which is my own fault. Also, the three of them were obviously buddies. Having said that, Brian was the friendliest by a very long way – he was approachable and went out of his way to try to help me become a part of the band. Freddie, on the other hand, was very deep.'

Freddie's ideas for Queen alarmed Barry from day one. He'd have had us all wearing women's clothes – and I wasn't having any of that! Freddie wasn't as outrageously camp as he later became but it was still there in those days. He'd paint his nails, curl his hair with heated tongs and everything. When I saw him at that game, I thought, wait a minute, what's goin' on 'ere then?' Freddie's heavy sense of imagery confused Barry, who felt bands should be dirty and sweaty and not tarted up to the nines. But he had to admit that Queen got far more work than any band he had previously been used to.

Barry's first appearance with Queen was at Imperial College on 23 August 1970. This gig was meant to be their springboard to fame, and Freddie had employed a dressmaker friend to run him up something special to wear. Following his rough guidelines she had made him a black figure-hugging one-piece outfit boldly slashed to the navel, with a wings effect at ankles and wrists. Freddie proudly dubbed it his mercury suit, and immediately had a white version made up as well.

From the start Queen went to extraordinary lengths to please their audiences. For this gig they laid on, free of charge, soft drinks and home-made popcorn which had been transported earlier by the bucketload from Freddie's flat to the college. They were very keen to make people realize that they were different from run-of-the-mill groups.

In September Brian made a return trip to Tenerife with Ken Reay, but now he was finding it much harder to leave his musical life behind, even for a short while. Ken confirms, 'Yes, he was forever talking about Queen and showing me photos of them in their stage clothes. He'd fish out this acoustic guitar, and if we weren't working of an evening he sat outside on the steps of the observatory and played. It's laughable now, but I used to listen to him and think to myself, that boy will never make it! It just goes to show how much I knew!' Back in London Freddie and Roger had closed their market stall for a day as a mark of respect towards Jimi Hendrix, whose sudden death from drugs had just been announced. Hendrix had been a vivid inspiration to them all, and Brian took the news of his death badly.

But there was scant time to brood. Queen wanted to play as many gigs as possible, and they were landing them mainly courtesy of their friend from Ibex days, Ken Testi. Ken was now studying at St Helen's College of Technology on Merseyside where he was social secretary. One of his jobs was to book bands for college dances, and he was crucial in putting work Queen's way. Says Testi, 'There was a public call box at the end of Freddie and Roger's row in the market, and I'd phone them there to tell them I'd fixed them up with a gig. Sometimes it took forever to get an answer, then whoever did pick up the receiver had to run like hell to tell Freddie or Roger to come quick before all my money ran out. There was no other way of contacting them. Fred told me they were ready, and I promised I'd try to book a few gigs at a time to make it viable for them to come all the way to Liverpool. I remember they were very pleased when I got them a gig at the Cavern.

Barry remembers that particular gig vividly. 'It was an amazing place. Nothing more than a hot, sweaty basement, really, with water running down the walls from the heat of all the people squeezed in there – but it had something, there's no denying that. I blew up somebody's amp that night. There was this other band's gear set up and my own amp had packed in, of course, so I gaily plugged into this guy's amp which promptly exploded!'

The constant trips to Liverpool often involved some hair-raising escapades on the road. 'I nearly killed Queen once,' confesses Ken. 'It was one of those trips when I'd been driving virtually non-stop for about forty-eight hours and it wasn't all motorway then. Anyway, it was on the M1 and there was an elevated stretch with fields falling away either side. It was very misty that night. The mist had risen to the level of the motorway at either side and it was like driving across clouds. I was so tired that I dozed off for a second at the wheel. Next second I was awoken by a piercing scream from Pat McConnell and found I was halfway across the hard shoulder. Without being dramatic, Pat's scream saved us all from certain death that night.'

In January 1971 Barry decided he had had enough adventures with Queen and left. Like Ken Reay, he didn't think Queen were going to make it – but that was not the reason why he left. 'We weren't earning anything to speak of, and I'd had enough of never having a shilling in my pocket,' he says. 'Also we were more or less performing all of their own compositions, and I wanted to play different music as well. When she discovered I was leaving, Freddie's girlfriend Mary Austin said to me, 'It's a shame you're leaving now. You're just getting to know them.' This was true, because I'd begun to hang out with Roger, but it wasn't enough and anyway I'd made up my mind.'

Barry played his final two gigs with Queen in early January – one at the Marquee, then another the next day at Ewell Technical College in Surrey when Queen were support band, along with Genesis, to the Kevin Ayres and the Whole World Band. Says Barry, 'Peter Gabriel fronted Genesis in those days, and in the classroom we were using as a dressing room Gabriel was trying his damnedest to get Roger to leave

Queen and join Genesis. But Roger wouldn't have it.'

Relief that Roger had refused to be poached away was quickly replaced with frustration that they couldn't seem to hold on to their bass players for love nor money. Someone called Doug was hired to fill the spot temporarily. Two gigs later he overstepped the mark, cavorting about on stage like a lunatic, and that was enough. Doug was jettisoned next day; it seemed they'd never meet the right guy.

That last gig with the excitable bassist at Kingston Polytechnic, on 20 February 1971, was in support of two leading progressive rock bands, Wishbone Ash and Yes, who shared top billing. Wishbone's Andy Powell remembers Queen's performance, and in particular Brian's, very well. 'That was the first time I heard him play,' he recalls, 'and his tone immediately grabbed me. Brian has his own style and sound, so you can always tell his work. Even in 1971 he had incredible finesse, amazing fluidity.' He continues, 'What Queen was playing then was, in my opinion, progressive music. A little later they became a glamour band, but at that time what they were doing was similar to us. Although, having said that, they did have that edge that was a bit more mainstream. I think you could tell they wouldn't stay playing progressive rock for long.'

Former Kingston Poly student Tony Blackman remembers how they looked that night. 'They were all dressed completely in black and their clothes were extremely tight-fitting. There's no doubt that they were projecting a very effeminate image. A gay image was not the done thing then, and yet these guys were going out of their way to flaunt it.'

When Queen were not performing, they enjoyed going along to see other bands play. Not long after they had ditched Doug, Brian and Roger were at a dance at Chrissy's college. It was here that they were introduced to a bass player by the name of John Richard Deacon. John, then studying electronics at Chelsea College, had been born on 19 August 1951 in Leicester. He had begun playing the guitar at the age of seven and formed his first band at fourteen.

Brian couldn't believe his luck. He pounced immediately and asked John if he would be interested in auditioning for Queen. A few days later, having heard him play, Brian, Roger and Freddie got down to some serious discussion. Apart from John's obvious skill on bass he had a placid, unflappable nature – a valuable asset – not to mention his electronics wizardry. Besides, it felt right. And so in late February 1971 the Queen line-up was finally complete.

Months of intense rehearsing followed, so that by the summer they would be ready to accept bookings for gigs. But Brian had to miss much of this preparation because his astronomy work took him once again to Tenerife, this time with a fellow research student, Tom Hicks.

Says Tom, 'Our job was to look at dust in the solar system, which entailed carrying out experiments and observing for time spans between one hour and all night, depending on the time of year. The hut – known as ZL, for zodiacal light – had one room which we used as a kitchen, and two bedrooms with bunk beds. The fourth room was the lab where all the instruments were. Some of our equipment was quite crude in many ways. We used one device called a coelostat which was really no more than a set of mirrors that directed light through a hole in the wall into the laboratory.'

Typically Brian and Tom would spend about six weeks at a stretch at ZL. 'We'd go out ideally before a full moon,' says Tom, 'and set everything up. Then we'd start once the full moon was past. At first we'd be working two hours, then three, then all night. At the dark of the moon you could work from, say, 10 p.m. to 11 a.m., or something like that. We got very disorientated at times – we'd be having bacon, eggs and beer for breakfast!'

The research grants which Prof. Ring managed to obtain were quite generous, so they could afford to enjoy themselves a little when they were there. Sometimes Brian and Tom would trek down to the coast or take trips further up the extinct but still smoking volcano to peer into its bowels. Says Tom, 'Brian used to produce this cheap little Spanish acoustic and proceed to thrash out all these wild rock chords on it. It was very strange hearing hard rock on a Spanish guitar. Brian wasn't around a lot with Queen when they first started up because he was out in Tenerife so much, yet I would swear that what he was playing ended up on their first album.'

Whilst in Tenerife they were given support and assistance from the University of La Laguna, in particular by Prof. Francisco Sanchez Martinez and Dr Carlos Sanchez Magro. 'Carlos took Brian and me out for a meal one night and afterwards Brian was driving back,' recalls Tom. 'Their roads in those days were very primitive – they just had one new motorway. Suddenly we saw these lights coming fast straight at us. We were driving up the motorway the wrong way! Thankfully there were no barriers at the sides and in a split second Brian see-sawed the wheel, pulled us on to the rocky verge and cut the engine. We escaped by a whisker!'

Being supervisor to both students, Ken Reay would join them there for spells and the three of them built a Fabry-Perot Interferometer which they used in their work. 'Brian was the one most involved in building this,' states Ken. 'It was also Brian who was heavily into carrying out the observations, data reduction and recording. He put in a lot of hours.'

Returning to London, Brian swapped his cramped lodgings at ZL for a miniscule bedsitter in Earls Court which had to house not only a bed but also his precious AC30 amps and piles of academic books. If he was in the room, only one other person could hope to stand up. There was a phone on the landing for communal use and the kitchen was part of an old corridor, partitioned off.

On 11 July, fortified by popcorn made by Brian in that seedy Earls Court kitchen, an Imperial College audience saw Queen play their second gig with John on bass. John wasn't sure about the reaction he could expect, since Queen had played so often at the college with other bassists – but he needn't have worried. It was a good night, made even better when record producer John Anthony, who had worked with Smile two years before, turned out to have been in the crowd. As he was leaving he promised to give them a call.

Money – or rather the lack of it – was a perpetual worry, so Roger decided to register for a degree course which would make him eligible for a grant. In the autumn of 1971 he enrolled at North London Polytechnic to study plant and animal biology. Brian, too, had recently stopped giving tutorials at Imperial and, although his fees had amounted only to a couple of hundred pounds a year, he still missed the cash. Bookings, while important for the experience, were essential for the money they brought in.

Roger now managed to arrange what was grandly called a Cornish Tour, which would carry them through August into September. It was quite an eventful trip. Arguments with pub landlords over the volume at which they played were an almost nightly affair, fees had to be wrested from reluctant hands after some performances and, taking exception to the 'dodgy' way Queen looked, some of the locals could turn nasty. On at least one occasion a posse with its blood up piled into an old banger and gave chase after Queen had fled the rowdy pub in their van. With Roger's knowledge of the area, though, the band easily outran the mob and lost them in the honeycomb of narrow country lanes.

Exhilarating as these escapades were, Queen saw themselves as too big for this particular pond. Brian felt that their best shot in moving upstream lay in persuading the music moguls to come and see how good they really were. So, despite their previous failure, he set about arranging for another private performance at college. This time they invited representatives from many of the London agencies who booked bands for major venues; several turned up on the night, but once again no bookings were forthcoming.

Fortunately Ken Testi was still working on their behalf. By this time he had left Liverpool and returned to London. 'I was sharing a flat in Wimbledon with Paul Conroy, who's now with Virgin Records,' he says. 'Paul was a booker for an agency and I used to pester him to book Queen. Lindsay Brown was another booker I knew and I used to hassle these two to death. They did indulge me a few times, which was really just out of the goodness of their hearts because they were supposed to be working for their agencies. But they did what they could, and at the time that meant a lot to Queen.'

Queen's first real break came via a friend of Brian's, Terry Yeadon, who in the autumn of 1971 was involved in setting up a brand-new recording studio in Wembley called De Lane Lea. Terry knew Brian from his Smile days. He says, 'I was a DJ in Blackburn in the mid-sixties and then came to London to work at Pye Recording Studios at Marble Arch as a maintenance engineer. In about 1969 a mutual friend asked me to come and see Brian play, so I went to one of Smile's gigs at Imperial College. I thought they were pretty good. We got chatting, and Brian asked if there was any way Smile could get some recording done. Pye knew nothing about it, but along with Geoff Calvar, who was a disc-cutting engineer, I recorded Smile on the side. We recorded two tracks, 'Step on Me' and 'Polar Bear', and Geoff did acetates. At that point Brian asked if I'd like to get involved with them, but I was busy at Pye and made all sorts of excuses not to.'

He goes on, 'Come 1971 I'd moved to De Lane Lea and Geoff and I were putting together this new complex in Wembley. We'd built three studios, but thought we had a problem with isolation. We were carrying out tests like firing pistols and shotguns and recording in the next studio to see if it picked anything up, but we weren't satisfied and reckoned that what we really needed was a rock band. There's nothing to compare with a rock band playing at full blast! By a happy coincidence Brian tracked me down again right then and told me they'd got a new vocalist and a full-time bass player. That's just what Geoff and I had been looking for, and so we worked out a deal.

Terry first put Queen into his biggest studio, which could hold up to 120 musicians. He says, 'There was just them set up in the middle. Brian took along his AC30 amps but they were no good for our purposes. We needed more power and so De Lane Lea hired a whole load of Marshall stacks. Queen played, while Geoff and I were in studios two and three testing. The problems with new studios are endless, especially to do with acoustics. We'd been having trouble with sound being carried through the air conditioning ducts and such like, and so testing took a while.' He adds, 'When it came to recording their demos, we did that on four-track in studio three, which is the smallest and was always going to be the rock and roll studio.'

Queen were ecstatic at being given this opportunity: not only could they record with the latest equipment free of charge, but they might even meet the people whom they'd been dying to come into contact with for so long. The producer/engineer they were set to work with was called Louie Austin, and all four threw themselves enthusiastically into the task. There were lots of hitches, but it turned out to have been well worth the effort when they listened to the end product – a demo of four of their own compositions : 'Liar', 'Keep Yourself Alive', 'The Night Comes Down' and 'Jesus'.

What the experience at De Lane Lea also did was cement in each of their hearts and minds just how much their future *had* to lie in music, to the extent that they now had little time for anything else. Brian was committed to another trip to Tenerife, but was aware that he was fading fast from the academic scene in preference to what was going on with Queen. At this point Roger decided to give up the market stall, although Freddie remained there for a while, joining forces with Alan Mair who had a boot stall on the corner of their row. Geoff Higgins recalls, 'Fred had only been at the new stall a morning when he discovered that if he moved the till a shade, he could see right into the changing rooms of the dress shop directly opposite. He'd spend all day watching women undressing and trying on clothes and no one ever suspected a thing!'

Around November – for the regular income if for no other reason – Brian took up a full-time post teaching at Stockwell Manor School, a coeducational comprehensive which served the north Brixton area. Brian was popular with his class of thirty pupils, all of whom could relate to this new breed of teacher. In his stylish clothes, with his long hippy hair and fine-boned, almost vulnerable good looks, he made a healthy target for schoolgirl crushes. And for the boys? Says Brian:

'They never knew at the time that I was in a band and used to say, "Hey, you should play in a group, sir!"'

At the end of 1971 Queen were still being allowed the use of the De Lane Lea studios. This was immensely important because, although they had a following, they still needed that vital link to the record companies which the band were convinced would stem from working there. That faith was justified when, one day while they were playing, the studio received a visit from two men – John Anthony, who six months previously had promised to ring Queen, and College staff engineer at the then highly influential Trident Studios, Roy Thomas Baker. Roy and John were impressed by what they heard and were happy to accept a Queen demo tape after the sessions. Norman Sheffield, co-owner of Trident, listened to the tape, but sadly was not prepared to do anything more than say he found it interesting. So once again all the boys in Queen heard only a deafening silence.

Having got the bug, Queen now decided to take their demo and try their luck around the record companies – a bold move, for which they enlisted the help of their mate Ken Testi. Says Ken, 'It was high time. For too long Queen hadn't seemed to be going in any real direction. So I just got out the Yellow Pages and started looking up record companies. I tried making appointments over the phone and largely got the heave-ho, but some did agree to see us.' According to Ken's diary those record companies included CBS, Decca, Island, A&M, Polydor and MCA. It was a thankless task: many turned them down without even letting Ken beyond the reception desk. 'I've got a record of the names of all those people who told Brian and me that Queen were no good,' adds Ken.

Nevertheless in the new year one record company sat up and took notice. Tony Stratton-Smith, head of Charisma Records, decided he liked what he heard and wanted to sign Queen. Almost immediately he put a deal on the table – a deal which, for all their frustration, Queen turned down. There were two reasons. First, the money on offer wasn't a lot and they desperately needed to replace their equipment. But, more important, Charisma was a small label and they all felt that they could benefit from big muscle behind them. They liked Tony, but there's no room for sentiment in business and the fact that he didn't have the right resources made them shy away from him. Finally, Tony's biggest involvement was with the band Genesis, and Queen had a lurking suspicion that they would always play second fiddle.

Ken Testi reflects on the courage of that decision at the time: 'It simply boiled down to the fact that Queen had complete faith in themselves. They didn't fear that the first deal offered could have been the last – no way. Their confidence was enormous and that was one of the things that was so attractive about them. They were waiting for the right pieces to fall into place. It was just a matter of time.' Meanwhile, Ken had arranged with the Red Bus Company in Wardour Street for Queen to play a one-hour support session at Kings College Hospital in Denmark Hill on 10 March for a fee of £20. Freddie's playlist for that night ran: '1. "Son & Daughter" 2. "Great King Rat" 3. "Jesus" 4. "Night Comes Down" 5. "Liar" 6. "Keep Yourself Alive" 7. "See What a Fool I've Been" 8. "Stone Cold Crazy" 9. "Hangman" 10. "Jailhouse R" 11. "Bamalama".' Says Ken, 'All the companies who had shown interest in Queen turned up. Stratton-Smith was there too, and I think he still thought he was set with Queen because there was a row between them. Three or four other companies made encouraging noises as well, but as it happened, nothing came of it. The first six songs featured on the playlist for that night would end up on Queen's debut album more than a year later.

Right then, they could think of little else than cutting that first LP. They still had high hopes of Trident. Certainly Norman Sheffield remained interested, but he felt he needed to see them perform live before he would consider making a commitment. Propitiously the band were booked to play at a hospital dance in mid-March and so, at Roy Thomas Baker's urging, Norman's brother and business partner Barry went along to weigh them up. Queen were in their element that night, the audience reaction was enthusiastic, and any reservations that Barry had harboured evaporated. He offered them a contract with Trident Audio Productions on the spot; two months later, however, nothing had been signed.

After their experience with Mercury Records, neither Brian nor Roger was prepared to lose control of Queen's destiny; Freddie and John went along with this. As a result Queen made certain stipulations about the terms of any agreement: they demanded three separate contracts, individually covering publishing rights, management and recording. Trident did not take kindly to this, but considered Queen worth accommodating and agreed to draw up the necessary documents. But still they remained unsigned.

Next Trident set about kitting out the band with brand-new equipment and instruments, with the exception of Brian who wouldn't part with his Red Special. A full-time manager, American Jack Nelson, was employed to handle their daily affairs. Unknown to Queen at the time, Norman had been trying to sell them as part of a package deal, along with Eugene Wallace and Mark Ashton. But Nelson, who had been acting as adviser to the Sheffields in setting up their company, had been immediately attracted to the Queen tape and promptly took it to every good business manager he could think of, trying to get them to sign the band up. No one wanted to know, so he took on the job himself.

Brian watched these developments with increasing optimism. He felt so close to everything they had been working towards for so long that nothing else mattered now. He had long since drifted away from work on his PhD, which seemed a huge waste of his talents to his supervisor. Ken Reay explains, 'We did still keep a desk there for Brian for a while, and occasionally he'd drift in and do some work, but music was tugging him away all the time. It's a real pity that he didn't just give it that little extra push. I read the manuscript of his thesis and helped with corrections. His work was of very good quality. If he had just gone to the bother of getting it typed up and submitted he would have got his doctorate and become Dr Brian May.'

It was the same story at Stockwell Manor, where Brian had been teaching all year. Mike Winsor, science teacher there at the time, clearly recalls. 'Brian was obviously contemplating a full-time career in music. He was a conscientious teacher, a likeable colleague and had very good relations with his pupils, and some of the staff thought he really ought not to throw that away. I remember Mr Simon, then head of the maths department, who was an old-fashioned teacher nearing retirement, vigorously counselling Brian one lunchtime to consider *very* carefully the wisdom of leaving the teaching profession with "its prospects, security and pension" and taking a real risk in a notoriously unpredictable business like music! I couldn't help but be reminded of this some years later,' adds Mike, 'when Brian, along with the rest of Queen, was cited in the *Guinness Book of Records* as being one of the highest salary earners of that particular year!'

Jack Nelson, meantime, had been busy trying to interest the music giant EMI in giving Queen a recording deal. Ten years earlier the Beatles had been turned down by Decca before being offered to and promptly signed by EMI. History looked to be repeating itself as Decca were given the chance of Queen and rejected them before Nelson approached EMI. Only this time EMI too rejected them. – not, however, because they didn't want Queen. They just didn't want the other two passengers whom Trident insisted they also sign up. Neither side would budge, and so EMI pulled out.

The whole band were disappointed at this turn of events, but Trident were unrepentant and set them to work on their first album. Unfortunately, however, Queen were allocated what was called downtime, which meant that they would only be allowed the use of a studio as long as no other artiste required it. This meant hanging around for hours on end, often days, hoping to snatch some time here and there behind the backs of, say, David Bowie, Elton John and the Stones. Queen did not think much of this demoralizing treatment, but were in no position to complain. One day when they were sitting about waiting for their chance to nip in and lay down some tracks, producer Robin Cable was working in an adjoining studio experimenting with a Beach Boys number, 'I Can Hear Music'. Cable had previously overheard Freddie singing and now roped him in to perform the song for him. Freddie promptly took advantage of the situation by enlisting first Roger and then Brian, until Robin suddenly found Queen commandeering his whole production. The result stood up well, though, and Robin promised that if he ever did anything with the song he'd let them know.

About this time Roger graduated from North London Polytechnic with his degree in biology; John had also got a first in electronic engineering. For his part Freddie, the former graphics student, decided to design a special logo for Queen. This time it befitted their image and incorporated all their birth signs.

Although September was almost out, still no contracts had been signed with Trident; but after considerable pressure from the band the company did agree to start paying them a weekly wage. After some stiff negotiation £20 each was the figure finally settled upon. It didn't go far since London was an expensive place to live in, but it was something and they had to be happy with that.

On 1 November Queen at last signed with Trident Audio Productions. The band were to record for Trident, who in turn would procure the very best recording and distribution deal they could wrest from a major record label. In fairness, Trident were taking a chance: no other independent production company to date had taken on full responsibility for a rock band.

Five days later Queen were booked to play a gig at the Pheasantry, an enormous club in Chelsea's King's Road. Trident had invited as many record company executives as they could entice to attend. Technical problems with the PA, however, threw a spanner in the works; although John Deacon's electronics expertise rescued them from total disaster, when they came to play they were full of nervous tension and it showed.

Queen's first album was completed at the end of November. It had not been conceived under the greatest of circumstances and, although Trident professed themselves pleased with it, the band were not happy with the mixes and also discovered that one track had been overdubbed on to the wrong backing tape. Roy Thomas Baker and Brian insisted on having more time to rectify this error and indeed to tidy up the recording in general, with the band having a little more control over the general sound. By January 1973 the album was finally ready, but still they had no record company to press and distribute it for sale. Undeterred, Jack Nelson soldiered on and in the end it was Ronnie Beck, an executive of Feldman Music Co., who played a crucial role in getting Queen to the attention of the right person.

Roy Featherstone, one of EMI's top executives, had been wading through the piles of hopeful tapes proffered to him at the annual Midem festival in Cannes in the south of France, but had found nothing to excite him. Then Beck suggested he listen to the Queen tape – and Featherstone was blown away. Beck, working on the age-old maxim that nothing makes someone jump quicker than to think that a rival is after the same product, quickly spun Roy the story that a couple of other record companies were showing interest in the band. Featherstone immediately cabled Trident, urging Queen not to sign anything until he had had a chance to speak to them.

The timing was perfect, for things had just begun to look up all round – Queen had managed to get themselves booked for a special session of a BBC Radio 1 programme, *Sounds of the Seventies*. Brian was delighted. This meant big exposure of a kind they had hitherto only dreamed of. The session was recorded at the BBC's Maida Vale studios with producer Bernie Andrews and went out on 15 February 1973. The listeners' response was so positive that EMI dithered no longer and immediately set about signing up Queen.

It has to be said that potentially Trident could have cost Queen dear at this juncture, because once again they put EMI over a barrel and insisted that Queen came as part of a package. EMI were very reluctant: they only wanted Queen, and their frustration ran high. The procrastinations caused Queen weeks of worry before they finally found themselves in the EMI offices in March, to sign their first recording contract. The deal was for the UK and Europe and constituted grounds for delirium to everyone – except Brian, who was inwardly worried. He still hadn't forgotten Mercury Records and the way things had turned out there after a rosy beginning.

With this deal sewn up, all eyes swept across the Atlantic to the American market. In April Queen performed a showcase gig at London's Marquee Club for the purpose of impressing Jack Holtzman, managing director of Elektra Records in New York. Holtzman had expressed an interest in signing the band, and Jack Nelson had promised him a live performance to help him make up his mind. With so much riding on that one gig it would have been easy to blow it, but that night Queen excelled themselves and Holtzman went away well pleased; their coveted US contract was effectively in the bag.

Throughout the spring Queen played gigs just as they had done in the past, but now bolstered with the confidence that only signing with a major record label can give. They were blossoming out, experimenting with their stage clothes and using dramatic make-up to accentuate their features, and the clever use of white and ultraviolet lighting added to the overall uniqueness of their shows. As before, Liverpool was a favourite stomping ground. Here they had become almost a cult, with a large proportion of the audience imitating the band by dressing in all black or all white.

Once their old Ibex friend Mike Bersin came to see them backstage. 'I went into the dressing room,' says Mike, 'and walked in on Freddie pacing up and down repeating, "What can I say? Give me something to say." Then someone handed him a copy of that day's *Liverpool Echo*. Still pacing up and down, Freddie furiously flicked through it. I really didn't know what was going on, but then he said "OK" and put it down, and I went out front to watch Queen perform. Right away Freddie walked up to the mike and said, "Good evening, Liverpool." The audience that night was typical – kind of rough – and Freddie looked out and simply added, "Nice one, Kevin" – a reference to striker Kevin Keegan, who'd scored a vital goal for Liverpool Football Club that week. Well, the whole place erupted! That was them on Queen's side. That's the sort of care Freddie always took.'

By May 1973 the British music scene had dramatically changed. The independent progressive and hard rock of the beginning of the decade had been infiltrated by the gentler urgings of folk-rock from the likes of Lindisfarne and Canadian singer-songwriter Neil Young, by the American balladeer heart-throb David Cassidy, by the bizarre Alice Cooper and by David Bowie's alter ego Ziggy Stardust, complete with orange hair and skimpy kimono. But the new music had gathered momentum and gone full commercial conveyor-belt glam rock, with bands like Sweet, Slade, T-Rex and Mud dominating the charts.

Robin Cable chose this moment to unearth the single 'I Can Hear Music', which Brian, Freddie and Roger had recorded with him the previous year and which EMI had been persuaded to release. With the imminent launch of the debut album no one was prepared to use the Queen name, and so they chose to send up the chart-topping Gary Glitter. Famous for his extravagant silver-sequinned costumes and six-inch platform silver boots, Gary was widely considered to be the king of glam rock – although he personally refutes this opinion and says Marc Bolan had seized that crown a year earlier.

Says Gary, 'This title "glam rock" was more of a phrase coined by journalists, anyway. I guess it was really theatrical rock. Instead of having the attitude "Let's not bother dressing up or anything, we'll let the music speak for itself", people like Freddie, Bryan Ferry, Bowie, Bolan and myself *liked* dressing up, being theatrical and having fun. It had a little bit more to it than just playing, you know. Bands like the Beatles had stopped making a statement through their clothes – they'd begun wearing chunky sweaters and sporting beards. Our attitude was that we had the opportunity of being up there on stage, so let's get dressed up and enjoy it. The press love to put people into categories – and yet bands like Queen, us and Bolan would appear in anything from heavy metal magazines to teeny mags to *Gardener's World*. We'd spread right across.'

The decision to release the single under the name of Larry Lurex was not the band's. 'No, we had no control,' confirms Brian. 'We all had a small session fee and Robin, along with Trident, owned the record. It was they who decided to put it out. By then it was already more or less unimportant for us. All we were concerned about was our album.' No offence had been intended to Glitter, and none was taken by him. Gary laughs, 'My reaction was that it was great! It's the highest honour for any performer to have people copying you. It's a form of flattery – let's face it – and Queen only meant it in fun, which is what music should be.' But the joke seriously backfired. Determined to be upset at what they saw as satire, people refused to buy the record and DJs wouldn't play it:

the whole thing went by almost unnoticed.

It was easy to forget their gaffe, however, because the band were now immersing themselves in the design of their first album cover. They enlisted a photographer friend, Doug Puddifoot, and set to work in Freddie's flat. As they sifted through old photographs for ideas, Freddie kept trying to veto all suggestions because he didn't look fabulous enough. Nevertheless, Brain and Freddie carefully cut the best of the pictures to shape for the collage which they had decided should go on the back of the cover.

Several thoughts for the front cover ricocheted around until they came up with the concept of evoking a sense of Victorian times, using sepia tinting against a maroon oval background. It was good, but meantime Brian had had what he felt was a better idea. Photography had always interested him and he was forever experimenting with effects. He stretched coloured plastic over the camera lens and had the band's photograph taken through that, which produced a weird, distorted look. Finally they submitted all their ideas to EMI for consideration.

Next they were required to select the track which they felt should become their first single. They decided upon 'Keep Yourself Alive', penned by Brian with 'Son and Daughter', also Brian's composition, on the B-side. It was released in Britain on 6 July, and Trident promised that European release would quickly follow. The record received mixed reviews from the music press. With no yardstick to go by, Brian didn't know whether to be pleased or not. He had no idea what lay ahead with rock critics.

What Brian did know, even then, was that the real importance lay in radio play. Where music papers' readership numbered thousands weekly or monthly, millions listened daily to radio. So it was extremely disappointing that, although the single was sent out to all local and regional radio stations for inclusion on their playlists, none except Radio Luxembourg picked it up. Licensed commercial radio stations would not appear for another few months and BBC Radio 1 – which therefore enjoyed a virtual monopoly of the pop airwaves – sadly rejected Queen five times on the trot. Not surprisingly 'Keep Yourself Alive' failed to chart.

The album followed one week later, on the 13th, and was entitled *Queen*. Early pressings of albums, called white labels, are doled out in advance for promotional purposes. They carry no band name because the labels and sleeves are still being printed, and so to be of any value they must be accompanied by the group's publicity material. EMI sent a white label to BBC Television – but unfortunately forgot the publicity bumph.

Luckily, though, Queen themselves had sent an advance copy direct to BBC DJ Bob Harris, presenter of one of the seventies' most popular television rock programmes, *The Old Grey Whistle Test*. The programme's unusual name originated from an old Tin Pan Alley phrase which referred to the time when there were literally songwriting factories. Writers worked from 9 a.m. to 5 p.m., five days a week, churning out songs. On Fridays, the best of these would be tried out on the cleaners who were dubbed 'the old greys'. If the 'greys' could whistle a tune after just one hearing it was thought to be a potential hit!

Queen certainly passed the test for Bob Harris. He recalls, 'The first moment I played the white label I absolutely loved it. I thought the track "Keep Yourself Alive" was wonderful. We decided to put it in the programme the very next week, accompanied by some black and white footage. *Whistle Test* often used old cartoon footage, and in this case we used a cartoon from the thirties of an overcrowded train hurtling out of control down a really steep hill, with loads of people clinging for dear life on to the sides. The exciting imagery, I thought, matched the raw excitement of Queen's music.'

That, enthusiasm, alas, was not shared by the general public, and initial sales were much slower than anyone had hoped for. But it was a start, and within a month Trident had bundled Queen into Shepperton studios to make a promotional film for despatch to Europe and America. For good measure they now took on board an experienced freelance publicist, Tony Brainsby, to handle the band's public relations.

'When Queen came to see me at my office,' explains Tony, 'it was the first time we'd met and they made a very deep impression. Obviously Freddie with his black nail varnish and everything stuck out the most, but I'm not really talking visually. Of all the bands I've looked after, only two had a particular effect on me. One was Thin Lizzy and the other was Queen. They knew their own identity in ways that are very hard to convey – they not only knew exactly what they wanted but also that they would be big, and it was just a process of trial and error in finding their way. Someone doing my kind of job is halfway there when a band have that kind of belief in themselves – coupled of course with the talent to back it up, which they had in abundance. That kind of conviction is what makes stars.'

After that meeting Brainsby went to watch Queen perform at one of the London polytechnics, which confirmed his instincts. 'They were playing standing on the floor for that gig,' he recalls. 'What I mean is, there was no stage and the band were at the same level as everyone else, which can be quite a disadvantage. But Queen were remarkable that night, and I knew what I was seeing was real talent.'

Tony was also quick to form opinions on the personalities of some of his new charges. 'In those days Freddie was a very inwardly aggressive and angry man in the sense that he knew he should be a star and he wasn't – yet. It's not a side of him that too many people were allowed to see, but it was definitely all the way through him. He felt that stardom was his by rights, and he was extremely frustrated at the time it seemed to be taking for him to reach it. He had an incredible need for acceptance. When I bumped into him years later, in the mid-eighties, he had mellowed enormously. But ten or twelve years before it was a very different story and that aggression, that energy was what gave him the fight.'

'Yet although Freddie's voice was unique, Queen's identity struck me right from the start as coming from Brian and his incredible guitar sound.' He continues: 'Brian was always very quiet and extremely modest – a rather intelligent guy, too, of course. It was Brian who gave me the chance to create Queen's first major press because of his Red Special. It was a great angle – here we had not only a brilliant guitarist but someone who got all those sounds out of a home-made guitar, for God's sake! It was a heaven-sent instant introduction into all the important music mags, and made a great talking point which started to get them noticed.'

Britain at this time was plunged into economic crisis. A miners' strike led to a series of enforced power cuts and the country was put on a three-day working week. In the summer of 1973 when Brian was on the look-out for work, jobs were understandably scarce. But he did manage to find something part-time.

That didn't matter too much, though, for soon he and the rest of the band were hard at work in the studio on the second album, and this time there was no question of being put on downtime. Round about now, too, his former astronomy colleagues Ken Reay and Tom Hicks had submitted to the Monthly Notices of the Royal Astronomical Society the paper on which they had all jointly worked. Says Tom, 'Brian had done a lot of the early work, then Ken and I continued when he drifted away. So when we submitted the paper to the RAS it was in our three names.

Papers have to be refereed by other scientists, who make comments on it, and if they decide the work is good enough to be published they accept it. And they did. We were delighted.'

September marked the US release of the *Queen* album on the Elektra label. It attracted fairly good radio exposure and as a result cracked the top hundred in the US Billboard chart – no mean achievement for a first time British band. But 'Keep Yourself Alive' failed to chart in the States, just as it had failed in the UK.

Again undaunted, Jack Nelson stubbornly beavered away at forcing Queen upon the public's awareness. Now he decided he needed to get them out there to be seen on tour. He knew Bob Hirschmann, manager of the then highly popular band Mott the Hoople. Hoople, named after the 1967 novel by Willard Manus and fronted by lead singer Ian Hunter, had had a hit the previous year with 'All the Young Dudes' and had recently followed that up with 'All the Way from Memphis', currently sitting at number ten in the UK singles chart. Jack wanted Bob to take Queen on as support band for Mott's forthcoming British tour but Hirschmann was highly reluctant, unsure that Queen had the bottle to handle the job; a £3,000 contribution to sound and lights persuaded him to swallow his doubts and allow Queen to be the opening act.

'Before that tour with Hoople,' recalls Tom Hicks, 'Queen played a warm-up gig at Imperial College. It was a free concert for the physics students and I went along to see Brian. I was knocked out by the difference in their playing, and it was deafening too – the loudest band on the planet. I tell you, you heard it through your chest that night and that's not a joke!' Their performance earned them a glowing review from journalist Rosemary Horide, who ended with the prophecy that on the Mott tour 'Queen could turn out to be a bit more than just a support band.'

The month-long tour, which included a quick raid across the border into Scotland, kicked off on 12 November at Leeds Town Hall and was quite an experience for the band. Brian's incredible virtuosity was of a kind that audiences had rarely seen before. By clever use of echo on his guitar he managed to create the impression that two guitarists were dueting, which caused many people to swivel in their seats as they searched in vain for the other musician. Their last date was on 14 December at the Hammersmith Odeon in London, and it was here that Brian's parents first saw him perform with Queen. They were astounded at the response their son and the band elicited from the thousands of young people corralled in the theatre.

It had been a whopping success as far as public acclaim was concerned, but most of the music press either panned them or just ignored them. Queen tried not to let it matter, telling themselves that what *did* matter was that Hoople had liked them and, on the strength of that UK tour, had invited them to be support band on their forthcoming tour of the States.

As the year drew to a close sales of their album had picked up, and the feeling at street level was that Queen were one of the most exciting prospects on the horizon. It was a pity that the press were so blatantly out of touch. They were nothing but hostile now and didn't seem to realize that the more they poked sticks at the band, the more Queen played up to it as their only defence against the more personal and hurtful slurs cast upon them.

Tony Brainsby holds forthright views on the subject of press criticism. 'Queen were accused of being a hype band. The reason was that their management had a lot of money behind them and also that I got them a lot of press coverage, concert bookings, interviews etc. If you're a success too quickly, you're automatically accused of being a hype band even if, as in their case, you're bloody good. What people forget, too, is that Queen had a huge following even before they made hit records. When you're getting fan mail and phone calls at that stage, you know you've got something special on your hands. The quirky thing is that the vast majority of their early fans were mums. There was one really old lady in particular who was so besotted with them that she'd write and ring all the time!'

He continues, 'The press saw Queen, particularly with Freddie being the way he was, as an easy target. You get some journalist who wants to make a name for himself and he'll latch on to an easy band to attack. In those days, of course, it was considered essential to have the music press on your side. Papers like *Disc*, *Melody Maker* and *NME* were far more important and influential than they are today. It's my belief that they felt Queen were in danger firstly of being too big and secondly of achieving it too quickly, and that's why they went for them. Of course it hurt the band. Brian, like the others, was always extremely anxious about their press image and what was being said about them. But they were also extremely excited when good things happened – like the first time there was a pop poster of them in, say, *Jackie* magazine, which used to be a landmark in any band's career. So it wasn't all bad.'

Queen played their final gig of 1973 on 28 December at the Top

Rank Club in Liverpool, supporting 10cc. Ken Testi had secured them this booking months earlier – one of the last things he had done for Queen before they'd parted company. After being signed to EMI Brian remembered how much Ken had helped them in the past and asked him to come on board as a salaried member of the team. Ken would have dearly loved to accept the offer but family commitments prevented him. 'It was a tough break for me,' he admits. 'It seemed that it was everything my life had been leading up to at that point, and I had to turn round and say no. But the simple fact was, my mother and family needed me more.' When Queen turned up at the Liverpool Rank they discovered that a local band called Great Day was also on the bill; among its line-up was Ken Testi. It was a good night.

That Christmas show ended a special year for Queen. 'Britain's Biggest Unknowns', they were dubbed. Not for much longer.

4

QUEENMANIA

For Brian 1974 began with health problems. At the end of January Queen were booked to headline at two gigs at a three-day open-air music festival in Melbourne, and like everyone else he had to have the appropriate inoculations. Almost immediately he became very feverish and his arm began to swell up dangerously. It was quickly discovered that the needle used on him had been dirty and consequently he had developed gangrene. During the first crucial days it was touch and go whether he would lose his arm.

Apart from the obvious worry this caused it also meant that rehearsals for their first headlining foreign gig went out of the window. As far as Queen were concerned the festival was doomed anyway. They couldn't do a thing right. For a start, they discovered that severe umbrage had been taken by the other acts on the bill – as well as the promoters – that a British band which nobody had heard of was head-lining over their own established groups. Then Queen's specially designed lighting rig, with which they had hoped to wow the audience, proved to be a major bone of contention. Queen had brought over their own crew to make sure that the complicated apparatus was worked properly, which upset the backstage people on site. Done out of their fee, the local technicians went out of their way to make life difficult. On top of this, to get the most out of the lighting effects, the band had to wait until darkness fell before going on stage, by which time the audience, impatient at the delay, was derisively slow-handclapping. Then the compere deliberately encouraged the discontent by introducing Queen as 'stuck-up pommies'.

As if all this wasn't enough, when they did take the stage Brian was in considerable pain and Freddie had an ear infection for which he had been taking antibiotics which were making him very sleepy. He couldn't hear himself sing, which put him off. Then in the midst of it all the lights gave out – quite clearly the result of sabotage.

Amazingly, though, through their music Queen forced their way across the barrier of hostility to reach a fairly large section of the audience, who by the end of the performance had made up their minds that they liked these 'stuck-up pommies' after all – very much. No one was more surprised than Brian when the last note rang out and they were greeted with a healthy roar from the crowd demanding an encore! It never happened. Before Queen could obligingly strike up, the compere rushed on and within seconds changed the audience's collective mind to holler instead for one of their own home-grown bands.

The awful sting of humiliation was complete the following day when the press joined in, slating them right royally. It was the last straw. Brian's arm was still worrying him and Freddie's ear infection had worsened, sending his temperature soaring. They cancelled that night's performance, ignoring the wrath of the promoters, and boarded the first plane home. On the long flight Brian had plenty time to nurse his aching arm and morosely reflect on just how much the whole fiasco had cost them. Not only had they had to pay their own return fares but the experience itself, so early in their career, had been painful in every way. 'None of us thought it was disastrous,' admits Brian. 'We just thought – one day we'll be back. And we were.' But at the time they acquired bad relations with the Australian press to add to the growing army of hacks already against them in Britain.

But the punters weren't against Queen. In February *NME* readers voted Queen the second Most Promising New Name. That same month Elektra released 'Liar' as a second single from *Queen*, but it didn't do anything. All eyes now turned to the release of the next single, scheduled for later in the month.

By now Ronnie Fowler, head of EMI's promotional department, had entered the fray. He had played a white label of the new single and adored it. Without a care for the fact that he was running up huge expenses, he set about pestering the living daylights out of anyone he felt could help give Queen the big push they desperately needed. He had Queen on the brain and expected everyone else to be the same. When Robin Nash, producer of BBC TV's *Top of the Pops*, rang him to ask if he could suggest anyone to fill a last-minute vacancy on that week's show, Ronnie went in with both feet and offered Queen.

Nash asked to hear a demo and one was immediately rushed round; he liked it. The only problem was, since artistes usually mimed to specially recorded backing tracks of their songs, the demo wouldn't do. This was Tuesday and the programme went out on Thursday. That night Ronnie contacted Who guitarist Pete Townshend, whom Fowler knew was recording in London right then, to ask if Queen could borrow studio time to record the necessary backing tape. Next day the four turned up flushed at the BBC studios to pre-record their appearance on the show.

On 21 February 1974 Queen appeared for the first time on *Top of the Pops*, performing 'Seven Seas of Rhye' – a single which hadn't yet been officially released. That evening Brian, Roger, John and Freddie all congregated on the pavement outside an electrical shop window, waiting to watch themselves through the glass on the bank of display televisions inside. With the momentum begun, next day Ronnie and Jack Nelson went all out to capitalize on the previous night's national exposure by hitting Radio 1 with white label copies of the single. EMI rush-released it on the 23rd, and by the second week of March it would scale the singles chart to a startling number ten.

By now their second album, *Queen II* (originally going to be called *Over the Top*), ought to have been in the shops, but it had been held up by a spelling error on the cover. In normal times this would not have constituted much of a delay, but Britain was still staggering along on a three-day week and now there was an oil crisis too, which meant that even more working time was lost due to strict government restrictions on the use of electricity.

They turned their minds to their forthcoming first British headlining tour, and started to consider what they would wear. To date they had made do with whatever they could lay their hands on at Kensington Market, and enlisted the services of their seamstress friend, but for Brian and Freddie the time had definitely arrived to splash out on professional clobber. They chose zany top fashion designer Zandra Rhodes.

'They came to me, I think, because they'd seen some of the outfits I'd designed for Marc Bolan and liked them,' says Zandra. 'At the time, too, I was seen as a very colourful bird of paradise with my bold make-up, freaky hair and flowing scarves everywhere, and I think they were drawn to that imagery.' She continues, 'Brian was very sweet. He's so tall, and I still have this clear mental image of him stooping right over to save braining himself on the low ceiling as he and Freddie tramped up the rickety winding staircase to my Paddington workshop.'

Having safely negotiated the stairs, Brian and Freddie discovered there was a price to pay for their desire to shine on stage. 'Well, obviously they had to try things on,' explains Zandra, 'and so they both had to strip off in front of me and my machinists. We were used to it, but they weren't! Poor guys, they were so shy – especially Brian.'

Zandra turned out some truly stunning outfits, indulging freely in yards of sumptuous satin, silk and velvet, all beautifully embroidered in minute detail. 'Everything was very positive in those days. What's called the seventies' style is really late sixties' fashion. We'd thankfully evolved from the dreary miniskirt into fabulously free-flowing skirts, flares and loads of scarves. Colour was vital, too.'

After rehearsing hard, their first headlining UK tour began on 1 March 1974 at the Blackpool Winter Gardens. Topping the bill was very different from playing support. In fact it was quite hard going, especially for the first couple of gigs, because Brian's arm was still hurting him and they didn't have a support band. Then a Liverpool group, Nutz, joined them for the remaining dates. It was during this tour that the audience began the habit of singing 'God Save the Queen' while awaiting the band's arrival. In time it also became a regular thing for Queen to close their shows with the National Anthem.

'Seven Seas of Rhye' entered the UK singles chart five days into their tour, sending the band into transports of delight. While it zoomed up to sit at number ten, on 8 March their second album, *Queen II*, was finally released on the public. On that album, a copy of which they sent to Bob Harris along with a note thanking him for his support, there appeared for the first time ever a white and black side as opposed to the traditional A and B. Within a week it was clear that the vast majority of their audiences had bought the album, for whenever the band played one of their new songs lots of people knew the words and were able to sing along. It was even more heartening when within two weeks it cracked the top forty in the album charts.

True to form, however, most of the music press slated it. Queen were ruthlessly criticized for having no depth and no feeling, and one writer went so far as to condemn them as the dregs of glam rock. Fortunately the punters who paid to see Queen perform didn't agree and came away from gigs thoroughly exhilarated. The meaty, mesmeric bass work from John and the driving surge of Roger's drums, coupled with Brian's powerful lead and Freddie's vibrant flamboyance, pumped adrenalin straight off the electrified stage into the faceless throng crowding the gloom beyond the footlights.

Occasionally, though, that adrenalin spilled out in negative ways. After a gig at Glasgow University, itself blighted by backstage problems, their next appearance of the tour was on 15 March at Stirling University. All went well with the actual performance and even the first three encores. However, when Queen refused to return for a fourth a small section of the overheated mob grew ugly. Within minutes a rash of fights had broken out. The police were called and Queen were locked in a kitchen for their own safety, while out in the hall a pitched battle raged. Two members of the audience were stabbed and two of the road crew also required hospital treatment – one for cuts, the other for concussion.

The upshot of that disturbance was that Queen's Birmingham date at Barbarella's two nights later was postponed until early April. They picked up their tour again at the Cleethorpes Winter Gardens and the press promptly jumped on their backs, running lurid headlines accusing Queen of inciting riots. That wasn't a reputation that the band wanted to court, so it was most unfortunate, when, in the last week of their tour after a gig on the Isle of Man, a party thrown in the hotel spun out of control. Slinking shamefaced off the island the following morning, they were quickly cheered by the news that *Queen II* had rocketed up the album charts to number seven. What's more, their first album, until now lethargically received in the charts, had managed to hitch itself up on the back of its successor's popularity to a respectable number forty-seven.

By the end of March people were being turned away at shows, as Sold Out signs sprang up nightly. Possibly the new adulation was temporarily going to their heads – in particular Freddie's – because during the day of their final gig, on 31 March at the Rainbow Theatre in London, a row erupted in the band. At one point Brian turned on Freddie and told him roundly that he was behaving like an old tart.

Unused to Brian losing his temper, Freddie took the attack to heart and stormed off. At first his absence was treated as a joke, but as time went on they started to get worried. Acting on a hunch, during the sound-check Brian turned up the volume on the mikes and began taunting at the top of his voice, 'Freddiepoos? Where are you?' Freddie burst furiously back into the theatre, and after glaring silently at each other they got back to work.

Paradoxically, although they shared a determination to succeed, Brian admits that in these early days the band had very little idea of what kind of long-term future they would have in the notoriously fickle music business. Their first ambition had simply been to make a record and have something tangible that they could say they had done. Having achieved that goal, their next aim had been to play some of the concert venues that were familiar to them. One of those was certainly the prestigious Rainbow, and so that night's gig was a culmination of their latest dream.

The capacity crowd loved them. John Harris had experimented with the hall's acoustics and devised a much better method of balancing the sound. The band played out of their skins, and for the first time Roger had poured beer on to one of his drums so that every time he hit it, it sent up a wild, frothy spray. It might not make a blind bit of difference to the sound but it looked great, as did Freddie in one of Zandra's extravagant white outfits. He called it his eagle suit, and every time he spread his arms, unfurling a mass of silky white pleats like wing feathers flexing ready for flight, it was as if the audience too spiralled higher with enthusiasm. It was the first time Queen had headlined at a major London venue and the panache with which they pulled it off astounded many vultures among the press. But once again Rosemary Horide, not in the least surprised at the tour's success, gave them a glowing review.

With the bit now well and truly between their teeth Queen were counting off the days for 12 April to arrive, for this was the date that they were to leave Britain to begin six weeks in America as support act to Mott the Hoople. They were pinning a great deal on this US tour. They already knew they got on well with Mott and, after their experience on the British tour, were looking forward to having a good time. But Queen were to find life on the road and the gigs themselves very different in the States – a lot tougher than back home. Each audience had to be won over from a cold start, and even getting to venues took longer than they had been used to. But it was all excellent experience.

In an attempt to tell America who the band were, Elektra released *Queen II* there three days before they flew out. But at their first gig, at Regis College in Denver on the 16th, they were met with a neutral audience. As usual, though, their music did the talking and the crowd quickly warmed to them.

At 1 May Queen were set to perform at the Harrisburg Farm Arena, in Pennsylvania, where they discovered that a second support act had been booked to play as well as themselves – the American band Aerosmith. A row broke out between the two groups as to who should be first on stage. It grew quite heated and Brian, tired of the squabbling, threw in his particular towel and wandered away backstage. There he met Aerosmith's lead guitarist Jo Perry, who was also cheesed off with the bickering. Since neither man gave a damn who got to play first, they left the others out front to get on with it and opened a bottle of Jack Daniels to christen their acquaintance.

The two guitarists found they liked each other a lot – and they liked the smooth-textured Tennessee whiskey even better. By the time an agreement was reached on that night's line-up Brian and Jo could scarcely stand straight, never mind play. Some desperate sense of self-preservation kept Brian from crumbling and he swears he played the entire performance from memory.

Next day he was amazed to be told that he had come out of his customary shell and had injected his playing with loads of fiery, spicy action – everyone thought he had been brilliant. Jo became a life-long friend, and from then on Brian followed two golden rules – to pile on the action and to steer clear of anything stronger than a pint before a gig.

The following week, during their New York gigs, Brian began to feel ill. He kept quiet about it at first, but inwardly he was worried. He'd never felt like this before. On 12 May, their final night in New York, Brian collapsed. On the assumption that it was exhaustion, he was strongly advised to rest before their next gig, which was in Boston.

Queen had already gained a reputation in that city for being hot stuff and they had been looking forward to appearing there. But when Brian woke up in the Parker House Hotel he knew something was dreadfully wrong. His whole body felt like lead, his head like a medicine ball, and when he dragged himself to a mirror he was shocked to discover that his skin had turned a ghastly yellow colour. A doctor was called immediately. The others waited anxiously, worried about Brian's health and concerned that they might have to call off the Boston gigs. In fact they had to cancel the whole tour, for Brian was diagnosed as suffering from hepatitis. That was the end of Queen's brave hopes of taking America by storm.

The highly infectious Brian was smuggled on board a plane back to Britain and ordered to stay in bed for the next six weeks. Elektra contacted everyone who had been in contact with him so that they could be quickly inoculated. The infection was attributed to the dirty needle with which Brian had been inoculated for the Australian tour, and which had already nearly lost him his arm due to gangrene. Now no one could be sure that he would ever fully recover from the hepatitis. Brian himself, however, was more concerned at the thought that he had let the band down badly.

While he was confined to bed he turned his time to good use by writing songs, for Queen were due to start recording their third album in the summer. Early in June the band took themselves off to the Rockfield Studios in Wales to rehearse, pen new material and lay down backing tracks. Brian had convinced himself that he was fit, but kept disappearing to be sick. He couldn't eat a thing and felt thoroughly miserable. Quite clearly he was still far from well.

As already arranged, they next began work at Trident Studios. For about three weeks everything went well; then Brian suddenly collapsed again. This time he was rushed to King's College Hospital where he underwent an emergency operation for a duodenal ulcer. Recently they had planned an American tour for September. Now, again because of him and his need to convalesce, it had to be scratched. This time he was devastated and, being an inveterate worrier, felt the band really might want to replace him. But he underestimated not just their friendship but also their enormous respect for his musicianship. The other three simply carried on at the studio under the aegis of producer Roy Thomas Baker.

When Brian got out of hospital he threw himself into the studio in London with a vengeance, finishing off songs such as 'Brighton Rock', 'Now I'm Here' – which he had written in hospital – and one called 'Killer Queen'. Working with him here was Gary Langhan. 'I was tape operator and assistant at Sarm Studios,' explains Gary, 'and Queen had chosen to finish off their new album there. My first meeting with Brian was when we were mixing the track 'Now I'm Here'. Brian is the ultimate professional, but he finds it *so* difficult to make a decision! Part of my job as tape op was to make sure that everything in the studio was working OK and that everyone had what they wanted, which included getting refreshments. Time and again Brian wouldn't be able to make his mind up whether to have tea or coffee, so you can imagine what it was like when it came to working on tracks! There is one thing, though. When it came to records, once he'd made a decision it was always the right one.' That first encounter for Gary began a long association with Brian and Queen.

In its first six months the *Queen II* album notched up enough sales – over 100,000 copies – to earn them a silver disc. Now Queen were beginning to be noticed, and requests for major radio and television interviews began filtering their way. Requests also came from the press, but were treated with caution given how savagely they had been treated by journalists to date.

'Killer Queen' was released on 11 October 1974 and by the 26th had stormed its way right up the charts to number two. Musically it had been a year of lightweight rock typified by Sparks, Leo Sayer and Mud; it had also seen the emergence of a new pop phenomenon in the shape of the Bay City Rollers, a Scottish band whose music, powered initially by unlimited hype, was aimed squarely at Britain's teeny-bopper market. 'Killer Queen', which Freddie once described as being 'about a high-class call girl', was in a category all of its own, yet it was held off the top by David Essex. The year before, the cheeky-faced Essex had portrayed the fictional doomed rock star Jim McLaine in the Puttnam/Lieberson film *That'll Be the Day*. His hit 'Gonna Make You a Star' was his first number one, and it staunchly refused to give way to Queen's latest single.

David says, 'Funnily enough "Killer Queen" is my favourite Queen record. With their stacked-up voices and guitar work it was extremely well produced – very clever. Everyone knows now that they were a highly innovative band, but it was obvious even then. I'd say Queen were probably the best British band to come out of the seventies.'

No small part of this success was the result of their stage image – an amalgam of appearance and props. As well as elaborate costumes, all four wore their hair long – Freddie adopted the popular feather-cut style. Then at a college dance one night Freddie had been wielding a microphone stand when its weighted base had accidentally dropped off, leaving him with only half the shaft. Finding this lighter portion much easier to play around with on stage, he had stuck with it. By the time he sensually caressed one arched palm up its chrome length during the opening lyrics of 'Killer Queen' on *Top of the Pops*, it had already become his trademark.

Were Queen a glam rock band, or not? At first they came in for criticism over the homosexual overtones they exuded, as if they had been the first to project this image – in fact the glam band Sweet had already been flaunting a bisexual image for some time, and far more blatantly. Looking back on the time when 'Killer Queen' exploded on to the charts, Sweet guitarist Andy Scott told Radio 1 DJ Alan Freeman, 'Maybe Queen were influenced by the Sweet – I'd like to think they were – but we opened the door and were left holding the handle because they rushed through like the wind!'

But with Queen, image and material were different concepts. Considering the general calibre of songs released by glam bands – songs such as Sweet's 'Blockbuster', Slade's 'Cum On Feel the Noize' and Mud's 'Tiger Feet' – it is inconceivable that they could seriously be equated with the sophisticated yet uncluttered composition of 'Killer Queen'. Gary Langhan heartily endorses this opinion. 'No way for me were Queen glam rock. For a start there was a far greater content to their records. I spent *days* with Brian working on the harmony structures, the guitar solos etc., for "Killer Queen". It was meticulous.'

Such care handsomely paid off as far as Brian was concerned, although initially he had had reservations about releasing it as a single. He now admits, 'I was always worried. When we put out "Killer Queen" everybody thought it was very commercial. I was worried people would put us in a category where they thought we were doing something light.' Yet at the same time this song unquestionably felt like the turning point in their career. To him it completely reflected Queen's kind of music – and of course it was a hit! Spurred on by this success, he was looking forward to 30 October and the start of their nineteen-date British tour, which had been arranged to compensate for the aborted US trip.

This time they intended to treat their audiences not only to a spectacular light show but also some firework effects, the likes of which no other band had contemplated. Unfortunately it left them wide open to attack from the press again, this time for being over-theatrical, but it was a big hit with the fans who considered themselves thoroughly entertained. Brian was at last fully recovered and went all out to prove it. Experimenting with ambitious stage wear only rivalled by Freddie's he rushed back and forth across the stage playing better than ever, mirroring the enthusiasm of the fans who had now started charging to the front in their desperate attempts to make closer contact with the band.

At Glasgow's Apollo Centre on 8 November – the same day that their third album, *Sheer Heart Attack* was released – the audience went way out of control and suddenly seized Freddie, dragging him clean off the stage into the seething, hysterical mob. Security dived in at once to rescue him, but in the ensuing melee fights broke out; the result was a few broken heads and damage to several rows of seats. Originally Queen had been booked to play just one date at London's Rainbow Theatre on 19 November, but such was the demand for tickets that promoter Mel Bush hastily organized a second night. Both gigs were captured on film, as vague notions of making a feature film of the band had now begun to take seed in some minds. Recording the shows also meant that they could perhaps later release a live album.

Although it was evident from the sell-out tour that Queen had finally arrived, their already poor relations with the press degenerated even further. It was a vicious circle: they were all understandably loath to cooperate with journalists who had done their level best to scupper the band's chances of success. But this reluctance only served to supply the press with more ammunition, and the insults flung at Queen promptly increased. Some reporters even went so far as to invent quotes.

By the end of 1974 it wasn't only with the press that Queen's relations were strained. In late December, after taking Europe by storm with more sell-out gigs and rocketing album sales, they returned to Britain to begin long and largely frustrating meetings with Trident over money. Their salaries had more than trebled by the time *Sheer Heart Attack* was released, but they felt this still wasn't enough and nowhere near commensurate with their success.

At this point Brian was living in a tiny and depressingly dingy room in a large and rambling house in Queens Gate, South Kensington; the only access was via the steamy boiler room in the basement. In fact, all the members of the band were living in insalubrious conditions. Freddie's bedsit was so damp that fungus hung off the ceiling and water constantly streamed through the wall. John was engaged to be married to his long-time girlfriend Veronica Tetzlaff, and felt they should be able to afford better accommodation. It didn't seem right to any of them that they were forced to exist in such spartan circumstances. In addition, they resented the fact that they couldn't pay lighting and sound companies, and the mounting debts affected them greatly.

Norman Sheffield, however, proved intractable and the situation became so bad that Queen contacted music business lawyer Jim Beach to find out how they could sever their connections with Trident. He took a fine-tooth comb through the terms of the three contracts which all four had signed in 1972, and then instigated what turned out to be lengthy negotiations with the Sheffield brothers.

Relieved to have handed over the fight to someone else, in January 1975 Brian took a short but well-earned rest in Tenerife. In the middle of the month 'Now I'm Here', the fourth single from their latest album, was released and John and Veronica got married. Trident were still refusing them more money, but Jim Beach kept a careful rein on everyone and encouraged the band to channel their energies into their imminent two-month American tour, due to start on 5 February at the Agora Theater in Columbus, Ohio.

This was Queen's first headlining US tour, and from the moment they boarded the plane they were gripped with nervous excitement. It was notoriously difficult at that time for British bands to achieve success in the States, and those who did had to work very hard for it. According to Tony Brainsby, it all went back to the sixties. 'In those days US bands couldn't get *arrested* in America!' he says. 'British bands were the only ones that counted, and I think the early seventies saw a backlash reaction to this. The Americans were getting their own back by being deliberately reticent about, and cool to, any British band trying to break into their market.' In Queen's case their image created an extra stumbling-block. American rock audiences were used to no-frills jeans and T-shirt machismo, and at first Queen's foppish finery was anathema to them.

During the flight, however, the band kept reminding themselves that 'Killer Queen' had reached number five in the US charts, so there ought not to be any real grounds for concern. They were right. The American rock critics severely clobbered them, determined to compare them unfavourably with Led Zeppelin, but tickets for each scheduled gig sold like hot cakes and several extra dates had to be hastily arranged to meet demand.

But the pace was crazy – at times they played two shows in one day, and not surprisingly within the first three weeks Freddie developed problems with his voice. By the time the Philadelphia show was over he could scarcely speak and a throat specialist from the University City Hospital was called in to examine him. Throat nodes were suspected, caused by him having strained his voice, and he was advised not to sing. Next night, regardless, he went on stage in Washington so as not to let the audience down, but it was obvious that he was struggling. He came off the stage in agony.

The following morning while Freddie consulted a Washington specialist, the rest of Queen waited anxiously for the diagnosis. Brian must have felt that America had put a jinx on them. Problems with his own health had cut short their first assault on the country and prevented their second from taking place at all. Now, on their third attempt to win over US audiences, it was Freddie's turn to be laid low.

Fortunately, it transpired that Freddie's condition, although very painful, was no more than severe laryngitis. Surgery would not be necessary – with antibiotics, painkillers, rest and the cancellation of the next six gigs the doctors said he would recover. It was a blow, but one they just had to take. When the shows did resume, however, it quickly became clear that the rest hadn't been long enough and Freddie relapsed, resulting in yet more cancellations. The entire tour was conducted on this on/off pattern, but even so they managed to perform thirty-eight gigs in the space of eight weeks.

During this tour the band were approached by Don Arden, a showbusiness manager who waved under their noses the carrot of a highly lucrative deal if they could break free from Trident. Developments in that quarter were frustratingly slow, but Arden claimed he could change all that if Queen would allow him to contact Norman Sheffield direct. The band agreed, and at first it appeared to have been the right decision. Norman and Barry agreed to let Queen go, and Brian, Roger, John and Freddie all signed a letter that authorized Arden to act on their behalf.

To get away from all these machinations, when the US tour ended they took themselves off to Hawaii to relax and recover their mental as well as their physical strength. There, they speculated on their forthcoming Japanese tour. They hoped to be given a warm reception – they simply did not anticipate blind hysteria.

As Queen stepped off their Japanese Airlines jumbo over three thousand teenagers, many clutching bouquets of red roses, screamed and waved from the airport rooftops. More fans strained dementedly against barely adequate security barriers inside the terminal building itself. Staring at all the banners, record sleeves and crumpled glossy publicity shots being thrust feverishly in their faces as Queen were shepherded through, Brian was thoroughly bemused. He couldn't believe that all these kids were actually chanting for them. 'We couldn't take it all in,' he says. 'It was like another world.'

The first concert, in Tokyo's Budokan Martial Arts Hall on 19 April, was a sell-out and the hysterical scenes at the airport paled into insignificance compared to the delirium exhibited by their audience that night. Brian recalls, 'They said, "The audience will be very quiet, but don't worry!" This was the start of something new in Japan. It's still with us in various ways.' Although the band's amps were working at full blast their music was completely drowned out by the screams, and finally the crazed crowd lost control and rushed the stage. In the stampede normally sturdy seats began to buckle like balsawood and to collapse under the sheer weight of the lunging bodies. For Queen it was a shocking, though strangely exhilarating, sight. Sensing that they were dicing with disaster, Freddie suddenly stopped the show and appealed to the frenzied fans to calm down. It took a while, but eventually it worked.

The whole twelve-day tour was a blistering success of a kind that Queen had never experienced before. This was Queenmania! Everywhere they went they were treated with enormous deference by their hosts and showered with expensive gifts. Brian believes that all this unvarnished adulation brought out a new strain of confidence, making them a little more extrovert in performance. On their final night – again at the Budokan – when the band came on stage for their encore they were dressed in traditional Japanese kimonos. The delighted audience went berserk at the compliment.

Someone who fully understood the impact that Japan had on Queen was Bay City Roller guitarist Eric Faulkner. That March Britain had witnessed the peak of Bay City Roller mania when the group seized the number one spot with 'Bye Bye Baby'. Love them or hate them, there was no denying the delirious mass adulation that these tartan-clad lads commanded – an adulation that Queen envied. Says Eric, 'Japan is like a separate planet for bands. They go absolutely mad for Western rock over there. In fact their own bands don't get a look in unless they are lookalikes of Western bands. It's crazy! At one time there was a Japanese lookalike Queen, Bay City Rollers and Status Quo. The press hysteria stories precede you, and by the time you arrive they're ready to swallow you whole! It's an unforgettable experience.'

As for the mania, Eric freely concedes, 'Of course you enjoy it. That's what you've worked for. There is a sense of deep satisfaction when you make it, but if it gets beyond that to the mania pitch you have to take it with a very big pinch of salt. If you believe it, you'll go clean off your head.' He goes on, 'This idolization stuff, though, is weird. Fans hang on your every word. You definitely get a sense of power. You just have to wave at a particular section of your crowd and there's a major freak-out, and you think, God! What's happening here? It's a strange world. You end up looking out at it from the inside – that's if you can see past the wall of bodyguards. I don't know about Queen envying us. But, to be honest, if I could have spoken to Brian then, I'd have told him he wouldn't want to go through what we went through.'

As well as giving them the opportunity to experience the effects of being hero-worshipped, Queen's first taste of Japan had also instilled in them a fascination for the country's culture, as their publicist can vouch. 'They were all smitten,' says Brainsby. 'Couldn't wait to buy all things Japanese. But Freddie was the most affected in the long run. He once spent all his Japanese royalties on Japanese antiques and artefacts – and why not? It had been such a thrilling time for them. Japan was the first country to fall. They made it big there before making it big in their own country. So of course it made a huge impression on them.'

Their feelings of exhilaration, however, were soon knocked out of them when they returned home. The Trident deal had fallen through. There was nothing for it but to let their lawyer haggle his way through the mire.

Meanwhile Brian busied himself with work on their fourth album. They had all benefited from their recent experiences and the new material, reflecting this stimulus, looked to be the most promising yet. Incessantly he sought new ways to extract ever more sophisticated harmonies and effects of all kinds from his guitar, and Queen steadfastly refused to fall back on the synthesizers favoured by many bands at this time. True sounds from real instruments had no equal, and what Brian managed to create on his Red Special was already becoming the envy of many of his fellow musicians.

It was in the summer of 1975 that two musicians took that envy one step further. The group Sparks, fronted by former child models Ron and Russell Mael, had enjoyed a handful of chart hits and the brothers approached Brian in the hope of luring him away from Queen – who, they maintained, were drying up. Brian knew Ron and Russ and was flattered by the proposition. He didn't, however, remotely consider accepting the offer. Queen meant far too much to him and his commitment was solid.

Now, at last, some major progress was being achieved in breaking the deadlock with Trident, and in August severance agreements were finally prepared for signature. EMI were to be given more direct control in the publishing and recording fields, while Queen, unshackled, were free to seek new management. The downside was that they had to cough up £100,000 in severance fees to Trident, plus the rights to 1 per cent of album royalties. Says Brian, 'We effectively had to trade the first three albums' sales up to that point for our future.' In addition, Jack Nelson had recently arranged another American tour and the tickets had already been sold. As a result of the change of management the tour was scrapped, which meant a substantial loss for everyone. So, what with the loss of future royalties, Queen were in the ironical situation of being effectively broke again. Not only that, but the cancellation of the US tour heralded rumours that the band were about to split up. Speculation gathered momentum, inferring all sorts of bitter internal feuding – none of which was true.

It was a difficult time all round, and they were not out of the wood yet. Management was clearly going to be a tricky issue for some time. Don Arden's promise to take on this role after they got rid of Trident came to nothing, so they set about drawing up a short list. Led Zeppelin's manager, Peter Grant, came first, but he wanted Queen to sign to Zeppelin's own production and record company, Swan Song, which was unacceptable. The second candidate, 10cc's manager, proved elusive to trace, despite Jim Beach's best efforts; so they turned their attentions to John Reid, who managed the hugely successful Elton John. Reid expressed an interest, and by the end of September 1975 he had become Queen's new manager.

Freddie's feelings on parting from the Sheffields were graphic. He announced, 'As far as Queen are concerned our old management is deceased. They cease to exist in any capacity with us whatsoever. One leaves them behind, like one leaves excreta. We feel so relieved!'

John Reid's first act was to hire a day-to-day personal manager for Queen, a former colleague called Pete Brown. Says Pete, 'That was me for the next seven years. I'd go everywhere with them, to recording studios, gigs, on tour – the lot.' He jokes, 'I can always remember Freddie saying, "I decided John Reid was the right person for the job of our manager the moment he fluttered his eyelashes at me!" Seriously, Queen really were in dire need of help then. Their finances were in a total mess.'

Reid's first step in this direction was to help Jim find £100,000 for Queen to pay off Trident before the November deadline. That meant nailing a music publishing deal – and fast. EMI stepped into the breach and offered to advance them this sum against future royalties. Next, an enormous party was thrown at the London Coliseum. It was ostensibly to celebrate the new partnership, but in a blaze of publicity, during the course of the party Queen were presented with a slew of gold and silver discs for the sales of 'Killer Queen' and their first three albums.

Their fourth album, meanwhile, was very much in the making. This time they used six separate studios in all. Pete Brown recalls, 'Once, three of them were working in three different studios at the same time, which had never been done before.' By October the band had unanimously agreed that the track they wanted to do as their next single was a composition of Freddie's called 'Bohemian Rhapsody'. John Reid was flabbergasted – it was an unheard of six-minute-long number and distinctly operatic. Pete states, 'A lot of us thought Queen were quite mad considering this track as their single. I tried to dissuade them, saying it was far too long, and privately John Deacon agreed with me. But Brian, Freddie and Roger were emphatic. They felt very strongly that they needed to establish their credibility and completely dug in their heels.'

Gary Langhan remembers that resistance well. 'I suppose you could call it arrogance, but only in that it stemmed from total belief in the number. Their attitude to it being twice the usual time slot allocated to each record on radio was: well, if that's the case then the DJs will just have to play one less record that day. And if they play "Bohemian Rhapsody" three times a day that's just three less other records on their list.' He goes on, 'I was standing at the back of the control room the day "Bohemian Rhapsody" was completed, and I knew I was hearing the greatest piece of music I was ever likely to hear. There's two feelings you get in your body about a new number. One's in your head, and that one can fool you time and again. But the other's in your stomach, when you *know*. That time, it got me right in the pit of my stomach. Queen knew it too.'

Initially John Reid, however, had reservations and felt it should be edited down or they would never get any airplay. But once he became aware of the band's utter conviction he too fought tooth and nail to keep it at the original length, and that is how the single went to press. Subsequently, the story goes, Freddie went to see Kenny Everett, a DJ friend he had cultivated a few years before, taking with him an advance copy of the disc to see what he thought about it; Brian, however, maintained that Kenny came to the playback. Either way, at first Everett had doubts, but as soon as he heard the single his response was rapturous: 'It could be half an hour long – it's going to be number one for centuries!'

'Bohemian Rhapsody' had not yet been accepted by the radio station's playlists, but the renegade DJ was not renowned for abiding by the rules. Pete laughs, 'Oh, Kenny was great. For two days he played "Bo Rhap" on air practically non-stop. He'd say, "Oops, my finger's slipped!" and he'd play it.' Within minutes of its first spin the radio station switchboard was jammed with calls from listeners demanding to know when they could buy this great new single.

On 31 October 'Bohemian Rhapsody' was officially released, and this time it sported a picture cover. For four years Queen had skiffed in and out of musical styles, never quite being progressive, never quite being glam rock, picking up experience, absorbing influences even if only to discard them, and always carving a new unlabelled vein of their own which defied definition. Now the stunning marriage of rock and opera knocked the music industry sideways.

It was really like three songs merged into one. From a simple ballad beginning it segues into complicated multi-tracking harmonic operatics – over 180 vocal overdubs – before bursting into out-and-out foot-stomping heavy rock. It was the most positive statement of their creativity yet, totally impossible to compare with anything else around, and it provoked an equally positive reaction – you either loved it or loathed it. The vast majority loved it, and it swept the country. This time reviewers were split in their feelings about it, but practically unanimous that it would never get played on radio in its entirety. They were wrong. By the time Queen began a lengthy UK tour in mid-November 'Bo Rhap' – as it had affectionately been dubbed – was rising steadily up the charts from its starting point at number forty-seven. The band desperately wanted the song to feature on TV, in particular *Top of the Pops*, but because of the highly technical make-up of its recording it would not be easy to perform live. So they approached director Bruce Gowers, who had made the film *Live at the Rainbow*, with a view to finding out if they could make a promotional film which could be shown on TV instead. As they were already booked into Elstree Studios on 10 November to rehearse for their tour, they decided to make the film that day too. The whole thing cost in the region of £4,500 and took just four hours to shoot and one day to edit. It became the first pop video of all time when it was premiered on *Top of the Pops* on 20 November – a memorable event in music, pioneering a whole new genre in rock.

The public reacted strongly and sales of the single catapulted above 150,000. The sheer unique brilliance of both the number and the prototype pop video captured the nation's imagination and dominated debate in the industry, although not everyone felt equally enthusiastic about it. DJ John Peel says, 'I liked Queen when they started out, although I have to admit they are not one of my favourite bands. I took the mickey out of them one night on *Top of the Pops*, and quite soon afterwards something appeared in a newspaper saying that Freddie Mercury and Roger Taylor were going to punch me out if they ever saw me. Thankfully, they never did. But seriously, when they first appeared I thought they were unique and sounded like nothing else ever had. Most people came to class "Bohemian Rhapsody" as the beginning of Queen – but for me it was the end of Queen. After that they became too bombastic in style for my taste.' Brian has his own views: 'What we actually became was successful. It's not cool to be successful in England.'

The day after that TV debut, the album from which 'Bohemian Rhapsody' had been taken was released. It was called *A Night at the Opera*. Four days later the single was number one in the charts. Years later Brian would look back on the album and declare, 'This can be our *Sgt Pepper*!'

The whole band was on a high as they gigged all over England. Then after a night in Newcastle on 11 December they were leaving for Scotland and their Dundee Caird Hall date on the 13th when the bubble of euphoria burst. Their coach was stopped on the motorway by a police roadblock which was waiting for them. 'To put it bluntly, they were looking for drugs,' recalls Pete. 'An ex-member of the crew who had been given the sack – by the PA company, not Queen themselves – had decided to get back at the band. So he'd anonymously tipped off the police, claiming Queen were all high on drugs and stuff. It was a load of rot, but the cops mounted this enormous roadblock sealing off every exit route – it must have cost them a fortune.' He continues, 'No one had anything, of course, but I remember this definite sinking feeling among us of: Oh God, I hope some silly sod in the entourage hasn't got anything, however small. But no one had.'

For Pete, who was responsible for ensuring that the band got safely to each destination in time for their gigs, the biggest worry was the potential delay. 'During all the time I worked with them Queen had never cancelled a show, and I was more concerned about that than anything else,' he admits. 'The cops hauled us all in – the PA company, the lights, the lot – for searching. It was obvious that they thought they had a real scoop. They treated us OK, I guess, because they must have realized quite early on that it was all a hoax. They rifled through the whole bus – noses into the ashtrays and everything – and couldn't come up with so much as a joint. Their disappointment was so strong as to be almost laughable.' In the end the police released them, incredulity vying with rage at whoever had cost them a small fortune, not to mention acute embarrassment.

By this time it was clear that 'Bohemian Rhapsody' was destined to hold on to its number one slot for Christmas – a distinction much coveted by every band. As their tour drew to a close in the run-up to the holiday, occasionally they found time to go and take in other gigs. Pete vividly remembers Queen's visit to the Brighton Dome to see Hot Chocolate, led by singer Errol Brown. 'We'd all gone to see Hot Chocolate perform. They were a great band and their number "You Sexy Thing" was sitting at number two. Afterwards we were all in the restaurant of the hotel we were staying at and suddenly Errol burst in, heading straight for Brian and Freddie and roaring at the top of his lungs, "You bastards! My main shot at a Christmas number one! You bastards!" God, it was so funny!' While it may not have looked like it to onlookers, there was actually a warm camaraderie between the two bands and it wasn't long before Brown allowed himself to be mollified with a beer or two.

Queen's 1975 Christmas Eve gig at London's Hammersmith Odeon was televised live by *The Old Grey Whistle Test* and picked up for live simultaneous broadcast on Radio 1. *A Night at the Opera* reaped its just deserts when, after notching up sales of over a quarter of a million, it went platinum; the festive season was complete for the band when, on 27 December, it reigned supreme in the UK album charts. This year Queen had scaled unprecedented heights, and for the first time Brian felt that, while they might not know where their career would take them or for how long, one thing was certain – they were definitely going up.

5

WE WILL
ROCK YOU

Brian began the new year by settling on a date with Chrissy for their wedding. They had been together for seven years, and for a lot of that time they had been inseparable. Queen had always placed a big drain on the time they could spend together, and now that the band's career was clearly set to soar those demands were about to increase drastically. In the next four months alone they were to plough their way through three major tours all over the world. Since their concert-giving calendar slowed down after April, Brian and Chrissy decided to get married in May.

While Chrissy began her preparations for the big day, Brian knuckled down to serious rehearsals for the first of those tours: a thirty-two-date whirl around North America. Confidence was high. They had already mopped up a heap of awards at the music press annual polls, and on 20 January when they flew to New York 'Bohemian Rhapsody' was sitting for the ninth consecutive week at number one. This was an achievement unequalled since the American vocalist Slim Whitman's 1955 hit 'Rose Marie'. With the UK million seller under their belt, coupled with the half million copies of *A Night at the Opera* already snapped up, Brian was relaxed and looking forward to the challenge of their third US tour. Their team – in particular a new addition in the shape of Gerry Stickells – had worked hard at the organization. Gerry had formerly been tour manager for Jimi Hendrix, among other stars, and was very experienced. His influence in the years to come would become vital to the smooth running of Queen's life on the road. As the aircraft's wheels touched down at Kennedy Airport, the only prayer Brian needed to send up was that no one would be taken ill this trip!

Their opening gig was at the Palace Theater in Waterbury, Connecticut, where they brought the house down; this set the pattern for the entire tour. The schedule, intended to take in practically every state in the USA, proved to be arduous but breathlessly exciting and at times hair-raising. Everywhere they went they were mobbed both on stage and off. Female fans in particular were astounding in their ingenuity at discovering, despite security precautions, not only which hotels the band were booked into but even which room belonged to whom. On arriving at their hotels all four invariably had to run the gauntlet of their crazed admirers, and sometimes even the width of pavement between car and entrance could be deadly. One week into the tour Freddie, leaping from a limo in New York, realized that he had committed the cardinal sin of sporting a long flowing scarf around his neck. He was nearly choked to death as two frantic girls, each desperate to claim a piece of his clothing, pounced on the scarf ends and simultaneously pulled in opposite directions!

During their four days in New York Brian discovered that Ian Hunter was recording at Electric Ladyland Studios with producer Roy Thomas Baker. He, Roger and Freddie went along to catch up with their two friends. Inevitably they got down to jamming, and all three ended up playing and singing backing vocals on the track 'You Nearly Done Me In' from Hunter's solo album *All American Alien Boy*.

By the time Queen hit Chicago in late February all four of their albums were in the UK top twenty – an amazing feat which added spice to their performances in that city. But Chicago holds very different memories for their personal manager Pete Brown, 'We'd been there for two days and it was time to leave. It was my job to settle hotel bills and get everything moving. This particular day I tried to use the Queen credit card, but they said it was over-extended and wouldn't take it. This was a Sunday and I had to organize all the luggage, make sure we made the airport in time etc., and I just didn't have the time for hassles. I argued and said I had to be going, so they would just *have* to take it. Suddenly the guy at the desk pulled a gun on me. I said, "I've got all the time in the world, mate!".' Pete goes on, 'Eventually I managed to get the promoter down to the hotel and he paid cash, but it meant we'd missed the flight.'

Still shaking from the heart-stopping experience of staring down the barrel of a gun, Pete then had a frantic time trying to organize alternative transport. As the hours slipped by, his nerves systematically shredded. He had been working with Queen long enough to know that they demanded super-efficiency from their staff at all times and rarely tolerated being let down. Even though in this case it patently wasn't his fault, Pete was sweating by the time he got himself in order. He says, 'I managed to scrape up a fleet of station wagons and we got there in the end, but all along I was convinced I was for the sack.'

The US tour ended on 13 March, and a week later they took off to start their second Japanese tour – a shorter stint this time. Brian and Freddie had taught themselves a smattering of the language so that between numbers they could communicate in some small way with their ecstatic audiences. The fans loved them all the more for it.

No more than a week again separated that tour from their second incursion into Australia. Perhaps it was fatigue or an understandable wariness after their disastrous Australian debut two years before, but a tangible tension emanated from the band. Again it was their long-suffering personal manager who bore the brunt. Pete explains, 'In Sydney, Queen were playing at the Hordern Pavilion. We arrived to find that the theatre could only be reached through a huge fairground. I didn't think there was any way I could get all the cars through, so I asked the band to get out and walk. Freddie's response was, "My dear, I can't possibly walk anywhere!" So there was nothing for it. We had to drive through the crowd at the fair at two miles per hour so as not to run anyone over – limos and champagne all the way. Needless to say, this didn't go down well with the Aussies, and immediately they started shouting at us through the windscreens – things like "Pommie pussies" and worse – sticking two fingers up at us and banging clenched fists on the car windows as we went by.'

Pete goes on, 'When we eventually got there Freddie was so cold with anger that he broke a mirror over my head and then ordered me to go and get a brush and shovel and sweep the glass up at once. It was the humiliation he had suffered, you see. He had to take it out on someone, and I was nearest. Freddie could reduce me to tears at times, but I did understand.' In fact their Australian tour turned out to be as successful as they had by now come to expect. Their single and album were both riding high at the top of the charts, and so when they arrived back in Britain on 25 April they had forgotten all about any unpleasantness and were well pleased with themselves.

Brian, of course, had more reason than the others to be happy. Just over a month later, on 29 May 1976, he married Christine Mullen at St Osmund's Roman Catholic Church in Barnes.

With the exception of Roger, who still enjoyed playing the field, stable relationships had for a long time characterized the private lives of the band. Right then Freddie, always complex in his relationships, was extremely close to Mary, John was blissfully happy with his wife Veronica, and now Brian and Chrissy had married. Perhaps this pervading sense of personal contentment was partly responsible for Queen's decision to release a gentle ballad as their sixth single. 'You're My Best Friend' was released on 18 June and was the first number written by John. Whichever song followed the inimitable 'Bohemian Rhapsody', it was bound to suffer in comparison; but the combination of Brian's rich chords, Freddie's husky delivery and the excellent harmonies which punctuate the song made it instantly popular, and it forged its way up the charts to number seven.

That summer Brian got down to working on songs for their new album, which they hoped to release before the end of the year. This was what they used to call 'routine time', and once they had each harvested their individual ideas they would all meet up in the studio. There, as soon as someone voiced his outline for a new song the others would promptly fall on it, convinced they could change it for the better. This way of working often produced lively debate and at time stubborn resistance, but they all considered it constructive.

At this time Virgin Records boss Richard Branson had an exciting new proposition. Says Branson, 'Basically I came up with the idea of trying to get permission from the authorities to stage a free concert in Hyde Park with the view of promoting some bands. The only thing was, at the time I couldn't afford to put the concert on myself. I knew Roger Taylor, and so I thought that perhaps it might be an idea if Queen put it on. I also thought that Queen might *really* break as a result of that kind of exposure. Having been to the Rolling Stones' Hyde Park concert in 1969 I remembered just what special kind of feeling and exposure a huge free gig like that generates.'

Queen went for the idea in a big way. They had been looking for a way to thank their loyal fans, and the concept of a free outdoor concert was ideal. Anxious to get the project moving, they and Branson decided to try to organize it for the following month, which meant approaching the London Parks Committee quickly. It was Branson who skilfully navigated the maze of stipulations laid down by the Metropolitan Police regarding the time the concert would start and finish, the facilities to be laid on for the public and the security arrangements for the band – all of which had to be agreed before the Committee would sanction the event. 'Once I got all the necessary permissions and the project was up and running, I handed it over to the Queen management,' adds Richard. The date was set for 18 September.

Keyed up at the prospect, Queen decided to arrange two special forerunner gigs for the beginning of September. The first was at the Edinburgh Playhouse Theatre, supported by the band Supercharge, and would take place during the Edinburgh Festival. 'Ask anyone who was there at the Edinburgh Playhouse that summer,' Pete Brown maintains, 'and they'll tell you it was a great experience. It's hard to explain, but it had a profound effect on everyone in Queen.' One of the highlights was undoubtedly when they performed a new hard rocking number of Brian's called 'Tie Your Mother Down'. It had the audience off their seats and jigging in the aisles.

Just over a week later Queen played their second gig, billed as *Queen at the Castle*, outdoors at Cardiff Castle. It had been a long, hot summer, but as the 12,000-strong crowd began assembling the rains came. By the time support acts Andy Fairweather-Low, Frankie Miller's Full House and Manfred Mann's Earthband played their sets, it was absolutely pelting down. The audience were bogged down to their ankles and soaked through as they waited for Queen to appear, but when they did there was nothing damp about the reception they got.

At Hyde Park on the 18th the sun shone bakingly once more as around 150,000 people converged on the area, bringing confusion to London's already congested traffic. Capital Radio was transmitting the event live, with commentary from DJs Kenny Everett and Nicky Horne; the giant outside broadcast trucks, the miles of cable and the army of agitated technicians milling about added to the general chaos.

Steve Hillage, Kiki Dee and Supercharge were the support acts. Says BBC Radio 1 DJ Bob Harris, compere that day, 'Supercharge's lead singer was a rather ugly overweight fella, and I remember he came storming on in a costume like one of Freddie's ballet dancer outfits. Not a pretty sight!' He goes on, 'That July Kiki had had a number one hit with Elton John called "Don't Go Breaking My Heart", and I know she had been desperately hoping to persuade Elton to come and perform it with her there. But he didn't, so that night she sang the number to a cardboard cut-out of Elton on stage instead.'

When darkness fell, Queen came on. Freddie greeted them with the words 'Welcome to our picnic by the Serpentine' before launching into 'Keep Yourself Alive'. In Harris's words, they 'were very special'. 'People had been gathering since about midday, and by mid-afternoon you could stand on the stage and, looking out, the crowd literally stretched to the horizon line. You could *feel* the anticipation,' he insists. 'When Queen walked on, to the strains of "Bohemian Rhapsody", the audience went wild. It was an incredible sight and as usual they gave 100 per cent. The never had that throwaway quality that some bands have. The light show was incredible, too.'

Everyone agreed that it had been a magnificent day, culminating with a truly scintillating performance from Queen. But when the band, highly charged, left the stage they had to ignore the deafening chants for an encore. The schedule had over-run by half an hour already and the police, having laid down hard-and-fast rules, were prepared to arrest Freddie if he so much as put one foot back on the stage. Bob confirms, 'In fact the police ended up pulling the plug on the power just to make sure, but still it had been a red letter day.' As to its wider effect, Richard Branson concurs, 'I believe it was a vitally important night for Queen and, I think, a turning point in their career.'

The next six weeks were spent working solidly on the new album, and in mid-October they pronounced themselves satisfied. They had lifted the name of their last LP from a Marx Brothers film and decided to do so again, calling this one *A Day at the Races*. John Reid organized a pre-launch press reception to be held on 16 October at Kempton Park racecourse near Sunbury-on-Thames, with two sixties' bands, Marmalade and the Tremeloes, providing the music. EMI sponsored a special race called the Day at the Races hurdle, and the turn-out for it was good. The race was won by Lanzarote, ridden by champion jockey John Francome, and before the off Brian had joined the others in placing his bet – they all backed Francome. All the proceeds from the meeting went to charity.

A Day at the Races was released on 10 December. The month before that, the track 'Somebody to Love' had been released as the first single from the forthcoming album. Again with the aid of a white label Kenny Everett had used his radio show to plug the single shamelessly, and it shot to number one in Capital Radio's own daily chart, Hitline. Officially released on 12 November, nationally it had to settle for number two. Although *A Day at the Races* was criticized by the music press for lack of inspiration, the fans loved it and it became Queen's second number one album in Britain.

By the end of the year Brian and Chrissy had bought a comfortable house in Barnes, John and Veronica moved into a house in Putney, while Freddie and Mary had found themselves a trendy flat in Kensington. But Roger went one better, opting to purchase a luxurious country house in Surrey, beautifully appointed and set in acres of garden and woodland. When he moved in he did not do so alone, for back in September, while traipsing back and forth to endless meetings on the organization of the Hyde Park concert, he had met Richard Branson's personal assistant, an enchanting Frenchwoman called Dominique Beyrand.

Brian didn't have much time to get used to his new house, because on 4 January 1977 he and the rest of the band were off on another States tour – their most extensive yet. It got off to a freezing start, for the country was suffering its coldest winter for a century.

Quite early into this tour they were joined by Thin Lizzy as support band. Formed in the early seventies and led by vocalist Phil Lynott, they had been a popular rock band in Ireland before notching up two UK top ten hits. Thin Lizzy's manager was Chris O'Donnell and he well remembers landing this support slot. 'Thin Lizzy had themselves been due to tour America,' he says, 'then one night Brian Robertson got involved in a fight at the Speakeasy Club. Some guy had been going to break a bottle over Frankie Miller's head and Brian had thrown up his arm to stop the bottle. It shattered, badly cutting his hand. Obviously he couldn't then play the guitar. So I sped off to America to see if there was some way I could salvage the situation – some way we could keep Lizzy's new album alive. It was there that I got a call out of the blue from Howard Rose, who was Queen's US agent then, asking me if Thin Lizzy would support Queen. Lizzy had been a big fan of Queen's since their conception, and I couldn't believe our luck at being offered the slot.' Brian Robertson's place would be taken by Gary Moore.

In 1973 Queen had had to pay Mott the Hoople to be support act on their British tour, but Thin Lizzy did not do so now. Chris is adamant:

'Lizzy never paid to support. Personally I don't agree with the practice. In the business it's called tour support money, because headlining bands try to sell the spot to help defray the cost of sound equipment and lights. The payback, supposedly, is the exposure, which can lead to the support band becoming big – but I'm very sceptical about that.' Brian, however, is equally adamant that Thin Lizzy *did* pay to support.

Thin Lizzy's lead guitarist was the easy-going, irrepressible Californian Scott Gorham, and he recalls the tour with deep affection. 'This was Lizzy's second tour of America. Before, we'd never toured with a British or European act – always American bands – and there's a whole different mentality there, especially with Queen. Once you get to a certain level in the rock world, it changes some people. A lot of bands get paranoid. They become obsessed with not letting the support act upstage them. They won't give you a sound check, a decent PA or anything, because they want to really keep you down. We didn't get any of that with Queen. They moved in right away and said, "Here's the PA. Now you'll need sound checks and lights, and what else?" Queen and Lizzy had this attitude that we'd set out as a British attack to conquer America.'

The two bands did get along very well, and not just because Queen were generous with their stage effects. Says Scott, 'I think it was partly to do with the fact that the bands were so very different. Lizzy was a sort of punk band with street cred, whereas Queen were very polished and sophisticated. I always think "pompous" is a really unkind word to use to describe their music, but it was certainly grand – so you see there was no competitiveness on that score. We were a great package.'

They also had great times and a lot of fun, Scott recalls. 'One night I was on stage, playing away, and in the heat of it all this thing whizzed past my face, just missing me by a fraction to thud into my 4x4 behind me. I looked round and saw it was a lemon. I took a second and thought: Is there a hidden message behind this piece of fruit here, or what? I mean, why not an apple or a lettuce? Why a lemon?

'We did our set and Queen were on. I went out front to watch them, and all of a sudden from the same direction of the audience a hail of about a dozen eggs went up in the air aimed right at Brian! Suddenly Brian's skating about and he lands right on his ass. I started to laugh real hard, then stopped myself: I thought: What are you laughing at? You got lemoned! I couldn't work out which was worse – an egg or a lemon!' Gorham goes on, 'Anyway, I looked into the audience thinking

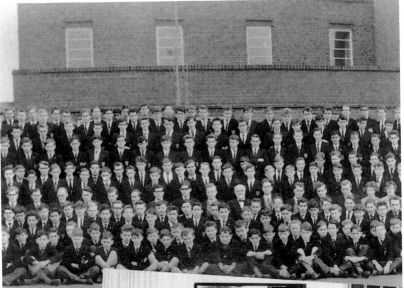

Above: Hampton Grammar School, March 1962. Brian third row from the back, fifth from right; Bill Richards, third row from the back, third from right; Dave Dilloway, third row from the back, second from right; Tim Staffell, third row from the front, second from left.

Above: Brian's first band, 1984 (left to right): Tim Staffell, Dave Dilloway, Richard Thompson, John Garnham and Brian, taken during the Top Rank Competition, 1967. Tim and Brian would soon quit to form Smile with Roger Taylor.

Left: A flying visit from Brian to the 30-years-on reunion of 1984 (left to right): Dave Dilloway, Richard Thompson, John Garnham and Brian. Tim Staffell gave it a miss.
(Richard Young/Rex Features)

Opposite: Heavy rock is a release of emotion for Brian, clearly seen on his face as he gets into his role for yet another celebratory Queen video – this time, *The Invisible Man*.
(Richard Young/Rex Features)

Top: 1971. Flaked out in the baking sun, Brian and his supervisor Ken Reay (seated) relax after another all-night zodiacal light study session at ZL Observatory, Mount Teide, Tenerife. Taken by fellow student, Tom Hicks.

Above left: While the expression belies it, Brian was thrilled to be reunited with his very first acoustic guitar.

Above: Trial and error. One of a series of attempts at producing the first publicity shot of Queen, taken in Freddie's Holland Park flat, London.
(Courtesy of Ken Testi)

Right: A large part of
Queen's success was
the result of their stage
image. The kimonos,
worn in tribute to their
wildly enthusiastic
Japanese audiences,
reflect the band's
reciprocal love of that
country. (Gems/Redferns)

Above: Voted in
February 1974 by
NME readers as one
of the Most Promising
New Names, fresh
faced and eager Queen
are set to embark on a
reign spanning almost
two decades.
(Rex Features)

Above: Ken Testi,
Queen's first manager,
1971, taken by Ibex
member Mike Bersin.
Ken was an invaluable
cog in the wheel of
Queen's early career.

Above: Brian's virtuosity as lead guitarist combined with Freddie's unique voice set the seal on Queen acquiring the handle of 'rock's untouchable live showmen'.
(Fin Costello/Redferns)

Right: Clowning around, although by the mid-eighties stresses and strains within the band began to tell on the four friends.
(Richard Young/Rex Features)

Opposite: Dubbed 'a giant prawn', in this specially designed costume for the video of *It's a Hard Life*, Freddie as ever outrageous and flamboyant stole the show.
(Richard Young/Rex Features)

There was
overwhelming grief at
Freddie's death in
November 1991 and
acknowledgement
from Brian, Roger and
John of the privilege it
had been to have
known Freddie and to
have shared his life.
(Top, Richard Young; right,
Graham Trott: both Rex Features)

there's a guy somewhere in there with a whole salad bar just waiting for us! We may not be getting paid much, but hell – we'll sure eat well! This was in one of those mega-dome places too, and what could Brian do but get up like nothing had happened – but he was wearing his flowing white top. Uh-uh, not any more. Man, I'm talkin' *yella*!'

But beyond the camaraderie there was a kind of rivalry. Lizzy already had a reputation for wildness, and their concerts were frequently violent. It had been quite clear from the first night that they would challenge the headliners by virtue of the sheer energy they created. 'We were out there to make Queen earn their money,' admits Scott. 'We were also out to win fans. Sure, we wanted to kick Queen in the ass – it makes you a better band – and we set out to make it as rough as possible for them to follow us. Man, once we were up there we wanted to blow those guys off the stage!' Brian recognized the threat but welcomed it. Not too long ago, they themselves had tried their damnedest to upstage Mott the Hoople. It was the duty of any self-respecting support band to try it on that way; there was nothing wrong with a dose of healthy ambition.

Ambition was something which Queen never lacked. On 5 February, when they played the highly prestigious Madison Square Garden in New York, the capacity crowd loved Queen as much as the band adored performing there. This, they felt, meant that they were now in the big league. Scott agrees. 'The building's not much in itself but you know you're there. It's Madison Square Garden. You've made it.' Pete Brown confirms, 'Queen were always setting themselves goals. To play Madison had been a goal and they'd sold out. It was a terrific night and afterwards they were delighted with themselves until somebody piped up that Yes had headlined three nights running. That was all it took. Freddie leaped up and roared, "Right! That's it! Five nights!" – meaning he wouldn't rest until Queen had bettered three consecutive nights at the Garden.'

This kind of fierce rivalry was not confined to vying with other bands, but was also prevalent within the group itself. Pete reveals, 'They were always *very* tough on each other. No one got away with a thing. For example, John didn't feel comfortable in certain outfits but he had to wear them because Queen had a very strong sense of the image they wanted to project. In some ways, they were all at one point pushed by the others into things that individually they didn't feel right about but would agree to because it was part of being Queen.' He continues,

'Their standards were the highest I've ever known. They encouraged each other all the time, drove each other relentlessly. If Freddie wanted to be seen as the best frontman in the world, then Brian had to be the best guitarist, John and Roger determined to prove themselves the best rhythm section, and so on. It was that enormous self-imposed pressure that made them unique.'

For Brian the two nights they played at the equally prestigious Los Angeles Forum more than equalled their night at Madison. Years before he had gone along to see Led Zeppelin headline at the Forum and had wistfully wondered whether he would ever stand where Jimmy Page had done. Each concert was a sell-out and left a lasting impression on him, even though the American critics tried to dampen things by running down Queen's performances whilst exalting Lizzy with great reviews. 'We didn't take a lot out of that,' confesses Scott. 'Papers all over the place were saying we were out there killing Queen, and it just wasn't true.' He adds, 'Brian would come back to our dressing room after our set to say to me or Gary, "I feel you guys are killing me out there." I'd go out front when Queen were on and think: So what show's he lookin' at, then?'

Just when the tour looked to be illness-free, as it entered its final stage in the second week of March Freddie's voice packed in. He never gave less than his all on every performance, but these tours of forty-odd dates were far too arduous, sandwiched as they usually were between European and Far East tours. Strain was again diagnosed, and two shows were cancelled so that Fred could rest. He went sightseeing in Hollywood while Brian headed back to San Francisco to look up some friends before they regrouped for the last half dozen Canadian gigs.

Earlier in the month Brian's number 'Tie Your Mother Down' had been released in the UK as their latest single, but the furthest it got in the charts was a disappointing number thirty-one. Come spring 1977 the British music scene had been infiltrated by a new and abrasive form of expression known as punk.

Purporting to reflect the cynical seventies, bands like the Clash, the Jam, the Stranglers and the Boomtown Rats sprang to prominence. They all did their very best to be as outrageously rude, crude and uncouth as possible, expressing anti-royal sentiments, gallows humour and general apathy with life. But one particular band, the Sex Pistols, managed by ex-New York Dolls manager Malcolm McLaren and fronted by Johnny Rotten – so named, it is said, because of his rotten teeth –

has since been credited as almost single-handedly launching punk, or New Wave, music in Britain.

Punk's roots had undoubtedly been laid in America a couple of years before, but the Sex Pistols earned the dubious honour of being the grossest and most spoiled band in the UK. Suddenly Britain's high streets saw teenagers emulating these new anti-heroes by clomping about in heavy Doc Marten boots and sporting short spiky hairstyles, scruffy slashed denims and leather jackets hung with chains, while their noses were lanced through with earring studs. The music press immediately latched on to this new fad and over-reached themselves, announcing that rock was dead and that groups such as Led Zeppelin, Genesis and Queen were passé. Brian viewed this latest movement with interest: new musical styles, however weird, always intrigued him.

There was hardly time to bother about their new rivals, however, for after a much-needed respite in April the band took off again, this time for Stockholm to commence another European tour. For the opening night at the ice stadium Freddie excelled himself by exploding on stage poured into a replica of a costume once worn by the famous dancer Nijinsky. He even managed to upstage himself later by returning for the encore encased in an outrageously loud silver lurex leotard which blinded the audience as soon as he shimmied under the huge bank of sodium lights.

After-gig parties had long since become the norm with Queen. Brian maintains that they were held partly to dispose of the incredible levels of adrenalin still pumping after a show. To these shindigs flocked any showbiz celebrities who happened to be in the area, local stars and, more often than not, less salubrious gatecrashers. At one party held on board a yacht during this tour the band were presented with thirty-eight silver, gold and platinum discs, commemorating their enormous popularity in the Netherlands.

Then it was back to work, opening a two-week UK tour which culminated in London at Earls Court where they played two nights in June. That year marked the Silver Jubilee of Elizabeth II and so Queen, already famous for their elaborate lighting rigs, smoke bombs and fireworks, decided to honour the occasion with something extra-special. For £50,000 they had built for them a rig in the shape of a crown, which ascended from the stage, awash in a sea of dry ice, at the beginning of each show. Some 25 feet tall and 54 feet wide, it weighed two tons and made its spectacular debut at Earls Court on 6 June.

Queen's display of lavish grandeur in this year of drab punk gave the music press yet more ammunition against them. A couple of weeks later *NME* fired a salvo in an article claiming that 'A rock gig is no longer the ceremonial idolization of a star by fans. That whole illusion, still perpetuated by Queen, is quickly being destroyed and in the iconoclastic atmosphere of the New Wave there is nothing more redundant than a posturing old ballerina toasting his audience with champagne.'

The article, which included a lengthy interview with Freddie, was titled 'Is This Man A Prat?' The gloves-off attack in the headline was echoed loud and clear throughout the entire two pages, but Freddie was more than a match for journalist Tony Stewart, busy erroneously predicting the artistic decline of Queen in that summer of 1977. By the end Freddie had lost his patience. Goaded into replying to the desperate accusation that he only went to play the piano at gigs so that he could make another entrance centre stage afterwards, he bluntly rasped, 'The reason I go to the piano is to play the fucking thing.' The time would come when Queen would refuse press interviews altogether.

Gary Glitter believes he knows one reason why the music press gave Queen such a hard time. 'Freddie used to say it like it was, and I think the press were probably very surprised. He was proud to be gay and yet was backed up by a band very obviously not gay. Again it's the pigeonhole syndrome – like the name Queen. Also, back in the early seventies it was very difficult to say the things Freddie would say about being gay. Males too were suddenly saying, "Yes, we really do do the washing up and the hoovering. We're not into this macho crap." But in the final analysis it's in the groove on the record and what you do on stage. So they said sod it to the music press, and they didn't like it.'

The 'groove on the record' with which Brian was currently involved was their new album, on which he had been working at Basing Street Studios in London. Since the days when he had grappled with his first oversized guitar one of his heroes had been Lonnie Donegan. In August, when these sessions switched to Wessex studios, he found Lonnie too busy working on a new album. Thrilled to be asked to guest on a couple of Donegan tracks, Brian appears on both 'Diggin' My Potatoes' and 'Rolling Stone', recordings not yet released.

There was never, however, a great deal of time to indulge in solo ventures, as Queen's recordings demanded so much time; by October, their thoughts had turned to the release of their next single. For the past four singles Bruce Gowers had filmed their promo videos. This time, however, Bruce was unavailable and so they turned to Derek Burbridge. The new number was an arm-locking anthem called 'We Are the Champions' and just the sound of it lent itself to being filmed before a live audience. So they hired the New London Theatre and recruited hundreds of 'extras' from their own fan club. It wasn't done to avoid expenditure – they really wanted to involve their fans, for whom they had genuine respect, in their work.

Bob Harris had already started work on a Queen documentary and he went along to the filming of this video, again acting as compere. He recalls, 'Nowadays they're all into rent-a-crowd set-ups for videos, but it wasn't done then for bands to ask their fan club members to come along and get involved. For me it was just another facet of Queen. I've known many a group to be very blasé about, not to say exploitative of, their fans, but Queen really care very much for the people who buy their records and videos and attend their gigs, and they're obsessed with ensuring that they always get value for money. Obviously they wanted an enthusiastic audience to create the right atmosphere, but they didn't automatically expect them to go mad and be great. As it happened, the fans *were* great. The band took time to chat to them, and this just bowled the kids over.' In fact the footage required for the video was shot in a very short time, but as a thank you the band carried on and played an impromptu gig for their fans.

Freddie's 'We Are the Champions' was released on 7 October with Brian's punchy, uncomplicated 'We Will Rock You' as the B-side. Elektra liked both numbers so much that they chose to release them a couple of weeks later as a double A-side. To date Queen singles hadn't set the US charts alight, but Elektra felt that this time both numbers would come in for considerable airplay. They were right – it was a huge success.

In Britain the fans were as appreciative as ever and it went to number two. No one in the band was surprised that the critics hated it. *NME* – sometimes known in the rock fraternity as 'enemy' – denounced it for, among other things, sounding as if it were intended to be adopted by football fans on the terraces. While this was meant as an insult, in one way the comment was right – the devotion of Queen's fans closely resembled the feverish loyalty enjoyed by top soccer clubs and their star players. It is hard to see what was wrong with that. American football supporters certainly felt no shame in adopting the rousing chant as a method of geeing up their teams. Reviews were less cutting, however, when the new album *News of the World* was released on 28 October.

A few weeks earlier Queen had put plans in motion to cut their last remaining tie with Trident. Financially they were now in a position to buy themselves out of that clause in the severance agreements which had allowed Trident a 1 per cent share of six future albums, and they were looking forward to finally being free.

Unfortunately, though, just as they were at last rid of Trident they found themselves facing a whole new set of management difficulties. Things weren't working out with John Reid. The main problem lay in the fact that Reid already managed Elton John and had had no idea, when he first took Queen on, how big they would become. Pete Brown is quite frank: 'Queen didn't feel that John Reid was able to give them enough of his time. It's important, too, to understand that the John Reid offices were really the Elton John offices. All the staff had worked for Elton previously and their loyalties lay firmly with him. Also, when Elton had picked Reid to be his manager he virtually plucked him away from Tamla Motown. Reid hadn't been a manager before and it was Elton who fixed him up with an office and so on. If Elton had a tour, therefore, that was a priority. With the personalities in Queen it's not hard to imagine how that went down!'

Once again Queen relied on the services of Jim Beach to find a way out that was acceptable to both sides. Dissolving their partnership with John Reid was not as troublesome as it had been with Trident, as was exhibited by the informality of the arrangements. Says Pete, 'It happened when the band were recording the video for 'We Will Rock You' in Roger's enormous back garden. It was absolutely freezing that day – something like a foot of snow on the ground. Filming always means an awful lot of standing around and everybody was very touchy that day. Anyway, in the middle of about the millionth take John Reid arrived, and he, Brian, Roger, Fred and John all piled into the back of Fred's car to sign the severance papers. I think they were glad to get in out of the cold more than anything else!'

On a more sober note, because Queen were in effect breaking their contract before the agreed expiry date there was a penalty: they had to part with a substantial sum of money to John Reid Enterprises as well as signing over a hefty percentage of royalties on existing albums.

Management was a major headache for many groups of this era, and yet the need for proper control was essential. The Bay City Rollers, for instance, had particularly unfortunate experiences in this department. Eric Faulkner explains, 'It's vital for a band to have the right people at the helm. People go on about it now, but even in the seventies it was run by businessmen who knew all the moves. Agreements tended to be frighteningly complicated and usually designed to take complete advantage of you. Half the time you couldn't understand the contracts, but you signed anyway because you thought they would give you what you wanted right then. Very few took the long view.' He adds, 'Nowadays there are books and other safeguards to tell up-and-coming bands what the pitfalls are and what to look out for. In those days there was nothing.'

But Queen *had* always taken the long view and, with the exception of the time when Brian, Roger and Tim had signed as Smile, the drawing-up of their agreements had always been a protracted affair precisely because they *did* understand the terms and would refuse to sign until they were acceptable. Yet still their management was up in the air again. After some discussion they now decided to manage themselves, with the help of Pete Brown, who had chosen to stay with them, Jim Beach, Gerry Stickells and a guy called Paul Prenter who had been hired by Reid. They were convinced they could make a good fist of the job.

With this all behind them Brian flew out to New Haven to join the others for their second American tour that year, which began on 11 November. When John arrived it seemed that at least one member of the band had let the punk tidal wave get to him, because he had swapped his long locks for the skinhead look. A highly practical man, John had decided that this hairstyle was easier to cope with; but the crew teased him relentlessly, nicknaming him 'Birdman' as in *Birdman of Alcatraz*. For this tour the band decided to bypass commercial flights and travel instead by private plane. Accompanying them on this trip was their friend Bob Harris. 'I was gathering footage for my documentary on them and so I filmed as we went. I did a long individual interview with Brian, Roger and Fred respectively, and a shorter interview with John. The idea was to knock these together with tour film and come out with a Queen retrospective at that point.'

On the opening night at the Civic Center in Portland for the first time ever on tour Freddie sang the tender ballad 'Love of My Life', a number for which Brian (on record) had specially learned to play the harp. The stage version was adapted for guitar in a different key. When the entire audience began to sing along word-perfect, Freddie stopped and let them take over. From then on it became a permanent feature at any gig in any country for the audience to sing this song back to Queen. 'Freddie was one of the most generous performers in the business,' says Bob. 'And it's not an ego trip when he gets the crowd to sing back to him like that. He actually wants the fans to communicate that closely with the band.' This proved to be the tour when Queen could say they had finally conquered North America. Their pride, delight and sense of fulfilment at this achievement put them all in excellent spirits.

December began with two nights headlining at Madison Square Garden in New York – not quite the five that Freddie had vowed to pull off, but still an improvement on February. For this gig Brian decided to invite his parents over, since they had never seen Queen perform abroad and it was, after all, Madison. Harold jokingly refused unless his son booked them on Concorde; much to Harold and Ruth's amazement, Brian did just that and brought them over in champagne luxury style. Years later, Brian reflected on this occasion, 'I suppose my Dad only came to terms with me being a rock musician when he saw me play Madison Square Garden. Until then it was, "That's okay, but you'll have to get a proper job later." The funny thing is, I think I still suffer from the same delusion myself!'

'A couple of days after Madison, Queen played a gig in Chicago in temperatures less than minus fifteen degrees,' recalls Bob. 'The stadium was the one used by the Chicago Bears and we were each presented with a team jacket. I wore that jacket until it disintegrated. It was beautiful!' Extremes in the weather were something the band had got used to by now, but they took the travelling DJ by surprise. He says, 'After that minus fifteen in Chicago just three gigs later we arrived in Las Vegas to be met with this wall of heat. It was in the mid-eighties.'

That Vegas gig, at the Nevada Aladdin Theater, stands out in Harris's memory. 'At the Aladdin the whole ground floor is covered with slot machines and the theatre entrance is right at the back. We turned up in four limos all lined up outside and were thrown for a moment because no one had expected this. Next second the first limo moved off and the others followed, and they slowly drove all the way through between the rows of slot machines to the theatre door at the back.' Shades of a certain Sydney fairground – only this time Pete had no fear of mirrors. . . .

The following night in San Diego, however, the gaiety vanished when John, somewhat the worse for drink, put his hand straight through a plateglass window. He needed nineteen stitches but still managed to play the four remaining gigs. It had been the first time Queen had taken on two major tours of America in one year, and by the time Brian flew back to Chrissy on Christmas Eve he, like his fellow band members, was worn out.

Once he had recovered, the details of managing themselves began to occupy Brian's thoughts. The band had already switched accountants to a firm which specialized in tax advice, but they realized they needed to set up a management structure. They turned for assistance to their new accountant, Peter Chant, as well as to Jim Beach. It was eventually decided that Peter would take over the business, tax and accounting side, while Jim, whom they trusted implicitly, was persuaded to relinquish his partnership in the west London law firm of Harbottle and Lewis and take over as manager in charge of the newly formed Queen Productions Ltd. While they were at it the band also set up Queen Music Ltd and Queen Films Ltd – the latter meant that they would be financing their own videos and as such could retain control of the rights whilst licensing them to EMI for promotional use. EMI in turn were invited to weigh in with a contribution to the cost of making the videos. It was a highly unusual proposition, but EMI agreed.

By this time Queen had earned so much money that British income tax regulations would cripple them were they to spend more than 65 days out of 365 in the UK. Chant's advice to them was to take what's called 'a year out'. In a perfectly legal interpretation of the tax rules he had set up a company structure whereby, when Queen played and recorded overseas, the proceeds went through an entirely different company from Queen Productions. After releasing their new single, 'Spread Your Wings', on 10 February in the UK, in April they took off for Sweden on the first leg of their European tour. John Harris, who had been with them for ten years, was unable to go because of illness and was sorely missed. It was during the short five-gig British tour which followed in May that Freddie's style was seen to be clearly undergoing a change. Famous for his flashy and revealing leotards, he had now taken to appearing on stage dressed in shiny black PVC from head to toe. Some people weren't too sure of this new Mercury – he looked too much like a biker.

Later that month Roger and John went to Montreux in Switzerland to begin working on new material while Freddie remained for a while in Britain. He had agreed with Roy Thomas Baker to co-produce an album which his close friend, actor Peter Straker, was recording. Brian, too, had no intention of straying far from home, for Chrissy's and his first baby was due at any time. James, or Jimmy as he is usually known, was born on 15 June 1978. Brian was thrilled, although in order to abide by the 'year out' regulations he had to leave within days of the birth. He flew to friends in Canada from where, after celebrating his thirty-first birthday, he headed to the Super Bear Studios in Nice. Once Roger, John and Freddie had arrived there too, intensive work could begin. The album was made partly here and partly at Montreux in Switzerland.

When developing songs in this hothouse atmosphere inspiration for Brian could arise from anything, any time. One track, 'Dead on Time', which would appear on their new album, features sounds which Brian had recorded during a terrifying thunderstorm. Whilst everyone huddled indoors and Montreux's power system was cut off, Brian dashed out in the torrential rain clutching his portable tape recorder. He was thought to be crackers at the time, but the results proved effective on vinyl.

The annual Tour de France bicycle race passed through Nice when Queen were there, and it is said that the delicious sight of all those body-beautiful, Lycra-clad guys crouched intensely over their handlebars, was responsible for Freddie's latest song, 'Bicycle Race.' Brian had been busy working on a number which he unflatteringly called 'Fat Bottomed Girls', and it was decided to hook up Brian's number with Freddie's.

It didn't involve a great leap of the imagination for someone to come up with the idea of staging and filming a girls' bicycle race for the accompanying video. Wimbledon Stadium was the venue, with sixty-five girls recruited through various model agencies. There was one last, ever-so-minor, detail: the girls had to be naked!

On 12 October 1978, the day before 'Fat Bottomed Girls' was due for release, the violence so prevalent in punk's image hideously spilled over for real when Nancy Spungen was found dead in a pool of blood in Room 100 of the Chelsea Hotel, New York City. Her boyfriend Sid Vicious, bass player with the Sex Pistols, was found blood-spattered and in a state of shock. He was arrested and charged with her murder.

Compared to Nancy's violent death, the press furore which erupted next day over the sight of a naked bottom on the cover of Queen's new single seemed pathetic – even hypocritical, considering the shelves of girlie magazines on sale in newsagents up and down the land. Brian certainly had little patience with the pious uproar. In an interview at the time he replied to the charge of sexism, 'I'll make no apologies. All music skirts around sex, sometimes very directly. Ours doesn't. In our music sex is either implied or referred to semi-jokingly, but it's always there.' He did concede that it had offended some of their fans, who felt it didn't match up to what they considered to be the band's spiritual integrity. Eventually the band caved in to pressure, and on later covers the rear end of the winning cyclist sported a carefully superimposed pair of skimpy black knickers.

Yet another US tour kicked off in late October. Its elaborate on-stage lighting rig and the entertainment laid on after the gigs at their by now infamous parties made it seem more extravagant than ever. On Hallowe'en their New Orleans bash – called a pre-launch for their new album, *Jazz*, and featuring such delicacies as a nude model hidden in a huge tray of raw liver – was so outrageous that it made the newspapers coast to coast in America and further afield too. Publicist Tony Brainsby, who after a three-year absence had been brought back to work with Queen on their latest and highly controversial single, says, 'The place had been made up to look like a swamp, hung with masses of creepy vines, dry ice smoke pumping everywhere. There were strippers, dancers, dwarfs, snakes – you name it. A whole bunch of us had been flown over just for that one night, that one party. Talk about jet-setting!' Ultimately Tony lost Queen to a former employee. He says, 'Roxy Meade started as my tea girl, then moved on to be secretary before becoming my assistant. She left after a while and set herself up in PR, and Queen went with her.'

Jazz was released in Britain on 10 November. Still unrepentant over the bike race scandal, Queen had inserted a free graphic poster of the race participants. America, however, banned the poster, considering it to be pornographic. One week later, while the band were performing the number in New York, they arranged for the stage to be briefly invaded by half a dozen naked ladies on bicycles, defiantly ringing their bells. Despite, or perhaps because of, the controversy the album survived in the charts for twenty-seven weeks, peaking at number two.

When the tour ended Brian flew back to his wife and six-month-old son in time for Christmas, but there was to be no let-up in the constant merry-go-round of record releases backed by tours. All too soon they were embarking on a two-month European trip. By now inured to music press reaction to their work, they were temporarily gobsmacked when both *Record Mirror* and the *Daily Mirror* actually liked the new single 'Don't Stop Me Now', released on 26 January 1979. A week later, on the evening Queen were due to appear at the Frankfurt Festhalle, news broke that Sid Vicious, due to stand trial in New York for the murder of his girlfriend, had died from a massive heroin overdose.

Through Switzerland, Germany and Spain they played nightly to wildly enthusiastic crowds, ending up in France for the three remaining dates of the tour at the Pavilion de Paris. On each of these three nights the front row was filled by the same contingent of British fans. Noticing this on the second night Freddie, much to their delight, affectionately dubbed them 'the Royal Family'. Then on the final night, seeing them once again perched there, he greeted them personally with the jovially blunt, 'Fuck sake, are you lot here again!'

The jocularity, however, didn't always extend to behind the scenes. During this tour Pete Brown had been kept on his toes organizing their comfort down to the last detail; it was no easy task to satisfy his exacting bosses. He reveals, 'One of my jobs was to ensure that the accommodation I fixed up for all four of them was of the exact same size, quality and style. The idea was that no one person was to have anything bigger, better or fancier than the other. It was a good enough policy in theory because they genuinely are a democratic band, but in practice it was a different story. That tour I couldn't seem to do anything right. Back in January Brian, I think for the first time ever, was very annoyed at me over the place I'd fixed him up with. Another time it was Roger with a list of complaints, but when we came to Paris I managed to upset all four at the same time. It was a horrendous task, though, trying to find four suitable houses – not apartments, mind you – of precisely the same dimensions and standard to please them all. Try as I might, I could never develop a thick skin and when they blew up at me it did hurt sometimes.'

Although Pete maintains he doesn't regret a second of his time working for Queen – indeed he is adamant that they were thrilling and unforgettable years – it is quite clear that the ruthless professionalism with which Queen attacked their music ran all the way through their organization. Without question they repaid loyalty in kind, but equally there was a distinct awareness among their staff that if anyone were less than committed to the band, there was no place for them in the tight-knit team.

The tiring life on the road gave way once more to two months recording, again at the delightful Swiss resort of Montreux. Each July the town stages its famous jazz festival, while in September it is the turn of classical music; in between are numerous free concerts. Brian loved working in that professionally stimulating yet personally restful environment. He also greatly enjoyed working at Mountain Studios themselves, so when Peter Chant suggested that Queen should buy the studios, they jumped at the idea. The Dutchman who had built them, Alex Grob, spent very little time at Montreux and was instantly amenable to Jim Beach's approach to buy out the shareholders.

At about this time the band were asked to write the music for a forthcoming feature film based on the comic book hero Flash Gordon. The idea appealed instantly and so Jim arranged talks with the Italian producer of the movie, Dino de Laurentiis. Dino had never heard of Queen – he is said at that point never to have heard a rock band full stop – but after listening to a sample of their work he commissioned them to write the soundtrack – a challenge which Brian found very exciting. Fired up with this pending venture Queen sailed through yet another Japanese tour, along the way receiving from their enormously enthusiastic fans awards for top group, top single and top album. During the tour they sang 'Teo Torriatte', a new song for which Brian had written a verse in Japanese and for which he took over on piano for the first time.

In the summer of 1979 they released the album *Live Killers* and the single 'Love of My Life' – both live recordings. Because EMI received the Queen's Award to Industry that year the record company decided to release a 300-copy limited edition of 'Bohemian Rhapsody' pressed on royal purple vinyl. The band themselves were for the most part holed up at Musicland studios in Munich. Unusually, they entered into these sessions with no preconceived ideas and therefore began each song from scratch. This time they found themselves teamed up with a new producer named Reinhardt Mack, universally known as Mack, who had already worked with ELO, Deep Purple and Led Zeppelin. Whilst they were in Munich, work also began on their film score.

Freddie at this time started to get involved in a new project that excited him very much. For a long time now he had been fascinated with ballet and had recently become friends with one of the Royal Ballet's principal dancers, Wayne Eagling. Wayne was involved in producing a dance gala for mentally handicapped children and wanted to widen its appeal. He went to see the Treasurer of the Royal Ballet School, Joseph Lockwood, then also head of EMI, and Lockwood suggested Freddie.

Wayne recalls, 'Freddie turned up for the first day of rehearsals wearing tights and ballet shoes, and we all took one look at him and nearly fainted. We were in the middle of rehearsing "Bohemian Rhapsody" when in walked the choreographer Sir Frederick Ashton. Frowning at Freddie, he enquired in a strangled voice, "*Who* is *he*?" A little embarrassed I explained that he was a rather famous rock star. Ashton snapped, "Well, he's got terrible feet!"'

At these rehearsals Freddie also met Derek Dean, another Royal Ballet principal dancer. 'We never stopped laughing,' Derek insists. 'He was so eager he'd try anything – in fact a lot of the time we had to hold him back in case he seriously hurt himself. Normally on stage he did his own thing, whereas here he had to be where he was supposed to be or he'd throw the whole company out completely.' At the dress rehearsal, Freddie may not have been much of a dancer, but his musical talents were undoubted. Recalls Wayne, 'All of a sudden he began to sing "Bohemian Rhapsody" without music. We just all stopped and looked at him, awe-struck by his wonderful voice.'

'Crazy Little Thing Called Love', an early Elvis-type number which Fred said he wrote in the bath and was premiered live at the dance gala, became Queen's fourteenth single when it was released early in October. For the first time it was also released as a twelve-inch single in Europe. The following month the band embarked on what they called their 'Crazy Tour'. Brian in particular felt that they had been playing what he called 'the big barns' for too long; although these gigs were enjoyable, he was worried that they could be losing contact with their audience. He explained at the time, 'Unless people can see you in their home town, it can almost seem like you don't exist. It's nice to be somewhere where people can actually see and hear you. The advantage of what we're doing this time is that, because our sound and lights systems are better than ever, we can really knock audiences in the stomach. The only real disadvantage is that not everybody can get to see us, but I think that those who do come have a much better time. It's great fun, too, because the reward is much more immediate.'

Gerry was appointed the task of seeking out venues that would never have dreamed of seeing Queen appear. The tour kicked off at the RDS Simmons Court Hall in Dublin, did two Glasgow dates and was then confined to England. The band's stage wear had somewhat changed. Brian and Roger remained much the same in style; but John, as befitting his sober short haircut, had recently adopted a conservative collar and tie, while Freddie was now never out of leathers and wore a leather and chain cap. His image was one that was closely associated in those days with gay men's clubs, although at the same time it was also very macho. This prompted a challenge from Judas Priest's colourful lead singer, Rob Halford, for Freddie to prove himself by mounting a powerful motorbike for a lap or two around the Brands Hatch circuit. Freddie's response was to accept on condition that his challenger first appeared with the Royal Ballet; Halford went curiously quiet.

The last gig of the year took place on Boxing Day at London's Hammersmith Odeon. It was a charity event in aid of the Kampuchea Appeal Fund and had been organized by Paul McCartney and his company MPL Productions. A series of concerts followed, involving among others Wings – rumours that the Beatles might re-form for the event had proved groundless – the Who, the Pretenders, and Ian Dury and the Blockheads. The concert was filmed for television and later appeared as an album.

As the seventies slipped away, Brian reflected on just how far he had come in the past ten years. At the close of the sixties Smile was breaking up and, although determined, he had been dejected and broke. Now wealthy, successful and famous – to date Queen had sold over 45 million albums worldwide – he wondered just what challenges the eighties would hold for him.

SON AND
DAUGHTER

Brian spent the first four months of 1980 in Germany at the
Musicland Studios, working on Queen's new album as well as
on the soundtrack for *Flash Gordon*. He found Munich a highly stimulating place and inspiration flowed freely in the
cosmopolitan atmosphere of a city noted for its uninhibited nightlife.
Back in Britain 'Save Me' had been released on 25 January, as usual
bombing out with the critics. However, since the band had long since
ceased to take any notice of their reviews this was of little consequence,
especially since 'Crazy Little Thing Called Love' had not only given
Queen their first American number one but had also reigned supreme
for seven weeks in Australia as well as hitting the top slot in New
Zealand, Canada, Mexico and Holland. Not bad for a 'tat band', as *NME*
persisted in dubbing them.

Working on two albums at once was at times a killer, and Brian had
scarcely a moment to lift his head. Freddie, however, managed a flying
visit back to the UK in March. He rarely made television appearances
but had agreed to go on his friend Kenny Everett's zany show. During
one sketch Kenny announced contenders for the 'British Eurovision
Violence Contest', and on walked Fred dressed in his new leather stage
gear. He promptly leaped on an unsuspecting Kenny, arms and legs

locking fast around the choking DJ as they engaged in a mock brawl on the studio floor. It was during this trip that Freddie saw and bought a sumptuous twenty-eight-roomed Victorian mansion set in a quarter-acre of manicured garden in Kensington. It would be several years before he took up residence there; for now he simply wanted the pleasure of owning it.

Back in Munich work continued on the albums. Queen were also to record a video to accompany the release on 30 May of their forthcoming single 'Play the Game'. This time, though, some of their fans felt that Freddie personally wasn't playing the game. His image had been changing from the one with which Queen fans had grown up through the seventies. Forsaking his leotards for leathers had been bad enough, but now many were shocked and dismayed to discover that he had had his once long, thick black hair cropped close to his head and had also grown a droopy, Latin lover-style moustache. Gone too was the familiar black nail varnish. To show their disapproval scores of fans sent in razors and bottles of nail varnish to the band's offices, but Fred refused to take the hint. The fans were further upset when *The Game* album followed on 30 June. The band had aimed this time for a more coherent, if sparse, theme, but for the first time they had used synthesizers – which on all their previous albums they had proudly boasted they did *not* use. Some of their followers from the early days felt let down, but the band were determined not to be hidebound by what had always been and felt they should experiment with new technology.

On the same day that *The Game* was released, Queen began a strenuous forty-five-date tour of Canada and the USA. This time they were at least giving themselves a couple of mid-tour breaks, during the first of which Brian flew home to his family. In the last five years Queen had gone on seventeen tours – in the case of the American/Canadian ones they lasted up to two or three months at a time. Because of their fame, everywhere the band travelled they were cocooned by airtight security and it was beginning to suffocate Brian, particularly since their decision the previous year to switch to private planes. Life got to be very claustrophobic for him, as Pete Brown recalls, 'Brian got to the stage where he just didn't want to use private planes any more. It was a case of arriving in a private plane on a private airstrip, being taken from the plane by limo to some sumptuous hotel, hotel to gig and back the same way. The rarefied atmosphere was driving him mad.'

Pete was all too aware of Brian's penchant for collecting things and recalls watching his boss in many of the world's top hotels, flit blithely between tables picking up sugar bags to add to his collection. 'Part of what was wrong with him,' Pete adds, 'was that there are no gift shops to browse in at private airfields and he didn't like that! But seriously, what Brian missed dreadfully was normality. He used to say to me, "What can I honestly say I know about anything, living the way we do?" Eventually he put his foot down and told the others that he wanted to fly commercial again. He told them, "I want to feel I've been somewhere!"'

The strain of their continually hectic schedule was being felt by everyone on the team. 'People think it's a glamorous life,' explains Pete, 'but it's damned hard work. Someone would ask me how Boston was and I'd reply, "Boston had orange curtains and a blue bedspread." That's what it was really like.'

In August their new single, 'Another One Bites the Dust', was released. The funky beat number, which proved to be another smash hit, had been written by John. Brian says it was a difficult number to pull off on stage, however, since it depended heavily on a combination of a strong throbbing bass line and a nifty piece of drumming; for all Roger's brilliance it was very hard to repeat the same tight drum snap as on the studio-perfected record. But since it quickly became a favourite with the fans, though, they persevered.

In America it was a colossal hit: thinking Queen were a black act, a New York City black radio station latched on to it in a big way and gave it massive airplay. Other major radio stations promptly followed suit and Elektra had no choice but to release it. Quickly rooting at number one, it presided there for five consecutive weeks and was one of just three Queen singles to go platinum in the States.

It didn't, however, spell success for everyone as Kent Falb, head trainer of the Detroit Lions American football team, explains. 'Early in the 1980 season defensive backs Jimmy Allen and James Hunter, along with tight end David Hill, heard 'Another One Bites the Dust' on the radio and decided to use the melody. They rewrote the words and made a recording of the song as a novelty tune which was unofficially adopted by the Detroit Lions. However,' he continues, 'at the time this was done the team had begun the season with four wins and no loses. As the season went along our fortunes declined, and unfortunately this tune ended up being used against us by numerous opponents!'

The band's longest and most gruelling tour ever finished with four sell-out gigs at Madison Square Garden – still not Freddie's goal of five, but a proud achievement none the less. By the time Brian returned home in early October he was exhausted and looking forward to relaxing with Chrissy, whom he had sorely missed on tour. It was very difficult juggling the band with marriage, since of necessity they were separated a lot. Time together had long ago become a precious commodity, and after completing work on the film score at London's Anvil Studios Brian tried to make the most of it before all too soon he had to jet off to Zurich at the end of November to rehearse for their European tour.

Four days into that tour 'Flash's Theme', written by Brian, was released as a single in Britain, backed by Freddie's 'Football Fight', also from the soundtrack album. Because Queen could not appear personally, a promotional video was shown instead on *Top of the Pops*. The new single reached number ten, considerably higher than its American counterpart. Elektra had chosen to release the single 'Need Your Loving Tonight', which barely scraped its way to number forty-four in the Billboard chart. The purpose-built, all-seater Birmingham Exhibition Centre had newly opened when Queen became the first band to play there on 5 December, just three days before the soundtrack album *Flash Gordon* was released to astonishingly rave reviews.

But their delight was turned to ashes next day when, as they were getting ready to go on stage at London's Wembley Arena, word flashed round the world that John Lennon had been murdered by an apparently deranged fan. Brian was devastated: Lennon had been their hero. Like every other rock star, suddenly he realized with icy fear just how exposed and vulnerable they were. That night, though, their thoughts lay with John and, as a moving tribute, Queen performed his 1975 hit 'Imagine', which reduced the audience to tears. Brian was so overwrought that he forgot the chords and got to the chorus too soon, which threw Freddie completely. But no one minded: the audience understood that the band's distress was as real and raw as their own.

Technically speaking, Queen had begun life in April 1970, but it wasn't until John joined Brian, Roger and Freddie in late February 1971 that the band was considered complete. They decided, therefore, that their official tenth anniversary year would be 1981.

That year also marked the beginning of their love affair with South America – near virgin territory for rock musicians. Always ready for new challenges, Queen had been looking for fresh venues for some time. Bands had played in South America in the past, but only as very low-key affairs; a spectacle such as a Queen show had never been attempted, and they were instantly attracted to the idea of taking on Argentina and Brazil. Jim Beach flew to Rio de Janeiro and set up a production office at the Rio Sheraton Hotel, from where he began liaising with local promoters.

While Jim was busy in Rio the band had to leave for Tokyo once more. Sharing their flight was the entire Nottingham Forest football team under manager Brian Clough, en route to Japan to play in the World Club Championship against the Uruguayan team, Nacional. Former Forest and England international Trevor Francis recalls, 'Queen were up front in first-class, whilst we were all back with the rough. I was absolutely passionate about music anyway, and when we discovered they were on the flight we couldn't wait for a chance to meet them.' He goes on, 'It was in Anchorage, when the plane was refuelling, that we got chatting. Somehow Brian and I seemed to pair off. I can't really remember now what we talked about, but he was very easy company and we got on very well. He gave me his home telephone number so that we could keep in touch and I invited him, if he had the time, to come to our game.' In fact the entire band had been invited, and Roger and John took them up on the offer. Sadly, the match ended in a 1–0 defeat for Forest.

Queen's stay in their beloved Japan was shorter than usual – five sell-out gigs at Tokyo's Budokan, and the Japanese premiere of *Flash Gordon*. The country's top music magazine, *Music Life*, presented Brian with an award for having come second in his musical category; Roger likewise came second in his, while Fred and John were voted top of their respective sections. Queen itself was awarded the best band award, and all this recognition provided a good boost for their first South American tour which was set to start in February.

Before the band could arrive, however, there were problems. For each Queen tour security passes were issued to the crew. They usually had a bit of fun with the designs – one for an Australian trip showed a sheep wearing black wellington boots on its hind legs. On this occasion, however, when their production manager flew into Argentina ahead of the crew and equipment he was stopped by customs, his luggage was searched and the tour passes were seized. The voluptuous pair of topless beauties pictured sharing a banana flouted the strict local pornography laws, and the poor man was forced to spend a laborious few hours at a desk carefully blotting out the offensive breasts with a black marker pen before he was released with the passes!

While the gear made its way to Buenos Aires and Rio there was time to squeeze in a brief vacation. Brian promptly paid a visit to Disney World in Florida. Roger opted for LA and Freddie went to New York, where he was busy purchasing an apartment. John, the most family-minded of them all, flew straight home to Veronica.

Because football is so highly revered in South America, before Queen were allowed to play in stadiums such as the enormous Velez Sarsfield in Buenos Aires artificial grass had to be laid over the hallowed turf. The fact that the country had never before witnessed such an invasion created problems for the promoters and Jim to sort out: the Argentinian intelligence agencies, for instance, were worried that terrorists might try to hijack such a high-profile event. Years later Jim confessed to having endured some hairy moments; when he turned up at the Morumbi Stadium in Sao Paulo in Brazil, for example, he was proudly advised by the head of security allocated to them that to date he had killed 206 people – presumably he felt Jim would think him very efficient at his job!

From the moment the band arrived at Buenos Aires they knew this was going to be special. They were met at the airport by hordes of screaming fans. In the past many false rumours had circulated that Queen were going to play there, and although the people thronging the airport were clutching tickets they didn't really believe it until the aircraft doors opened and the four walked down the steps. Even the Argentinian President, General Viola, marked the occasion by sending a government official to greet them and whisk them through the normally tiresome customs procedures. Television and radio kept up a steady flow of bulletins, and indeed their first appearance on the aircraft steps had been transmitted on the national news. From that opening night in front of 54,000 fans at Velez Sarsfield Queen became South America's most popular rock act.

From the outset Brian had been eager to perform in Argentina, but had realistically decided to settle for being received at best as a curiosity. He was astounded, therefore, to discover that the crowd knew the words to every song. Probably the high spot of the night was when Freddie began to sing 'Love of my Life'. As was his custom, he stopped halfway through; right on cue the audience took over and flawlessly sang the song back to them. It was an experience that Brian says he will never forget.

Two rather special parties were thrown in their honour. At the first, hosted at his home by the president of the Velez Sarsfield, were celebrity guests who included the country's legendary soccer star Diego Maradona. By the end of the evening Brian had swapped his Union Jack T-shirt for Maradona's football shirt. Then they were invited to meet General Viola at his official residence. Queen's tour was a major cultural event in his country and he wanted to show his recognition of this fact. Brian accepted his invitation in the spirit in which it had been extended, as did Fred and John; but Roger strongly disagreed with some of the General's political views and chose not to attend.

The tour then trundled from Argentina to Brazil, where they were booked to appear at the Morumbi Stadium in Sao Paulo – but it was a transition dogged by problems. Over 100 tons of expensive equipment had to be road-hauled through dense jungle between the two countries. Logistically speaking this was bad enough, but then on arrival at the Brazilian border the customs threatened to search every truck meticulously – a nightmare operation which would have taken weeks when they had just three days to get to their destination. Panic set in, but José Rota, the overall promoter, had contacts in customs and by pulling strings managed to get round the red tape. Even so, when the trucks were finally granted passage only thirty-six hours remained before the show.

Brian, meanwhile, blissfully unaware of all the drama, was relaxing with the others in Rio, a breathtaking city brimming with life. Rio has a rhythm all of its own, redolent of the carefree spirit of the Brazilians, and Brian was reluctant to give it up and move down coast to Sao Paulo for the gig. But the audience for that performance at Morumbi turned out to be 131,000, the largest paying audience for one band anywhere in the world to date. This momentum kept up until by the end of the tour the total attendance came to just under half a million people, grossing in the region of three and a half million dollars.

Looking beyond the dazzle of triumph, however, Jim had to keep his wits about him. It hadn't escaped his, or Gerry Stickells', attention that some of the gear they had been offered on arrival at the concert site had 'Earth, Wind and Fire' faintly stencilled on the sides. It must have been confiscated, under some probably flimsy pretext, from that band on a previous tour, and Jim was worried that the same might happen to Queen's equipment, especially since they had brought practically every piece they owned. Jim and Gerry decided to outflank their hosts.

To coincide with the end of the tour they flew in a specially chartered 747 cargo plane. After the final show the crew immediately set about stripping down the stage in record time and loading up the gear, hurrying it away to the plane waiting on the runway – all the while cutely overlooking the expensive artificial turf. As Jim later explained, 'By eight o'clock the following morning it had all gone, so when we finally met to negotiate some settlement and payment, they suddenly realized that their major leverage – which was the equipment – had left whilst they had been busy stealing the grass!' The experience had not put Queen off, though. Flushed with success, they flew home in the knowledge that they would be undertaking a second South American tour later that year.

On 22 May 1981 Chrissy had their first daughter, Louise. Again Brian was thrilled but, just as had happened after his son's birth, within weeks he had to leave Chrissy and the new baby at home to fly to Montreux where work had begun on the next album. By now the band's attitudes toward recording had taken on a new hue. In March Roger had released a solo single, 'Future Management', followed quickly by a solo album, *Fun in Space*. Now, while Queen were recording at Mountain Studios, he again branched out on his own and released a second single, 'My Country'. At about this time, too, David Bowie began dropping by the studios.

Bowie, a Montreux resident, frequently socialized with Freddie and Roger and quite often the singer would turn up unexpectedly while Queen were recording. One day in the summer of 1981 an impromptu jam session developed with Queen and David. Initially it was regarded as no more than that; but then, totally spontaneously, they found themselves writing something together. By the end of the day the song seemed to have some potential.

Work on the new album slowed down as their return trip to South America beckoned. But first Freddie decided to celebrate his thirty-fifth birthday, on 5 September, in spectacular style. He flew all his closest friends by Concorde to New York for a lavish party in Freddie's gargantuan suite of the Berkshire Hotel, which went on non-stop for five days! There was scarcely time to recuperate before the band regrouped in New Orleans to rehearse for their forthcoming 'Gluttons for Punishment' tour, as they had christened it.

Like their previous trip, this one too was fraught with problems. When they arrived in Venezuela on 21 September they discovered that the statesman Romulo Ethancourt was very ill. The local promoter explained that, should he die, the entire country would go into mourning and Queen's gigs would be axed. The first three concerts at Poliedro De Caracas went without a hitch, and then they had a day off. That evening Jim had arranged for Queen to take part in a live Venezuelan television pop show; Brian, John and Roger agreed to appear, but Freddie refused point-blank.

As it happened, the show was a shambles because earlier the programme had featured some lookalike stars. Consequently when Brian led the others on, and they were announced as Queen, the audience weren't convinced! Brian was beginning to feel like a prize prat when all of a sudden a panic-stricken man dashed on stage to the mike and began yelling frantically in Spanish. He was announcing that Ethancourt had died and that a two-minute silence had been ordered. A moment later another even more rattled man rushed on and announced, again in rapid Spanish, that Ethancourt wasn't dead after all. Total chaos erupted. Standing in the wings, Jim was desperate to tell his bemused band what was going on – but as it was live TV he could hardly march out and explain, and so he had to leave them to squirm helplessly.

In the event, Ethancourt did die later that night and Queen's next two shows were scratched. It got worse. The entire country shut down, which meant that the airports closed and the band couldn't leave. It was all very frightening – the volatile political situation could have resulted in a revolution, with them trapped in the middle of it all. Stories abounded of people vanishing off the streets, never to be seen again, and it wasn't at all hard to believe in that heaving cauldron of unrest. It was a great relief, therefore, when the airport reopened allowing them to get the hell out of Caracas and back to America.

On 9 October at the Estadio Universitario in Monterey Queen played their first gig in Mexico and went down a storm, but again their appearance was clouded by problems behind the scenes. Not only had Gerry ended up taking the calculated risk of offering a bribe to the Mexican border officials in order to speed up their entry into the country with the equipment in time for the gigs, but the local promoter managed to get himself arrested and Queen had to bail him out of jail. Then when the crew arrived at the stadium they were playing, on the outskirts of Mexico City, they discovered it was in a very run-down, dilapidated state. Finally, when Queen did take the stage that night the massive crowd began hurling rubbish at them.

Thoroughly dismayed, Brian came to the conclusion that for once the audience hated them. Then someone explained that this was the traditional local show of appreciation! But it still meant that performing in Mexico was a highly dangerous occupation. Brian's height made him a perfect target, and he spent the entire performance darting about to avoid being injured by the volley of shoes, bottles and acid-filled batteries which were homing in on them with alarming accuracy. Nevertheless, they played a second night – only to discover that, due to complicated tax problems, they were not going to be paid for it. That was it. Patience already at a premium, they unanimously decided to cancel the remaining shows and scarper.

Smuggled aboard a flight bound for New York instead of being en route to Guadalajara as they had promised the promoter they would be, everyone agreed never again to set foot in Mexico. It had been an incredible experience, but one which they had no wish ever to repeat. The promoter was not out of pocket because he had made more than enough money out of the two shows that Queen did perform. He was, however, stamping mad at being duped – but that was his problem.

The band was safely ensconced in New York in time for the UK release of their *Greatest Flix* video on 19 October, which was a compilation of all their singles videos since 'Bohemian Rhapsody'. It was the first time that such a collection had been released by any band, and they felt it was fitting as the first in a series of special releases to mark their tenth anniversary.

Whilst in New York Queen had grabbed the chance to work with David Bowie on the finishing touches to the song they had begun in Montreux, and now, rejuvenating the pop duet tradition, the single 'Under Pressure' was released. David's frank opinion of the number at the time was: 'It sort of half came off, but I think it could have been a lot better. It was a rush thing. I think it stands up better as a demo. It was done so quickly that some of it makes me cringe a bit.' Despite this, the combination of Bowie and Queen fans rushing out to buy the single enabled it to soar to the top, giving Queen their first number one in the UK charts since 'Bohemian Rhapsody' six years before.

The *Greatest Hits* album followed in November, as well as a book called *Greatest Pix*, a pictorial diary of Queen's first ten years together compiled by photographer Jacques Lowe. The video, album and book to commemorate their anniversary shared the same cover – a special portrait of them taken by the Earl of Snowdon – and, as usual, they had gone to great lengths to satisfy themselves that their fans were receiving top quality and value for money. It was largely this worry that sparked off the only matter to blight the few remaining weeks of this special year.

Throughout the seventies several books had popped out of the woodwork charting Queen's musical career to date, but none had been authorized by the band themselves. Like most bands they did not take much notice of these publications, but now, in the autumn of 1981, there emerged a book written by a Judith Davis which, in their opinion, purported to be in some way official. Since none of them had had anything to do with the author they were concerned that it might contain inaccuracies and so took the publishers to court. Although they won a temporary injunction against the book, they later lost the action, which meant that the book was published after all and they had wasted a great deal of time and money to no avail. They vowed never again to sue an unofficial publication.

None of this, though, was allowed to sour their celebrations, and shortly after they flew to Canada to perform two special gigs at Montreal's Maple Leaf. These shows were filmed by director Saul Swimmer, known for the Beatles' film *Let It Be*. The Queen concerts were intended to form a feature film to be released the following summer.

By early December Brian had returned to Munich, a city which he feels not only played an important role in his life but had become almost a second home to him. For some time he had suffered from a continual sense of claustrophobia; this was perhaps inevitable given the sometimes unhealthy nature of the rock business, and, even though the band had toured the world, they could never experience more than brief, sporadic contact with each city. But the time spent in Munich, Brian felt, was different. There was even time to get to know some of the locals and to visit nightclubs and discos like the Sugar Shack, which became a favourite haunt. Too much partying, however, soon began to take its toll, and for a while Brian turned up at the studio each day late and tired. He later confessed that, during that spell in Munich, for himself and for Freddie the 'emotional distractions', as he called them, became destructive.

Meanwhile, back in Britain Queen's music was being celebrated in their absence at an Albert Hall charity concert given by the Royal Philharmonic Orchestra and the Royal Choral Society in aid of leukaemia sufferers. The manager of the RPO at that time, Ian Maclay, remembers, 'The original idea for the concert came from a charity called the Solid Rock Foundation, which had Jim Beach on its committee. It was my job to coordinate the musical preparation and supply the orchestra. The RPO already had a reputation for appearing with rock and pop groups such as ELO, Frank Zappa, Procol Harum and Rick Wakeman. Now it was the turn of Queen's music.' Ticket prices for the formal event started at £50, and the two-and-a-half-hour concert raised a great deal of much-needed money for the charity.

By the end of January 1982 Brian had returned to Musicland Studios to continue work on their new album. Realizing that they had lost quite a bit of ground in their highly successful anniversary year, now there was a definite return to discipline. But Brian still found time to see other bands, and it was when the heavy metal band Def Leppard were playing in Munich that lead singer Joe Elliott first met Brian.

Says Joe, 'It was backstage. Queen were working on their album *Hot Space* at the time. Anyway, Def Lepp were supporting Ritchie Blackmore's band Rainbow – and Brian came along to see Rainbow, I assume. That first meeting was astonishing for me. The door of our dressing room opened and in walks this guy wearing a black jacket, black jeans and white clogs and he says, "Hi, guys. I'm Brian May from Queen" – as if we didn't bleedin' well know! He was so very humble, genuinely humble. I mean, he wasn't making a great entrance or anything like that. He was introduced to everyone and spent ages talking to us and listening to us. He was really sincere.' Joe adds, 'It's often made me laugh since. You get bands who are really nobodys and yet they get away above themselves, and here was Brian from Queen being like that. It was a good lesson in life to us, I reckon. For me Brian has been a yardstick in that way.'

Come March Brian flew to Los Angeles – where, partly as a tax write-off, he had bought himself a house – to discuss their pending European tour with the others. They also needed to film a video to accompany their forthcoming single 'Body Language', due for release on 19 April. The B-side was to be 'Life Is Real', which they had dedicated to the memory of John Lennon.

Before that, however, their contract with EMI for Britain and Europe was up for renewal. On 1 April Queen once again signed to the EMI label, this time for a further six albums including the one they were currently working on. The following day war broke out between Britain and Argentina over sovereignty of the Falkland Islands in the South

Atlantic. Since 1833 the British had occupied the islands, supposedly for the protection of the seal fisheries. Argentina had other ideas and continued to claim sovereignty over what they called the Islas Malvinas. Their invasion on 2 April resulted in a task force being despatched from Britain – just when Queen's appropriately titled hit 'Under Pressure' was at number one in the Argentinian charts. The Argentine Government were not amused and banned Queen from appearing in the country again; and, at least for the duration of the conflict, their records were banned from the airwaves.

The band themselves had just begun their European tour, but things weren't quite going to plan. Their new musical direction was not going down well with the audiences, who disliked what they saw as its unchallenging funky disco feel. Brian had been aware in Munich that the band had now moved more towards rhythmic rock. It was a new avenue for them and they had been curious to explore it, but clearly it had upset many of their European fans who preferred the familiar hard rock.

The clincher for those disaffected fans came when the album *Hot Space* was released on 21 May. It had distinctly deserted the hard rock image and for many it was a deep disappointment – Brian's usually dominant guitar work seemed suffocated behind a synthesizer-produced fog of electronic mishmash. A huge chunk of the band's support sprang directly from admiration of Brian's brilliance on guitar; now that this was missing, they felt adrift and confused. Brian himself harboured doubts about the album and publicly admitted that he personally wasn't terribly keen on it, although he offset this remark by defending Queen's decision to experiment with new musical forms.

It was while they were on the British leg of their tour that Brian's love song 'Las Palabras de Amor (The Words of Love)' was released. Queen's *Top of the Pops* performance of the number was their first in five years.

Just over a month later, in mid-July, the band set out on another of those gruelling Canadian/US tours, playing practically every night and in almost every state. It was a blindingly hectic time, punctuated as usual with extravagant parties. By this time Freddie was freely admitting that he had begun to hate the tours, and by the end of them he felt he never wanted to go on stage again. Brian must have felt the same. Yet despite this, with barely time to draw breath after the tour ended in September, they took off again for a six-date tour of Japan.

For Brian and Roger their arrival in Tokyo this time was met by a blast from the past – they were informed that Mercury Records had just released an album there entitled *Gettin' Smile*, featuring six tracks which Brian, Roger and Tim Staffell had recorded back in the sixties. Neither Brian nor Roger believed that Smile had ever recorded enough material for an album, and at first both were highly suspicious. However, having listened carefully to the album and having had the cover notes translated, they agreed it was indeed them and so they would not be taking legal action.

In December it was time to renew their contract with Elektra. But Queen were no longer happy with this record label: after some protracted and ultimately fruitless negotiations they decided to part company, opting in the interim to sign all their albums to EMI.

The end of 1982 heralded another kind of split – of the band itself. It wasn't the end of Queen – no one considered it in that light at all. But it had become increasingly obvious to each of them that the twelve continuous years of living in each other's pockets, of constantly recording and touring and being on the road together, were taking their toll. They frankly admitted that they were getting on each other's nerves and that serious arguments had become a far more frequent occurrence of late. So they decided to take a year off. Of course, as soon as news leaked that they would not be touring for the next twelve months claims of a dramatic bust-up were splashed all over the music press. In reality the feeling within Queen was a markedly more sober and reflective one – let's go our own way and then see what happens.

PUT OUT THE
FIRE

The decision to step off the touring treadmill for 1983 was the right one as far as Brian was concerned, and the opportunity to stand back and take a long look at themselves was very valuable. There had always been tension in the band. Often not one of the four liked the same things musically, and the resulting struggle to find some common ground led to forceful disagreements which had grown worse during the making of their last album. Brian admits that in these situations he is probably the most stubborn one of them all. Quite simply, he was tired – they all were – and the prospect of churning out yet another album just did not appeal.

Brian also believes strongly that a number of major groups have broken up prematurely simply because individual expression is suffocated. He is convinced that breathing space which gives freedom to expand beyond the group, particularly a long-standing group, is essential, and ultimately results in a return to a closer-knit, more productive and revitalized working arrangement. No thought entered Brian's head that Queen was over. Even with all the fights, what they had was too precious for that. But it might be interesting to see what he could get up to in the line of solo projects.

On that score Freddie had already stolen a march on him by booking time at Musicland Studios, where he had begun work on his solo album. Whilst in Munich he had also met Georgio Moroder, who had invited him to collaborate on some music for a film with which he was involved. Freddie jumped at the opportunity. John for his part was more than happy to relax at last into steady family life. By his own admission he had little inclination to make solo recordings, although he enjoyed meeting up occasionally with friends to make music.

Roger, meanwhile, was busy making mischief. As a way of livening up his short stay in Scotland with Crystal Taylor, his personal assistant, he tried playing tricks on residents of the Highland ski resort of Aviemore by posing as a door-to-door salesman, waiting to see how long it would take the householders to twig his true identity. But the joke was on Roger because no one recognized him! Deciding he had had enough practice on the artificial slopes he headed for the real thing in Switzerland, where John later joined him at Mountain Studios to help lay down some tracks.

Brian and Chrissy, meanwhile, had been enjoying a month in Paris. It had been a long time since they had been able to spend any uninterrupted length of time together, and the holiday went a long way towards unravelling some of the tension which had been building in them both. Surprisingly quickly, too, Brian found that ideas had begun to pulse through his brain for a solo album, and soon he was hankering to get back into a studio. When he flew to America, Chrissy went with him. So too did his Red Special, which caused some problems at Orly Airport when he tried to take it on board the plane as hand luggage. There was no way he was prepared to deliver it into the rough clutches of the baggage handlers, and because it was too big to be stowed away in the usual fashion he ended up having to pay for an extra seat. Still, it meant he could keep an eye on the precious instrument, so he didn't object.

Soon after his arrival in Los Angeles Brian met up with a friend, American vocalist Jeffrey Osborne. Osborne was in the middle of recording his forthcoming album at the Mad Hatter Studios and asked Brian if he would guest on a couple of tracks. Brian appears on 'Two Wrongs Don't Make A Right' and 'Stay with Me Tonight'; the latter made it into the British top twenty the following spring.

Having had his appetite whetted again for studio work, Brian lost no time in ringing round some friends who were staying in LA at the time to ask if they would like to knock about some musical ideas with him. In late April guitarist Eddie Van Halen, together with Fred

Mandell, a renowned keyboard player, bassist Philip Chen and Alan Gratzer, drummer with the band Reo Speedwagon, all showed up at Record Plant Studios to see exactly what he had in mind.

Brian's preferred way of working was not to set too rigid a plan at first but to encourage everyone to play whatever sprang to mind – be it jazz, blues or hard rock – while he kept the tapes running. Once settled in, however, he set about channelling the melting-pot of talent at his disposal away from indulgent twelve-bar blues towards something more specific. Brian had made his own arrangement of the theme tune to *Star Fleet*, which was his son Jimmy's favourite television sci-fi series at this time. As the day progressed the scratch band played this number, as well as an old one of Brian's, 'Let Me Out', which he had written some time ago and promptly shelved. Ending with a good old meaty blues jam, they had all thoroughly enjoyed the work-out. At this point Brian wasn't too convinced that he had anything; but, on the off-chance that he would think differently at a later date, before the guys left he secured their respective permissions to do a bit of work and future mixing on the tracks if he so desired.

Unknown to Brian, Freddie too was making his way to LA. He had been having a whale of a time in New York, frequenting his favourite riotous nightclubs until the early hours, after which, thoroughly spent, he would spend the rest of the day in bed. But now he had decided to abandon his nocturnal New York life in favour of sunny California, and had flown to Los Angeles to spend some time with his close friend Michael Jackson. Michael was recording his new album, the follow-up to *Thriller*, and they had decided to sing a couple of songs together with the thought that these might end up on their respective forthcoming LPs.

Quite soon after his studio jam Brian had to up sticks and fly back to Britain. Polydor Records had recently approached him with the idea of getting him to produce one of their newest signings, a Scottish group called Heavy Pettin'. In the past Brian had co-produced Queen records, but he had never produced anyone else. Willing to have a stab at it, though, he accepted and set to work at the Town House Studios in west London on the group's debut album *Letting Loose*. As a fail-safe Brian called in the services of Mack. That enabled him to try out new ideas, secure in the knowledge that an experienced producer was keeping watch and could bail him out if necessary.

Jim Beach knew all about rescuing his charges from trouble.

Above: Grosvenor House Hotel, London, 1992 (left to right): Brian, Bert Weedon (King Rat) and George Harrison attend the Annual Ball of the charitable Grand Order of Water Rats.

Right: Guitarist Gordon Giltrap and Brian, Workshop Studios, Redditch, July 1993. Brian got lost trying to find the place, then was mistaken by a passer-by for Prince!

Previous page: Brian
and Freddie on stage.
Right from the start
Queen bent over
backwards for their
audiences.
(Raj Rama/Rex Features)

Brian's relationship
with actress Anita
Dobson is now well
established.

Brian with Malcolm Thomas, co-founder of the British Bone Marrow Donor Appeal, of which Brian is the patron.

Above: At a Queen party in Marbella with his ex-wife, Chrissy.
(Richard Young/Rex Features)

Right: With his son, Jimmy, his eldest child.
(Richard Young/Rex Features)

Freddie in the role he loved – conducting the crowd. Audience participation was an integral part of any Queen performance. Brian and Roger also give their all.
(Suzi Gibbons/Redferns)

For Brian, Queen will
always be a huge part
of his life. But for now
he enjoys success in
his new career with the
Brian May Band.
(Michael Linssen/Redferns)

Although officially on holiday in Montreux, he was still on call. Needless to say, the culprit spoiling his break was the irrepressible Roger. Taylor's rampant enthusiasm for motor racing was well known and he had been invited to be a guest at the Monaco Grand Prix. Accompanying him were Crystal and Rick Parfitt of Status Quo – another car freak. It was a disastrous combination: hot sun, fast cars and free-flowing wine were sure to lead these three fun-lovers to trouble – and they did. Roger managed to get himself arrested, and it turned out to be a costly business. Not only did Jim Beach have to stump up a large sum of money to get him out of jail, but the authorities insisted that the drummer left Monaco without delay. Unable to book him on a regular flight, Jim had to charter a helicopter in order to comply.

Although, as planned, all four had pursued their own interests, along the way they had kept in fairly regular touch with each other while Jim kept tabs on them all. Lately he had come up with an interesting proposition. He had certain interests in the film world and had been involved in discussions concerning a film version of the John Irving novel *The Hotel New Hampshire*. Asked if they would be interested in recording the music for the film, Freddie and John flew to Montreal in July to meet director Tony Richardson. It was agreed that Queen would begin work on some ideas for their second film score.

Whether it had been a shrewd ploy of Jim's to bring Queen together, or just coincidence, it was this project which brought it home to all four just how much they had missed recording together. They set up a date for mid-August in Los Angeles, where work at the Record Plant Studios began almost at once with a renewed sense of vigour. It was the first time they had recorded together in the States, too, and they felt this would be a bonus – that fresh surroundings would engender a new approach. As work began on the album, Jim was busy negotiating his way through the maze of existing problems in finalizing their break from Elektra.

While in Los Angeles Brian got the chance to catch up with his friend Joe Elliott. Def Leppard were appearing at the Forum and Brian went along to see them. This time, though, he went one step further and, to Joe's delight, joined them on stage. Says Elliott, 'Brian got up with David Lee Roth and a couple of others and jammed with us. It was great. You know, Brian's really thought of now as the sixth member of Def Leppard. That night he played the old Creedence Clearwater Revival number "Travellin' Band", and it was out of this world.' He reveals,

'Brian had actually brought his guitar and amp with him, yet when we invited him up he was a bit unsure at first. But we dragged him up by his curly hair, did a sound check and we were off!' Later Brian confessed to having had great fun that night performing live with Def Leppard, and of being highly flattered at being asked to join them on stage at all. He said of the band, 'I was bowled over by them. Their show was one of the highest-energy things I've ever seen. They destroyed the place.'

Although that guest spot was relatively short, Brian was very much aware of what it felt like working with other musicians. He had been doing a lot of thinking, and lately he had come to wonder if he was even capable of functioning outside Queen. In a way that was partly what had been in his mind back in April when he had rounded up a few of his friends at Record Plant Studios to kick around some ideas. Now the fruits of that experiment were about to be tried out on the public as Brian's first solo single, 'Star Fleet', a cover version of the song written by Paul Bliss, was released in the UK in late October. Despite the fact that the number featured some powerful and impressive guitar work from both Brian and Van Halen, the disc received no daytime radio airplay; consequently, although it cracked the top hundred, sadly it stalled at number sixty-five and remained in the charts a mere three weeks. Brian was disappointed. Two days later Queen signed a new contract with America's Capitol Records; Brian also struck a separate deal with Capitol in connection with his intended forthcoming solo album.

Meanwhile, despite initial enthusiasm, work on the film score had taken a distinct downward curve. They had tried to tailor the music to the book, which everyone in the band had read, but marrying the two was not easy and, while they were happy enough with the music itself, it had dawned on them that it didn't match the film. At first they considered recording two separate albums, a Queen one and a soundtrack, but that notion soon fell by the wayside and in the end they felt they had no option but to pull out of the project altogether.

They concentrated instead on putting together a new album. The break from each other had done them a power of good and all four were fired up with enthusiasm, brimming with ideas and collectively determined as never before to put everything into this recording. Only one remnant from the film project survived on to the album – a track called 'Keep on Passing the Open Windows'; this was a phrase which the author had frequently used as a form of advice on how to avoid committing suicide.

Brian's debut solo album, *Starfleet Project*, was released in the UK 31 October 1983. It was in fact a mini-LP in that it featured just three tracks – the full eight-minute version of 'Star Fleet', Brian's old number 'Let Me Out' and the twelve-minute blues jam in which he and his friends had all indulged at the end of their day's recording at Record Plant. This was now entitled 'Bluesbreaker', and Brian dedicated it to one of his guitar heroes – Eric Clapton. The album reached number one in the British heavy metal charts.

London's Capital Radio had meanwhile approached Brian to see if he would be interested in participating in a proposed new series. Capital's Head of Music then was Tony Hale, who recalls, 'At the time we were recording what was called *Rock Master Class*. I presented and produced the programmes, which were to feature besides Brian, Rick Wakeman, John Entwistle, Steve Howe and Midge Ure. In essence each programme was an extended interview with the artiste in front of an invited audience of about six hundred people in the Duke of York's Theatre. Answers were played, as well as spoken. As part of the show two young players were taken through a piece with "The Master". For his programme Brian chose a Pavane. The two young guitarists were given tips and at the end of the show, along with Brian, they played the whole thing all the way through.' Brian's programme was broadcast live on 20 November 1983 and formed part of a successful series all round.

From the new album, due for release early in 1984, Queen had decided that 'Radio Ga Ga' was to be the first single. Written by Roger, it was a driving, rhythmic, very pop-oriented song. Its lyrics paid tribute to the solid consistency of radio as a dependable medium which would be there to fall back on once people tired of video's visual attractions. That's not to say, though, that they didn't want to film a video to accompany the single.

Lately these productions had become bigger and bigger affairs, but this one assumed epic proportions. After discussing the idea with director David Mallett they set about recruiting five hundred extras. Mallett looked no further than the loyal Queen fan club, and the fact that they could only give four days' notice didn't matter. By mid-morning on 23 November five hundred keen fans had turned up ready for action at Shepperton Studios. Donning white boiler suits which were then sprayed with silver paint, they were herded into regimental rows before a huge stage on which the band were lined up. At each chorus they had to raise their arms above their heads and clap their hands in a special routine. It wasn't complicated and the fans grasped their duty straight away, but the same could not be said of the band. One or other member managed to screw up each take by clapping out of time. However, when work finally finished at about midnight it proved to be one of the most ambitious and extravagant videos they had ever shot and it looked exciting. It had also been responsible for the birth of the famous hand-clapping sequence which would later be adopted by concert crowds around the world.

Just before 'Radio Ga Ga''s release on 23 January 1984, Freddie took off for Munich to carry on with work on his solo album. Deep down he nursed a definite penchant for ballads, and with this project it was something he could indulge to his heart's content. 'I write commercial love songs because basically what I feel very strongly about is love and emotion,' Freddie admitted. 'I'm not a John Lennon who sleeps in bags for I don't know how long. You have to have a certain upbringing and go through a certain amount of history before people will believe in what you're writing about.'

The new Queen single shot straight into the charts at number four and was the first one also to appear on the fairly new cassette single format. Also, again for the first time, it carried the Queen 1 personal catalogue number, and because it represented the band's return after a longish absence a lot of PR went into promoting it. Some things, however, never change and one hypersensitive reviewer on *NME* accused it of 'quite upsetting [his] afternoon'.

A certain fragility existed within Queen which no one, now that they were 'back together again', recognized until they all gathered in Italy in February to perform at the huge annual music festival in San Remo. No one is prepared to say what triggered the incident, but their first live performance together as Queen since 1982 almost came to grief when a fight erupted backstage between Brian and Roger. Some say it originated from an argument between the pair over material and/or something to do with the stage, but whatever the cause, the occasion undoubtedly released a great deal of pent-up emotion in both men. It had long ago been understood that Roger had a volatile temper, but Brian operated on a long fuse and the incident took the others by complete surprise. It was Freddie who saved the day – some say the entire future of Queen – by leaping between the battling pair and proceeding to take the mickey out of them both. For a moment the situation trembled precariously in the balance, but Freddie was so typically outrageous in his antics that neither Brian nor Roger could stop himself from bursting into helpless laughter. In an instant sanity returned, and nothing more was ever said about the incident.

Out front the crowd, oblivious to the carryings-on, had been enjoying throughout the evening a succession of bands, most of whom performed just one number. But now they had begun to chant for Queen – the main band of the night. The two thousand delirious Italians went berserk during 'Radio Ga Ga'. Keen to keep up the momentum, Capitol Records released 'Radio Ga Ga' in America on 7 February as their label's first Queen single, and it climbed to a respectable number sixteen in the US charts. In Britain by now it had reached number two, where it stayed, but in no fewer than nineteen other countries it captured the number one slot and remained there for some weeks.

Their new album was called *The Works* and it contained all the old Queen trademarks – lots of harmonies, careful production and clever arrangements. This time, too, the material was much harder and gutsier. Brian had fought to get it that way, firmly believing that they needed to do this in order to haul themselves back on track after the disappointment of *Hot Space*. *The Works* was released first in America on 24 February, then three days later by EMI in Britain, where it crashed into the album charts at number two. Brian was delighted, and even some of the reviews were good. In particular, Brian's 'Hammer to Fall' track came in for special praise for its meaty heavy metal sound – credit which Joe Elliott feels is well deserved. 'It's my personal belief that Brian was the big anchor of Queen. I don't mean to take anything away from the other three, but had it not been for Brian then I think they would have become a pop band and probably not so big as they are. Freddie, I feel, would have leaned more toward ballads and Roger to pop. I mean, "Radio Ga Ga" is a terrific Queen number, but very pop. The hard stuff is down to Brian. I think he kept a crucial and very unique balance in the band.'

Brian now felt effectively back in harness and was looking forward to working on the video for their next single. Before that, though, he had some spare time when his good friend Chris Thompson, former vocalist with Manfred Mann's Earthband, asked for his help. Chris was working on his new album and invited Brian to play on the haunting track 'Shift in the Wind'. It was subsequently released as a single, the proceeds going to the Save The Children Fund.

The second single to come off *The Works* album was 'I Want to

Break Free', directed again by David Mallett. This time Roger had come up with a rather startling idea for the video. He suggested they did a send-up of the longest-running British soap, Granada TV's *Coronation Street*, with each of them dressing up as a specific female character. Any idea that some of the band members resisted the notion of dressing in drag were well and truly dowsed when Freddie later told a television interviewer, 'People have asked me how I got the others to dress up. In fact they ran into their frocks quicker than anything!'

The video was to incorporate three quite different sequences. For one sequence Queen were filmed surrounded by a crowd of feet-shuffling miners hobbling slowly down some steps. This was filmed on the first day in a huge draughty warehouse at Limehouse Studios in London's Docklands and again featured four hundred volunteer fan club members, once more in boiler suits but this time sprayed with black paint.

The following day the second and main section was filmed in a studio in Battersea and proved to be much more fun. John was cleverly turned into the granny of the bunch, buttoned up to the neck, hatted and complete with disapproving scowls. Freddie proved hilarious in his loose interpretation of *The Street's* busty barmaid Bet Lynch. Sporting a pink skinny-rib sweater over a pair of enormous false boobs, and a saucy PVC miniskirt offering the occasional flash of white knickers, he nearly broke his neck teetering on an over-ambitious pair of six-inch stilettos. Roger for his part transformed himself into a convincing sexy schoolgirl siren of a type previously associated with lusty fifth formers in the St Trinian's films! And Brian made a priceless entrance scrambling inelegantly out of bed in what had to be a custom-made full-length pink nylon nightie, his hair a mass of curlers and cream daubed all over his face.

The final sequence involved Freddie only, working for a second time with dancer Wayne Eagling. Again he rehearsed with the Royal Ballet. Derek Dean recalls, 'He wanted to re-create the ballet *L'Après-midi d'un faune*, made famous by Nijinsky, so Wayne choreographed it for him. It begins with Freddie looking like he's sitting on a rock but it's really made up of a pile of bodies. Later there's a shot of Freddie rolling on his front on top of a line of rotating bodies along the floor. Now he *loved* that bit!'

The filming of that ballet sequence took a full day at Limehouse Studios, yet features for less than one minute in the final video. Before he made it, Freddie had shaved off the droopy moustache – which went down well with many of his fans. As soon as the video was released, however, it became more cannon fodder for their enemies in the press. It was quite clearly intended to be funny – outrageous, perhaps, but still funny – and Queen certainly weren't the first band to dress up for a lark: the Stones had caused an outcry by doing it in 1966. Yet still shouts of transvestism rang out, followed by hysterical claims that such blatant homosexuality could corrupt their young fans. It was utter rot. Fans saw it as the joke it was intended to be, and loved it.

At the end of that day Freddie, who had enjoyed himself enormously, asked Wayne if there was anything he could do in return for the dancer, who had refused payment. 'I told him I can't sing', says Wayne, 'but I'd love to sing a song with you. So Freddie and I wrote a song together called "No I Can't Dance". When we recorded it I got a taste of what Freddie felt like the first time he came to ballet school. I was never so nervous in all my life. If you feel inadequate you're like that, and believe me I felt inadequate! The thing was, though, I could sing with Freddie next to me. We had a great time.'

'I Want to Break Free' was released as a single in early April. Despite the slagging it got from the critics it reached number three in the UK charts, was a huge hit in Europe and went straight to the top in several countries. It was even adopted as a freedom anthem in some parts of South America. Later that month Brian again took time out to guest at Battery Studios for another friend, Billy Squier, who was working on a new album. Roger's thoughts too were trained on a new album – his second as a solo performer – and he flew off to Montreux to work on it.

At the beginning of the year Brian had been approached by Guild Guitars in New York with a proposition: his home-made Red Special had long since become world-famous, and Guild said they would like to make a replica for sale to the general public. Brian agreed, but only on condition that it was an exact replica. Guild were determined to do the task properly; besides getting Brian to provide details of its unique composition, they took X-rays of the instrument and Brian was invited to inspect developments regularly. Each time he came away pronouncing himself satisfied with the way it was shaping up.

In June Guild proudly launched the BHM1 in Chicago, with a party which Brian attended and at which he was presented with one of the first copies. Although the BHM1 went on to feature both on stage and in the studio, Brian's delight with Guild quickly tarnished. The price tag of £1,200 reflected the detailed care required to build each instrument, but it also put it out of reach of many people, and it just wasn't selling well enough. Supposedly to improve it, although probably to cut production costs, Guild made a few alterations. When Brian heard about these changes he immediately protested, but to no avail, so he withdrew his support and terminated the agreement. Passions of a far more serious kind stirred up a hornets' nest for Queen when they announced in July that, after their forthcoming European tour, they would be playing some gigs at the Sun City Superbowl in South Africa. This statement sparked off an immediate row with the Musicians' Union, as well as with many anti-apartheid groups and of course with the press. Brian came straight out in the papers stating, 'We've thought about the morals of it a lot and it's something we've decided to do. This band is not political. We play to anybody who comes to listen. The show will be in Botswana in front of a mixed audience.' But it didn't matter what he said; the controversy had begun.

Trying to ignore the reaction, the band settled down to filming the video to accompany their latest single, to be released on 16 July and called 'It's a Hard Life'. Brian had a £1,000 guitar in the shape of a skull made especially for the video, but it was Freddie who stole the show with an elaborate flame-red costume which made him look like a giant prawn.

In August they set out on what they dubbed 'The Works' tour. They were accompanied by a new keyboard player, Spike Edney, who had recently been working with the Boomtown rats. Says Spike, 'I was introduced to Queen through Roger's personal assistant, Crystal. He said they were looking to replace Fred Mandell and asked if I was interested.' He goes on, 'Queen asked me to an audition in Munich and I went thinking there'd be a queue, only to find I was the only one, which was all right.' It transpired that Spike knew Queen's material, as he puts it, 'in many ways better than they did themselves', which delighted the band. He would become a permanent fixture on stage with Queen for the next two years. On this, as in all subsequent tours, they were rewarded with the sight of every fan in the stadium doing the famous handclap sequence during the chorus in 'Radio Ga Ga'.

Brian's hard rocking number 'Hammer to Fall' became the band's twenty-sixth single and is redolent of what drives him most in music. He freely confesses that the heavy side of it is a release of emotion and that what he loves best about rock is its meaty sound. He had already tried his best to stamp some good old-fashioned rock into *The Works* album and, as usual, had been offered the band's ideas in return. But he once revealed, 'The pressure has always been against me, because not everyone in the band is into the same stuff as I am. I get the most pleasure out of the things that I can hammer down and get some excitement out of. Basically I'm like a boy with a guitar. I just love the fat, loud sound of it.'

Soon they were off to Bophuthatswana in South Africa: Queen were scheduled to play twelve dates at the Sun City Superbowl and the tickets had sold out in a single day. But on the first night the gig was barely fifteen minutes old when Freddie's old enemy reared its head and his voice, which had been threatening to act up, almost gave out. The band tried to plough on regardless, but it was no use. 'Fred was in agony,' says Spike, 'and after three songs he walked off stage.' A specialist was quickly flown out to examine him, and it came as no surprise when he was strongly advised to take a complete rest. They had no option, and Queen cancelled the following four nights. Adds Edney, 'It caused a big scandal because the tickets were sold and there was no time to reschedule dates, but it couldn't be helped.'

Already upset at the turn of events, Brian decided he would use the time to go and talk to some black South Africans for himself; he wanted to see life in this country as it really was. It so happened that in October Soweto, the black township on the outskirts of Johannesburg, is where the annual Black African Awards shows are held. Brian was asked if he would attend and present some of the prizes, and quickly accepted. The officials at Sun City tried their best to stop him, apparently fearing for his safety outside the complex, but he would not be thwarted and, with Jim Beach for company, went to Soweto.

That night made a lasting impression on Brian. It was a muggy night and warm rain fell on his face as he stood on the bare stage in the open muddy field before an audience of thousands, handing out awards. For all the dire warnings pressed on him back at Sun City, Brian met with nothing but warmth and unmitigated friendliness. Moved deeply, before he left he personally pledged from the stage that one day the band would come back to Soweto and play for them.

The rest of Queen also felt they wanted to help in some way. When they learned that a school for deaf and blind children in Bophuthatswana was struggling to survive, after talking it over with

EMI and the school patrons the band agreed to release a live album in South Africa with all the royalties going directly to the school. In no time at all it paid for a whole new wing to relieve the desperate overcrowding, and money still accrues today every time an album is sold.

Spike recalls, 'We'd all been very happy to have the chance to play South Africa. It was quite an experience. For one thing, it teaches you not to listen to people pontificating about something they really know nothing about. Personally speaking, before I went there I was very sure about what I felt about South Africa. When I came home I didn't know anything any more – the visit had altered my whole way of looking at things. For Brian and the others it was definitely an enlightening experience.'

Not everyone, though, was convinced that Queen, even though they had the purest of intentions, truly understood the serious political implications involved. Mandla Langa, cultural attaché with the African National Congress, is quite forthright. 'Queen came into the country at a time when people didn't need any external influence which could give respectability to the Pretoria regime. In addition, Sun City was always regarded as an insult to any right-thinking South African. To perform there, in the midst of poverty and rage, cannot be rationalized as Queen doing their bit through music to break down barriers. It must also be remembered,' adds Mandla, 'that the people who attended those concerts were overwhelmingly white, and that institutions such as the South African Broadcasting Corporation, revelling at their new-found connection with the Western world, would give maximum airplay time to Queen. Their music then – and possibly still now, because people have long memories – has never been embraced by black activists.'

Queen were placed on the United Nations blacklist of musicians who performed in South Africa, although their name was later removed. In Britain, the Musicians' Union were not impressed either. The MU had banned its members from playing in South Africa, and Queen had barefacedly flouted the rules. Brian went to face the Union's General Committee on the band's behalf and gave a lengthy and impassioned speech, detailing their reasons for the trip and stressing how much he felt they had achieved. He made no bones about the fact that they were totally against apartheid but that they didn't feel anything was achieved by just not playing there. Music, he maintained, should transcend all barriers unfettered by race or politics; by going there and speaking out against it, weren't they trying to do something practical about the problem? He received a standing ovation from some of the more enlightened members, but the Committee refused to budge and fined Queen heavily. The band grimly accepted the decision but stipulated that the money be donated to charity: it stuck in their craw to think it might go into the MU coffers.

With these problems behind them, in November they decided for the first time in their long career to release a Christmas single. Brian, Roger and John had some fun at Sarm Studios recording the number; then Brian and Roger flew to Munich, where Freddie was staying, so that he could complete it. 'Thank God It's Christmas' entered the British charts on 8 December. It only got to number twenty-one, but this was no great surprise, for this was the year that Boomtown Rats singer Bob Geldof, moved by the scenes of famine and suffering in Ethiopia on television news reports, had banded together several stars under the name Band Aid. In a glare of publicity they had recorded the number 'Do They Know It's Christmas', which was guaranteed to become 1984's Christmas number one.

In December Queen released a batch of singles which in reality were all individual tracks from one album. Critics immediately lambasted them for supposedly exploiting their fans' devotion. It was a sour note on which to end their first year performing as a band again.

SAVE ME

Any crisis of confidence had to be quickly pushed aside as, less than two weeks into the new year, Queen picked up the cudgels again and headlined at what was hailed as the biggest rock festival in the world. This star-studded event was held at a custom-built arena snuggling in the mountains at Barra da Tijuca near Rio de Janeiro and was the brainchild of Brazilian businessman Roberto Medina. Billed as 'Rock in Rio' and expected to surpass the famous Woodstock of 1969, besides Queen it featured among others Iron Maiden, AC/DC, Yes and Ozzie Osbourne. Def Leppard were also to have appeared, but had had to pull out at the eleventh hour due to a horrific road accident on New Year's Eve in which their drummer Rick Allen lost an arm.

Before a record-breaking crowd of over a quarter of a million, local Brazilian bands rubbed shoulders with the cream of the world's rock acts. It was the biggest audience Queen had performed to, and Brian could hardly believe his eyes when they walked out on stage to close the show in the early hours of 12 January. They were given a tremendous reception until they returned for an encore and broke into the number 'I Want to Break Free'. No sooner had Freddie appeared on stage wearing the top half of his outfit from the video, complete with tousled wig, than the audience began pelting the stage with trash. Once before a South American audience had bombarded them with missiles as a show of appreciation, but it wasn't only the velocity at which the crunched cans and rubble rained down on the stage which made Freddie realize that this was different. There was the sickly scent of real rage out there, and in a flash he shed the props, laughed loudly and carried on as if nothing had happened. The other encores went down a storm and the band came off stage on a high. Later, someone explained that 'I Want to Break Free' had been adopted as a freedom song by many in the country, and Freddie's drag act had seemed to demean it.

That evening EMI threw a lavish party for all the festival artistes at the opulent Copacabana Beach Hotel, which was relayed on live TV all over South America. It wasn't uncommon for high jinks at these shindigs to begin with guests diving fully clothed into a swimming pool, and that night Brian was one of the first in. Later, however, in the midst of all the decadent excess, word filtered to his ears that a very different party was being held nearby.

Hundreds of Queen fans, determined to be close to their band, had gathered for their own celebration on the ribbon of sandy beach opposite the hotel. They had embedded masses of slender candles in a sloping sandbank so that, when lit, they spelt out the name 'Queen'. Around this glow in the dark they were singing, playing drums and dancing to guitars. Their admirers the world over were very important to Brian, who left the hotel and headed for the beach. The fans couldn't believe their eyes when they saw his distinctive figure quietly strolling down to join them at the water's edge. He stayed for quite a time soaking up the atmosphere, sharing in the fun and thoroughly enjoying himself – in so doing making it an unforgettable night for hundreds of Brazilian Queen supporters.

The final night of Rock in Rio took place on 18–19 January, and again Queen closed the show. Brazil's Globo Television had recorded the whole festival; afterwards Jim Beach entered into negotiations to purchase the rights for Queen's performances, with a view to releasing it on video at a later date. 'The whole thing was treated as a two-week holiday really,' says Spike, 'with loads of stars hangin' by the hotel pools and all that. But what Rock in Rio did was reaffirm Queen's standing as South America's top band.'

Shortly after Brian had returned to Britain he was approached by Michael Stimpson, guitar tutor at Roehampton Institute. Michael was writing a book entitled *The Guitar: A Guide for Students and Teachers*, which explained various techniques including classical, lead, bass, folk, flamenco and jazz guitar. Aware of the enormous respect for Brian's skill on lead electric guitar, he asked him to write a chapter for the book. Says Michael, 'I wanted to include a chapter on electric guitar because one of the main fields of my work has been to encourage the acceptance and teaching of the guitar in a way which reflects its affinity with different musical genres. In other words, it was well overdue that guitar teaching in schools and colleges was moved away from a purely classical approach.' The book was published by Oxford University Press in 1988 and to coincide with it BBC TV made a short film about Michael's work, to which Brian contributed.

Brian thrives on new experiences and can rarely resist one, and in February 1985 he tried his hand on a two-hour stint as a guest DJ at London's Capital Radio. The original plan was that, although he would do the mouthing between records, an experienced hand would be in charge of the controls. But Brian got carried away and in no time was experimenting furiously, pushing buttons right, left and centre. He made more than one blunder during those live two hours, but it added to the sense of fun and the show had good listening figures.

While Brian had been busy writing and spinning records, John had managed to chalk up a drink-driving conviction for which he was fined £150. Roger had involved himself with producing firstly a single by actor Jimmy Nail and then, at Virgin Records' request, one by a new young Scots band called Sideway Look – although unfortunately the latter project fell through. Working subsequently with singers Feargal Sharkey and Roger Daltrey, however, made up for any disappointment. And Freddie was to be found staking out his pet London nightclubs. It was at one such club, Heaven, that he met a men's hairdresser named Jim Hutton who was then working at the Savoy Hotel. They had known each other vaguely years before, but this time the chemistry jelled and a relationship began.

By early April the band were on the road again as they took off for their first tour of the year. The first date, on 13 April, was at Mount Smart Stadium in Auckland, and because they had never played in New Zealand before Brian was excited at the prospect; but their anticipation was somewhat marred when they were harangued both at the airport and outside their hotel by groups of anti-apartheid demonstrators. Brian took it deeply to heart and, when he discovered that yet another noisy crowd of protestors were lying in wait for them outside the concert venue, he wished they would understand once and for all that Queen too were vehemently anti-apartheid. Having played in South Africa looked set to haunt the rest of their career.

One thing which happened during their stay in New Zealand briefly took Brian's mind off the Sun City repercussions. Their keyboard player, Spike Edney, was contacted by Boomtown Rats vocalist Bob Geldof. Geldof and former Ultravox singer Midge Ure had decided to try to follow up the charity hit 'Do They Know It's Christmas' with a massive rock concert, all proceeds from which would go to help the starving people of Ethiopia. Geldof had rung his friend to talk about Queen's possible participation in what was to become the legendary Live Aid concert.

Says Spike, 'Geldof rang me up saying he wanted Queen on the bill but he didn't want to officially ask them in case they said no, so would I speak to them about it.' Although the band were greatly taken with the idea, it seemed too unlikely a project ever to come to fruition and their response was to refuse. 'I know that Brian and Roger had been bitterly disappointed not to have been asked the previous year to be involved in the "Do They Know It's Christmas" single,' adds Spike, 'so I wasn't surprised that personally their first reaction was to be all for it. But when they thought about it Queen were sceptical of this thing coming off, and who could blame them then?' Spike though suggested Bob should try himself, which he did. In the end they said they would consider appearing if he and Midge did actually manage to pull it off.

A day or so later they headed to Melbourne for the first of their four dates at the Sports and Entertainments Centre. Singer Phil Collins was on his own tour of Australia at this time and two nights later Queen went to see his show. Returning the compliment, Collins arrived backstage on Queen's last night in Melbourne to catch their performance, although he annoyed Freddie by entering the dressing room before the show – always an intense time for performers and an area usually out of bounds to outsiders. That night's gig was a disaster – lights acted up and the sound was nowhere near its normal quality. Brian came off stage deflated, convinced that it had been dreadful for the capacity crowd. Nor was he persuaded by Phil's assurances afterwards, that despite everything, they had performed well.

Glad to leave Melbourne for Sydney, they had a few days' break before their four dates there and during this time Chrissy flew out to join

Brian. Together they flew up to the Great Barrier Reef where they tried their hands at scuba diving. Brian acquired quite an aptitude for the sport, but his enjoyment mainly stemmed from being able to relax for a short while in his wife's company.

Shaking off the misfortune of that last night in Melbourne, Queen's Sydney performances went without a hitch. While there they met up again with their former manager John Reid. His client Elton was also gigging around Australia, and on their only mutual night off they all teamed up. Brian and John Deacon trotted off with Reid to enjoy a civilized evening at the Opera House, while Freddie, Roger and Elton plunged unashamedly into the hectic Sydney nightlife.

Two days later, back in Britain Freddie's first solo album, *Mr Bad Guy*, was released on the CBS label. The content, mainly love songs, took the music press by surprise and, although he did find one or two allies, some reviewers were even more cutting than usual about it. Freddie didn't care. He was proud of the album and knew it reflected his personal taste, which is what he'd set out to accomplish – and to hell with the critics.

From Australia Queen flew direct to Japan to begin another brief tour. Here Brian – again prevailed upon to share his experience and musical expertise with eager students – happily spent what time he could spare talking to and helping pupils with guitar techniques at the Aoyama Recording School.

Once back in the UK in mid-May all four went their separate ways for a while. Roger and John opted for a holiday, while Freddie shuttled back and forth between his beloved Munich and London. By now his relationship with Jim Hutton had deepened to the point that they were almost inseparable. The major casualty was his physical relationship with his much-loved Mary Austin; it was over. But Mary was still very precious to Freddie, and occupied a place in his heart and life which no one could ever hope to rival. So, although they ceased to be lovers, he bought her a luxury flat near his own home so that she could always be near him. Mary too remained closely involved in the day-to-day running of his house, its staff and seeing to his business affairs.

Brian, meanwhile, spent time at home relaxing with his family and did everyday things like meeting up with friends, among them Def Leppard's Joe Elliott. Says Joe, 'I'd bought a house about twenty minutes walk from Brian's. Chrissy was from Leeds and my girlfriend was from Sheffield, which meant they found a lot in common. So the four of us would have dinner, the odd drink, or would just pop round to each other's for cups of tea and a chat. Brian's really good company. There's not any feeling of being threatened. There's no rivalry, which can happen sometimes. One night at dinner in a restaurant in Cobham the wine had flowed particularly well – the later it got, the looser tongues grew all round, and we very nearly set about making an album. The band was going to be Brian, myself and Rick Savage from Def Lepp, Jason Bonham [son of the late John Bonham of Led Zeppelin] and Spike Edney. Unfortunately my manager wouldn't allow it to happen, but I'd love one day to record with Brian.'

While individually the band were doing their own thing, Jim Beach was holding business meetings with top promoter Harvey Goldsmith. It looked as if this idea of a massive concert for Ethiopia was a goer after all. The intention was to stage it at Wembley Stadium in the summer; since April matters had progressed considerably and a parallel gig in Philadelphia was now planned. The event, now billed as 'Live Aid', would be, as Geldof dubbed it, a 'global juke box', and Queen decided they were definitely on. 'Absolutely,' confirms Spike. 'By now Geldof with his forceful personality had got the BBC to agree to set up a satellite link to the States, and it was frankly just too good a thing not to be part of.'

Harvey Goldsmith had been having problems with managers of various bands who were all hoping to close the event, so when Jim brought up the issue of Queen's time slot he let out a pained groan. Queen, though, were not expecting to be considered headliners – indeed if anyone were to be – and their preferred slot was around 6 p.m. Harvey was delighted. Actually it was quite a shrewd move on Queen's part, considering the Philadelphia link-up – the time difference would make them the first band to be seen on live TV in the States.

Excitement mounting, on 10 July they hid themselves away for three solid days of rehearsal at the Shaw Theatre in London's King's Cross. Each band had been allotted twenty minutes, and because Queen wanted to use their time to best advantage they decided to restrict themselves to their most famous hits. But of course there were several to choose from and lively arguments erupted over which ones to select, condense and hone to a slick twenty-minute spot.

Live Aid, on 13 July 1985, was an incredible day. Wembley Stadium was jam-packed and everyone was convinced that they were taking part in what would surely become an historic event. Even the sun made a guest appearance after a gloomy week of drizzle. At midday Status Quo took the stage and belted out their hit 'Rockin' All Over the World'. The atmosphere was already electric, intensifying as the hot afternoon unfolded and one top performer after another streamed on and off stage.

Following David Bowie's set, around 6.30 p.m. (the schedule was running late), by which time Wembley had been hooked up by satellite to the Philadelphia stadium, Queen came on. Brian was more nervous than he had ever been in his life. The sense of occasion – it was simultaneously broadcast live to over one billion people worldwide – almost paralysed him, but they all turned in an absolutely terrific performance. Queen in fact, no one would argue, stole the show that day. Geldof later admitted to emerging from the appeals box at Wembley, having just taken a telephone donation of one million pounds from a Kuwaiti businessman, and being stopped dead in his tracks wondering who had got the sound together. It was Queen, belting through a medley of edited versions of their most popular hits which had the crowd, Queen fans or not, with arms raised above their heads swaying like a giant barley field in a breeze.

A fellow performer that day, singer Paul Young, concurs, 'I'd always liked Queen anyway, but that was the night I said to myself: these boys really are fantastic. The sound they managed to get was amazing. There was just the four of them on there, with none of their usual trappings, and they *still* blew everyone away. Freddie also proved to the whole watching world that evening just what a showman he was.' Yet despite being told so by their friends backstage, it didn't hit them until some time later just how well they had gone down. Brian later admitted in interview, 'It was the greatest day of our lives, although we only played a very small part in it. I think it's the thing I'll remember above all, out of all the things we've done. It was an amazing day!'

Before Live Aid the band had again come to the point where they hadn't really wanted to do anything else for a while, and were unsure whether Queen had anything left to give. But having gone out on that Wembley stage without the familiarity of their usual lights and effects, and having found that they could still do it, had been a great boost to their confidence – just the shot in the arm that Brian in particular had desperately needed.

For a while after Live Aid all four again settled to pursuing solo projects or at least knocking about with ideas. Brian had been toying with the notion of recording a second solo album. But that's not to say that

Queen as an entity wasn't more alive and kicking than it had been for a long time, and, galvanized to harness this potent energy, they started planning a major 1986 European tour. They also desperately wanted to get back into recording, so it was quite propitious when director Russell Mulcahy asked if they would consider writing and recording some music for what was going to be his first major feature film. Queen agreed, on condition that one of their numbers was used as the title track. The film was *Highlander*, starring Christopher Lambert and Sean Connery.

September 1985 found Queen hard at work in the studio. One track emerged quite quickly and appealed so strongly to everyone that they decided it was a must as their next single. 'One Vision' was released on 4 November, only to be unreasonably targeted by the music press as Queen cashing in on Live Aid because of the sentiments expressed in the lyrics – that of the world pulling together in harmony. In the wave of moral conscience sweeping the country cries went up that Queen really ought to donate their royalties to charity, which was patently unfair. The band were no strangers to largesse and in fact the royalties from one number featured at Live Aid, 'Is This The World We Created?', was currently raking in money to the Save The Children Fund. Besides that Queen, like any other band, were in the business of making music and making money. Busy working on material for their new album while EMI released a special boxed set of thirteen Queen albums, Brian ignored the accusations – but they still hurt.

Also still hurting was the perpetual row over Sun City. Every so often something or someone would fan the flames, until at the end of 1985 Queen decided they had no option but to come out and make a full statement to the press. So in mid-December they reasserted their anti-apartheid stance, stating that they were apolitical and finally that they would never again visit South Africa. Brian was very upset at having to make this particular pledge because he remembered personally promising the crowd in Soweto that one day Queen would return and perform for them. However, it seemed the only way to get some peace and stop the continued attacks on them.

The intense work required throughout January 1986 on the soundtrack for the $20 million film *Highlander* came as a welcome distraction for Brian – something to concentrate his mind on. The songs were to be directly inspired by watching the daily rushes, and it was while he was driving home one day after sitting through one particular print that he began to hum into his tiny tape recorder the beginnings of a song which would later emerge as the beautiful and haunting 'Who Wants to Live Forever'.

To many, Brian's outstanding brilliance on guitar tends to over-shadow his very real talent as a songwriter – something that Brian himself is very modest about. When interviewed for a 1983 BBC Radio 1 series, *The Guitar Greats*, he had this to say, 'I'm not a very prolific writer and I can never just sit down and write a song. There has to be something there and usually I get a couple of lines of lyrics and melody together and then the rest of it's really working very hard, searching the soul to see what should be in there. But then some of the stuff I've done without taking it too seriously – I've been more pleased with it in the end.' However, Joe Elliott in particular feels strongly: 'Brian's "Who Wants to Live Forever" will become like the Moody Blues' "Nights in White Satin" – a classic. It's got that feel. I remember when he wrote it, he presented it to Freddie as a demo and Freddie said, "Hey, that's good! No, no, I'll just come in second" – meaning he thought Brian should take first lead vocal on it and that he would come in on the second verse.' He goes on, 'Mind you, I thought Brian's early stuff was great, too – like "White Queen" and "39", which I've always felt sounded sort of Lindisfarne-ish. The thing about Brian is, he's never afraid to experiment.'

When their album was finished, EMI and Capitol Records held conflicting views as to which single to release from it first. The American label opted for the powerful 'Princes of the Universe', while EMI plumped for the catchy 'A Kind of Magic', which was also intended to be the album title. The videos to accompany both were impressive. In the case of 'Princes of the Universe', Queen contacted *Highlander's* star, French actor Christopher Lambert, to invite him to take part in the video playing Connor Macleod, his character in the movie. Christopher had never filmed a pop video before but gave it a try and thoroughly enjoyed himself. For 'A Kind of Magic' the band went to film at the disused and freezing Playhouse Theatre in London's Charing Cross. In the video Freddie portrays a magician who strolls past three sleeping vagrants and, with a swish of his cane, transforms them one by one into performing rock stars until he summarily breaks the spell. With its clever special effects and animation it made for a very unique video, and when the single was released on 17 March it went straight to number one in thirty-five countries; in Britain it sat at number three.

Once again for a few weeks the band went their separate ways. John found himself inveigled into working on music for yet another film, *Biggles*, and ended up making a video in which the distinguished actor Peter Cushing made a cameo appearance. Roger had agreed to be a judge in a rock musicians' national talent competition, while Freddie occupied his time by dabbling in musicals.

Some months back Fred had been involved in writing and recording a couple of songs for his friend Dave Clark's production of *Time*, which would go on to run for two years in London's West End. He had recently got permission to use the stage set of the musical at the Dominion Theatre in Tottenham Court Road to make a video to accompany the single 'Time', although because there were two shows a day his time was restricted to early mornings.

One day Freddie returned to the Dominion for the evening show. On impulse, at the interval Freddie decided he wanted to distribute ice cream. Despite advice to the contrary he barged into the confectioner's stand and, after buying up a whole tray of assorted goodies, pulled on a white coat and walked out into the audience. At first no one took any notice of the man gaily handing out free ices, but then Freddie got carried away and began chucking them about willy-nilly. Cornettos, tubs and rock-hard ice lollies unceremoniously bounced off the head of many a punter or landed with a squelch on their laps, reducing the once orderly theatre to chaos when a few people started hurling them back at the madman in their midst. Soon everyone discovered it was Freddie Mercury, and when he made his escape, exhilarated by all the sheer silly fun, thunderous applause buffeted him all the way.

Unfortunately, life for Brian was now far from carefree: for some time his personal life had been heading inexorably for the rocks. There were various reasons for this situation, and it would seem that the blame, if that's the word, lay at both his door and Chrissy's. Brian had known for some time that things weren't right between them and that they had both been papering over the cracks, neither willing to accept that their problems were only multiplying. They had been married for a long time, had been together for even longer and had two beautiful children whom they both adored; none of that would easily be put under threat if Brian could help it. The thing was, though, he didn't quite know what to do.

In many ways, therefore, it was a relief when Queen had to knuckle down to rehearsals for their forthcoming European tour. But it was during a break in these, when Brian attended the London premiere of the film *Down and Out in Beverly Hills*, that fate brought him into contact with actress Anita Dobson, then starring as Angie Watts, the feisty landlady of the Queen Vic pub in the BBC TV soap *EastEnders*. Something clicked between Brian and Anita, and on impulse he invited her to come and see Queen when they performed at Wembley Stadium on 11 June.

At the beginning of June *A Kind of Magic*, the soundtrack album from *Highlander*, was released, entering the album charts at number one. Four days later the band took off for Stockholm to prepare for what they called their 'Magic Tour'. Much to Brian's dismay, regardless of the very clear statement they had issued six months before, when they arrived at the Rasunda Fotbollstadion in Stockholm for their first gig they were confronted by a pack of chanting anti-apartheid protestors. The audience, however, dispelled the sour taste by going wild with enthusiasm throughout the gig. At the end, already whipped into a frenzy of excitement, Freddie in a typical piece of theatre snatched their breath away. He vanished off stage while the music continued to swirl, egged on by the crescendo of Roger's drums, and reappeared, swathed in a red velvet, ermine-trimmed robe with a six-foot train, an elaborate crown on his head, and cradling his sawn-off mike stand as a sceptre, to accept the crowd's cheering homage as if he were King Mercury. Only someone with Freddie's delicious audacity could get away with it, and the audience adored it.

A couple of days later in Britain their new single, a gentle, lilting ballad called 'Friends Will Be Friends', was released. Brian, meanwhile, was spending a free day in a Dutch recording studio to prepare a demo of two songs, one for Japanese singer Minako Honda and the other for Anita Dobson, whom he found was more and more on his mind. The tour then moved on into France.

It was in Paris that Fish, then lead singer with the band Marillion, first got to know Brian. He says, 'Marillion had gone out to support Queen on the open-air gigs in that '86 tour, which in fact ended up being the last live dates that they'd do, and of course Freddie was Freddie and kept himself very much to himself. Brian and I got talking. It's funny, because normally I don't tend to get on with guitarists – not because I've got anything against them, but because of the personality types that guitarists normally are. Brian, though, isn't the stereotype egocentric guitarist who'll sit and discuss pick-ups for two hours!'

He goes on, 'Brian's a painful romantic and quite excruciatingly sensitive. He doesn't get angry. He gets hurt very easily. He was hurting that night we first got talking. It was in a Paris nightclub and he sat and talked to me about South Africa and apartheid, all the pros and cons of playing Sun City which Queen were still copping an awful lot of flak for. Brian was deeply hurt by the furore. We both agreed that the straightforward blacklisting by the UN was out of order. For me, musicians, lyricists, whatever . . . they can get away with stuff that politicians won't get away with, and they can actually change an attitude. For somebody to have the nerve to go there and stand on a stage in front of a massive audience and take an anti-apartheid stance – that does more, I think, than saying, "Right, we're not going to play your country." Anyway, that's what our talk revolved around for two hours solid, and I was quite impressed at how much Brian had actually thought it all through. But then he's that sort of person anyway. He churns things over in his head for hours and hours.'

Brian and Fish got on really well, and to some extent it helped with his personal problems too. 'Yeah, his marriage was in trouble at this point,' Fish admits, 'and Brian was really going through it. We talked quite a lot about it during that tour. He was questioning was it right, was it worth taking all this grief for. He was extremely tortured by it.'

After France the tour trundled on through Germany and Switzerland, then to Ireland and finally back to Britain with a solitary gig in the north of England before hitting a two-night slot at Wembley Stadium on 11 and 12 July. The extra date had had to be added to cope with the deluge of demand for tickets, which delighted promoter Harvey Goldsmith no end. He felt, 'It just shows that after fifteen years Queen are bigger than they've ever been.' Brian certainly found the adrenalin flowing again at its best, and the occasion reminded him of Live Aid. Anita Dobson turned up to watch him play, and both nights were complete sell-outs.

One special guest attending the first Wembley gig was Formula One motor racing champion Jackie Stewart, who had been invited along by John. Stewart had known the band since the mid-seventies. Says Jackie, 'It's a curious thing – music and motor racing. There always seems to be a link. George Harrison is a big fan of racing, and Paul McCartney used to come to the Monaco Grand Prix, as did some of the Stones. Roger, of course, is mad keen on cars and had been to quite a few races. I'd always enjoyed Queen's music and had been to a few of their concerts, but I suppose my first link came through John. I'd been on radio's *Desert Island Discs* and had requested "Bohemian Rhapsody" and "Killer Queen", as well as the national anthem which Queen play at the end of their concerts. Not long afterwards I got a letter from John Deacon inviting me to one of their concerts.' He continues, 'They knew a reasonable amount about my racing, and when mutual respect of each other's talents is there it sets up a bridge of respect. It's not the same if you just admire someone's talent – there's still that barrier there. But that's not what it's like with us.'

For Jackie that night's performance was exceptional, and to a great extent this was down to Brian. He feels, 'What Queen created was an extraordinary thing, and there are no copies – nobody else was able to do what they have done. I call them sound merchants. They conjure up an individual sound instrumentally, and for me Brian's contribution to that is immense. He is so unique and very identifiable. I don't care where you are, in which country or whatever, you can always tell when you're hearing Brian May.'

Although Queen's after-gig parties had long ago assumed the mantle of their own mythology, the post-Wembley rave-up at the Roof Gardens in Kensington High Street holds a special place – partly because, although they didn't realize it at the time, this tour they were halfway through was the last they would ever undertake. About midnight over five hundred people ascended to the beautiful restaurant landscaped like a garden. That night the guests included a host of celebrities, fellow musicians and friends like Fish and the fun-loving Gary Glitter, all of them in a state of eager expectancy. They were not disappointed. Says Gary, 'Queen without doubt gave the most outrageous parties I have ever been to, but this one was something else! For a start every girl, or boy for that matter, acting as a waiter had drawn-on suits – I mean body paint. At first you didn't notice that they'd actually got nothing on. Then you did a double take and thought, Wow! Only Queen would have thought to do this! A lot of people make a fuss about what goes on at Queen parties, but the bottom line is they go out of their way to make sure that everyone has as good a time as possible.' He adds, 'That was the night I met up with Brian again after all those years. Anita was there. They hadn't long met. Brian was going about the whole time asking everyone what they'd thought of the concert.'

After playing at Maine Road football stadium in Manchester, Queen flew to Germany for a gig at Cologne's Meunsdorfer Stadium on 19 July.

That night it was Brian's turn to get on stage with Marillion and play. Says Fish, 'Again it was a spontaneous thing. Backstage at gigs, no kidding, is the most boring place in the world, with everyone sitting around waiting to go on, and I just suggested it to Brian on impulse and he agreed.'

Vienna came after Cologne, followed by a trip along the Danube – in the Russian President Gorbachev's personal hydrofoil, no less – to Budapest where the British Embassy had laid on a special party in their honour. The gig at Nepstadion (the People's Stadium) was again a tremendous experience. Fans from all over the Eastern Bloc converged in droves to see Queen perform – eighty thousand of them to be precise, not including a further forty-five thousand ticketless fans who had flocked from Odessa, Minsk and Warsaw just to stand outside and listen. Freddie and Brian had attempted to learn a couple of verses of the Hungarian folk song 'Tavaski Szel', which Freddie sang that night to ecstatic applause, even if he was quite obviously reading the words off a note taped to his palm. It was the courtesy of trying which found its way straight into the audience's heart. They in turn paid tribute to Queen by singing back, in perfect English, the words of 'Love of My Life'. It was most definitely a night out for a mutual admiration society.

After France and Spain, the final gig of the 'Magic Tour' took place at Knebworth Park in Hertfordshire on 9 August. It was a huge event with a funfair and beer tents. Several delay towers were erected around the field to carry the amplification, so that those at the back could hear the performance properly. Traffic jams started building up early that morning and Queen were to have the biggest paying audience they had ever played to in Britain – somewhere close to two hundred thousand.

The band made their entrance in twin helicopters flying in parallel, one of which had been resprayed with the distinctive *Kind of Magic* images from the album sleeve. As the choppers weaved over the crowd to come in to land, the audience forgot the support act on stage and craned their necks back to squint up into the brilliant sun, waving and cheering on the arrival of their heroes. 'It was an amazing day,' recalls Spike. 'That extra gig arranged at Wembley could have run to another four nights – the demand for tickets was so great. The turn-out at Knebworth was just incredible, and of course the party afterwards had everything including mud wrestlers. What none of us knew at that time, of course, was that it would be their last ever gig.' That afternoon a baby was born in the audience, but sadly there was also a fracas in which a young Status Quo fan was stabbed and bled to death before he could reach hospital.

With the tour over, the discipline of life on the road was also over and, although they had all enjoyed it, in some ways it didn't come a day too soon. As at the end of 1982, friction and discord had been wreaking destruction on the band; all four felt they needed a break from each other, and so that summer they decided to take most of 1987 off. Brian once openly admitted, 'We did hate each other for a while. Recording *Jazz* and those albums we did in Munich, *The Game* and *The Works*, we got very angry with each other. I left the group a couple of times, just for the day. You know – "I'm off and I'm not coming back." We'd all done that. You end up quibbling over one note, and we always raved about money. A lot of terrible injustices take place over songwriting. The major one is B-sides. "Bohemian Rhapsody" sells a million, and Roger gets the same writing royalty as Freddie because he did "I'm in Love with My Car." There was contention about this for years.'

In Brian's case, coming home meant a return to his pressing domestic problems, compounded by the fact that Chrissy was pregnant again. John too had been facing serious pressures in both his professional and personal life and he desperately needed to get away. While Freddie, for reasons he kept very much to himself, suddenly decided he was at last ready to take up residence in the Kensington mansion he had bought on impulse years earlier. He needed to be alone, although some months later Jim Hutton would join him.

Brian's beautiful ballad 'Who Wants to Live Forever' was released as Queen's thirty-first single in September. A month later he and Roger attended the British Video Awards ceremony to receive an award for the best live performance video for *Live in Rio*.

In November the rock band Iron Maiden was staging a charity Christmas gig in aid of the NSPCC at London's Hammersmith Odeon scheduled for the ninth. They had already invited the spoof heavy metal band Bad News, which comprised four highly talented comedy actors – Nigel Planer, Rik Mayall, Adrian Edmondson and Christopher Ryan, better known as TV's *The Young Ones*. Says Nigel, 'It was our idea to invite Brian to be part of our routine. What we do as Bad News, you see, is on stage we go mental with our guitars making all these fabulous noises, but really it's a guest guitarist hidden off stage who's doing all the work. For the Hammersmith gig we'd asked Jimmy Page as well as Brian.' He goes on, 'That night Ade and I were doing our usual thing, then I switched off my amp and rushed to the front of the stage to fall to my knees and go through the big ecstasy thing, supposedly playing an intricate and absolutely fantastic lead guitar piece. The song was "Hey Hey Bad News", more commonly known as "Fuck Off Bad News". On cue Brian then walked out from behind the speakers, playing his guitar and showing me up. A big argument got up between me and him that he was paid a fiver to stay hidden, which got clean out of hand. It was really funny and the audience lapped it up. So did Brian.' In fact Brian had such a fun time with Nigel and the others that when they later asked him to produce their forthcoming album he instantly agreed.

Fun, however, was rapidly becoming a stranger to Brian. Depression was swiftly setting in as his problems with Chrissy worsened. By now he had agreed to be producer on some recordings for Anita Dobson, and through working together had unwittingly been growing closer to her. As the divide between himself and his wife widened, he felt himself gravitating towards the vivacious and warm-hearted actress, although he fought it as best he could.

Even before the affair actually began the newshounds leaped on his back, quick to sniff out potential scandal. Although both Brian and Anita issued emphatic denials, articles sprouted in the gossip columns. Brian's biggest worry was the effect it might have on his children, who he feared were already being tormented at school. He didn't expect Chrissy to understand how it had come to this; he couldn't really understand it himself. His was such a steady, dependable nature, and never in a million years had he envisaged himself embarking on an affair. Now his whole world was upside down and he didn't know where to turn.

9

NOTHIN' BUT BLUE

The first six weeks of 1987 were highly emotive for both Brian and Chrissy. Their third baby was due any day, and the natural tension of this time for any woman heightened her anxiety about her marriage. Brian remained at home trying desperately to sort himself out, although in his heart he must have known that ending his affair with Anita was something he could scarcely contemplate. Nor was that relationship probably plain sailing, considering the terrible emotional triangle they were all embroiled in. Brian's one source of pure happiness came with the birth on 17 February of his second daughter, christened Emily Ruth.

Having made the decision to take a break from recording as a band, the other three had for the moment gone their separate ways. Roger and John had opted to leave the cold British winter behind for Los Angeles and their respective homes there, while Freddie had dived straight into the Town House recording studios in London to work on a second solo album. His next solo single, he had decided, would be a cover version of an old Platters number, 'The Great Pretender'; he had extravagant ideas for the video and hoped to rope in Roger as well as his friend Peter Straker. Roger obligingly flew back from LA for the shoot, in which all three of them once again dressed up as women – only this time stunningly so. The single was released in mid-February and careered to number four in the UK charts, rewarding Freddie with his highest solo chart position yet.

Brian meanwhile had left the domestic chaos behind him and flown out to Los Angeles. Together with American rock singer Meat Loaf, he had agreed to work on the theme song for the Paralympic Games to be held in LA the following year. For this major sports event for physically handicapped people they penned a special number called 'A Time for Heroes'.

Heroic was the last thing Freddie felt in March as he paced about the room of his sumptuous suite at the Ritz Hotel in Barcelona in front of a watchful Jim Beach. A remark he had made the previous summer on Spanish television about wishing to meet opera singer Montserrat Caballé had culminated in the setting up of a meeting between the two stars. Freddie had aspirations of recording with the soprano – something that not many male rock stars would have had the guts to attempt – and he had written a couple of potential numbers on the off-chance that she would agree. Few people had the power to intimidate Freddie, but as time ticked by and the singer failed to turn up, any vestige of excitement rapidly evaporated, leaving him a complete bag of nerves despite all Jim's attempts to keep him calm.

Caballé, however, did arrive and lunch began. Jim tried valiantly to make small talk to cover the awful silence stretching between the two; Freddie didn't know at this point that Montserrat was just as much in awe of him as he was of her. After they had finished eating he suddenly sprang to his feet, curtly snapping that he had one or two songs with him and did she want to hear them or not! Mollified slightly when she quietly said she would love to, he played her 'Barcelona' and 'Exercises in Free Love'. She was so impressed that she eagerly urged him to write more material so that they could record an album together. Freddie was absolutely flabbergasted, but there was no way he would show it. With a careless flick of his wrist he tossed back, 'Oh, why not, dear?' Work on the album began in April.

Their strange alliance became quite a talking point in music circles, and when the island of Ibiza decided to stage a giant festival at the end of May to celebrate Spain having won the honour of staging the 1992 Olympic Games, Freddie and Montserrat were asked to close the event. Ibiza became the hideaway of writers and artists before the invasion of the sixties' flower children; for after-dark action anything goes and it is definitely not a place for the prudish. A favourite nightspot of Freddie's, the Ku Club, was the focal point of the festival and it was here that he and Montserrat finally performed 'Barcelona' against a sparkling back-cloth of cascading fountains and exploding showers of spectacular fireworks.

But behind the fame and glamour lurked a dark and distressing time-bomb. Although no one would admit it publicly – indeed would refuse to do so for another four and a half years – Freddie was ill. This was mainly what had been behind Queen's decision to stop touring, and also why Freddie had taken to living behind the ten-foot-high secure walls of Garden Lodge. At this point he was keeping the matter very much to himself, although it was obvious to those around him that something was dreadfully wrong. Already Fred's appearance, the way he dressed, had begun to change in a way that was hard to ignore, although he himself tried to shrug off questions by maintaining that a man in his forties would look ridiculous still running around in skin-tight costumes.

Fish remembers how upset and shocked he felt when he came across Freddie in Ibiza at this time. He says, 'Marillion were also taking part in this big TV thing along with Duran Duran and Spandau Ballet, and I thought I'd go down and see Fred and say how ya doin', you know? I got the shock of my life! He was really drawn. There were about three or four close friends in the room with him, and it was like someone had fuckin' died!' He continues, 'I think that this was actually when Freddie was told what was wrong with him, but at the time the people around him were saying things like he's got a kidney problem or he's got a liver complaint. Having glimpsed some of Freddie's excesses it was quite easy to put one and one together, but nobody talked about it. And of course Queen, as with any band which develops to that stage, had built such a strong perimeter fence that if they wanted to keep something inside it, they did. You *knew* there was going to be no leaks.'

Back in England Brian too was trying to create the impression that it was business as usual. He had recently teamed up again with Bad News, with whom he had appeared at the Hammersmith Odeon the previous November. To claims that Bad News had to pester Brian to fulfil his promise to produce their album Nigel Planer protests, 'Not a bit of it. It was us who got begging letters from Brian, urging us to let him do it! Actually it all started with Adrian. He came up with the idea of us recording "Bohemian Rhapsody", and immediately the next thought was, why not ask Brian to produce it for a laugh. From there, it went on to him producing our whole album.' Brian already loved their zany humour and he certainly needed some light relief in his life, so he was happy to get involved – even if it was an experience the like of which he had never had before.

'I have to say it was a strange marriage,' laughs Nigel. 'Brian being so very good and a proper musician on the one hand and us a bunch of louts out to have a laugh on the other.' He goes on, 'Recording comedy songs is really more difficult than you'd imagine. If you carry the comedy too far you lose the music. Carry the music too far and you lose the comedy. Of course during the recording we went into character. Mine is a bonehead called Den Denis, while Ade is Vim who has the biggest ego and is an incredible show-off. As Bad News we'd talk, swear and argue, and all the time Brian had the tapes running. Once we started we just improvised, and of course it got way out of hand. Every time I looked up at Brian in the box he was laughing like hell, literally falling about.' The recording at Sarm Studios began in May, and the album release was scheduled for autumn 1987.

Before that, on 6 July, Anita's single 'Talking of Love', which Brian had also produced, was released. The previous August she had done a single called 'Anyone Can Fall in Love', to the theme tune of *EastEnders*, and it had reached number four in the charts. Unfortunately, although 'Talking of Love' breached the top fifty a couple of weeks later, it dropped anchor at forty-three. Still, she and Brian flew to Vienna to make a video to accompany it. They continued to refute all the rumours that they were having an affair, even to the extent of denying it on a BBC TV chat show.

With Brian busy working on the Bad News album, Freddie recording with Montserrat Caballé and John touring the world, Roger found himself getting itchy feet. He wasn't taking too well to another year off from Queen and had decided to form a separate band. It had nothing to do with splitting from Queen, and indeed Brian, John and Fred all discussed his idea with him and were happy for him to go ahead, so long as it was understood that Queen work would always take precedence should the two ever overlap. Roger therefore placed a low-key advert in all the popular music papers, applying for musicians to join the drummer of a top rock band who wished to form a new group. But replies were thin on the ground, so the following week he tried a bigger, bolder box ad – this time tempting would-be applicants with the promise of them potentially becoming a star. Applications poured in.

Roger shortlisted them to sixty, then hired a Soho nightclub to hold four days of auditions, although he personally kept out of sight. Eventually Roger made his decision: Clayton Moss came in as lead guitarist, Josh Macrae on drums, Peter Noone (no relation to the Herman's Hermits singer) became bass player, and finally Spike Edney was roped in on keyboards. For Roger this was going to be very different from Queen, for he intended stepping out from behind the drums to hold down lead vocal as well as rhythm guitar. As rehearsals began they settled on a name for the band – the Cross; then they took off for Roger's holiday villa in Ibiza to record.

By now Brian's recording work with Bad News was finally drawing to a close. It had been an incredible experience and they had all become good friends. When the band were invited to take part in the annual Rock and Jazz Festival at Reading at the end of August, they invited Brian to come along with them. He agreed, again with no idea of what he was letting himself in for.

Bad News had played their first-ever gig at Donington Park in Leicestershire before an audience of sixty thousand and their reception had been volatile: while most people found their spoof heavy metal routine hilarious, other more dyed-in-the-wool heavy metal addicts thought it offensive and showed their displeasure by bombarding them with rubbish. During a subsequent television interview Rik Mayall recounted their effect on the audience, ending with the story that afterwards, among all the other garbage littering the stage, they had found a sheep's eye. With his particular brand of acerbic humour Rik looked deadpan into the camera and invited those attending the Reading festival to come and throw sheep's eyes at them.

Says Nigel, 'It was a great day. Brian came with us all in the coach, taking his kids along with him. In fact everyone took their kids. It was more like a creche than a heavy metal gig. We were definitely playing second fiddle to all these children. The roadies and backstage helpers were more interested in goo-gooing at the mess some baby had made than in seeing to us.' Of the performance itself he adds, 'The audience was just this seething horrible mass of pink! We did our usual act and Brian joined us on stage. We got pelted worse than ever that day. Plastic bottles of urine came flying at us by the dozen, and enough sheep's eyes rained down on top of us to turn the air black! But Brian was dodging away like an old pro, laughing his head off!'

Roger continued to forge ahead with his new band. To show their support Brian guested on one track, 'Love Lies Bleeding', of the forthcoming Cross album and for the same reason Freddie sang lead on 'Heaven for Everyone'. Virgin Records released the Cross's first single, 'Cowboys and Indians', on 21 September 1987, the same day that 'Barcelona' was released in Spain. Over ten thousand copies of Freddie's duet sold out within hours of going on sale and many Spanish record shops, caught short of stock, found themselves having to turn away disgruntled customers empty-handed.

'Barcelona' was released as a single in Britain on 26 October, much to the consternation of the music press who didn't have a clue what to make of it. Their reviews polarized from extolling Freddie's bravery and ingenuity to damning him as an out-and-out embarrassment to the rock world. It peaked at number eight in the UK charts.

Brian ended the year still engaged in the fruitless effort of trying to dowse the flames flickering in the tabloids around his romance with Anita. By now he was working with her on her album and this occupied much of his time. His thoughts were another matter, for deep down he knew he couldn't put off grasping the nettle indefinitely. It must have been a fraught Christmas in the May household as he mulled over his dilemma.

By January 1988 Brian was glad to slope off to the Town House studios once more to join up as Queen. The year apart had made them eager to record together again, and they had decided to make a start as soon as possible. Brian very much needed to find a focus right then, and work was safe as it could keep his mind off his troubled relationships.

As it happened, he wasn't the only band member with personal problems. Roger too was experiencing a strange upheaval. During the making of a video for the Cross's recent release he had met and fallen for model Debbie Leng. Dominique Beyrand, however, had been his live-in lover since 1976 and they now had two children. Faced with the situation that he and Debbie wanted to live together, the three came to a bizarre decision.

Roger and Dominique – they say to safeguard their children's future – got married on 25 January with Freddie and Mary as witnesses. Then just over three weeks later Roger moved out, away from his new wife and kids, and into a house he had bought nearby with Debbie. This provided the tabloids with a juicy story; for a while, everywhere the couple went they were pursued by a gaggle of snap-happy paparazzi.

Following the release of the Cross's debut album, *Shove It*, Roger embarked on his first tour without Queen. It was a success by any standards, in part because his fans turned out loyally just to see him. It wound up with a gig on 10 March at the Town and Country Club in Kentish Town in north London. Brian went along to provide moral support, as did all of Roger's family and friends; despite initial nerves, the evening went well.

But although enjoying Roger's gig that evening was something of a relief for Brian, it was no more than a transient one. Life had been extremely stressful for a long time and he was already at a very low ebb when in early summer he was hit by an enormous blow – the death of his much-loved father on 2 June. Harold and Brian had been so close and had shared so much. To lose him at any time would have been crushing for Brian but for it to happen right then, when he was already so desperately unhappy, was practically more than he could bear.

Not surprisingly, this traumatic event heralded the final collapse of the very shaky grip he had on his life and family. Following Harold's death the rift between himself and Chrissy burst open, and there was clearly no saving his marriage any longer. At the same time his affair with Anita had become such common knowledge that it would have been farcical to attempt further denials. No one but Brian can know how desperately torn he was at this time, but undoubtedly one of his greatest causes for anguish remained his children – he couldn't bear the thought of leaving them. His physical and mental health had been suffering for some time, but now he descended rapidly into bouts of dark depression, plunging so low that no one could reach him as he fought to work things out for himself.

After wrestling with his conscience, his feelings and those of all the people closest involved, he finally decided to leave his wife of twelve years and begin a new life with Anita. It was the toughest and most painful decision he had ever made, but he hoped that by making a clean break it would leave everyone knowing where they stood and might help to relieve the intense pressure. With their usual crass insensitivity those sections of the British press that had been making insinuations for months now tore into Brian tooth and claw, splashing his private business all over the front pages. Yet again his major concern was how his two elder children, now old enough to understand the slurs, would be affected by this cruel publicity, and he worried incessantly that their school mates would be tormenting and jibing at them.

It was a sorry summer that year for Brian – he scarcely kept track of what the others were up to, or realized that Queen videos were busy claiming awards. 'Bohemian Rhapsody' won first place in a 1988 BBC Radio 1 poll as the all-time favourite single. Life had changed so much in the thirteen years since it had been released.

With his mind in such turmoil it could hardly be expected that his new life with Anita would be a bed of roses either. It appears that the various and unavoidable tensions created around and within them led to arguments, some of them gleefully exposed in the press. By October one tabloid reported a blazing row between the couple after which Anita had, they claimed, furiously walked out on Brian, only to be reconciled with him the next day. About this time Anita was due to appear with singer/actor Adam Faith in a stage musical version of Faith's popular sixties' TV series *Budgie*. A soundtrack album was planned, and Brian was asked to guest on the track 'In One of My Weaker Moments'.

That same month Freddie and Montserrat Caballé were due to appear in Barcelona at an open-air festival to celebrate the start of the four-year run-up to the 1992 Olympic Games. They sang with the Barcelona Opera House Orchestra and Choir on a huge stage situated in front of the illuminated fountains in Castle Square. Two days later the album *Barcelona* was finally released.

In November Anita released another single, 'To Know Him Is to Love Him', which was a cover of the 1958 hit by the American group Teddy Bears. This was quickly followed by her album *Talking of Love*, on which Brian had been producer and which featured some of his most inspired guitar work. A great deal was invested in that album – much more than he could possibly have dreamed of when he originally agreed to produce it.

Since losing his father in June, Brian's chosen method to try and get his life back on track had been to throw himself into work – anything so long as it occupied his thoughts and time. He was still writing some material with the vague notion of compiling a second solo album, although to date his ideas had tended to be a confused kaleidoscope of musical styles and the distinct lack of direction to the album was also something of a problem. This, though, would take second place to any Queen projects, which included the album they were currently working on.

On top of this, he sorely missed performing. For Brian, touring was the best and most fulfilling part of being in a band. 'Suddenly life becomes simple again,' he once said. But Queen hadn't toured for two years now, and deep down he already knew that they would never tour again, although this was not yet openly admitted even amongst themselves. Already prying eyes were watching them and questions were being asked as to why Queen had gone to ground. It seemed inevitable that when the time came to field lies to the media over Freddie it would mean more pressure and more deceit.

To occupy his time and stimulate his brain in late 1988 Brian went through a phase of plunging from guesting with one artiste to another. He helped out the group Living in a Box on their single 'Blow the House Down' before working with Tony Iommi, lead guitarist with Black Sabbath, on their album *Headless Cross*.

Tony Iommi is probably Brian's closest friend and confidant, the one person to whom he knows he can always turn whatever the circumstances. It is, on the whole, a very private friendship. 'We've been friends for something like twenty years,' he explains. Tony firmly agrees with the characterization of Brian as being the worrier of the band, explaining, 'He and I can relate really well on that one because we are very much alike in that respect. He's the one with most of the work to do and always has been, who'll end up literally all day in the studio, holding it all together, no matter what happens.'

About that guest spot on Black Sabbath's album Tony goes on, 'Brian often comes to my recording sessions, just as I pop into whichever studio he is working at, and one day while working on *Headless Cross* I just said to him, "Bloody hell, come and have a play." He asked, "Really? Do you want me to?" and that was it. Except that Brian is the only other guitar player we've ever had play on any of our records. I'm kind of funny about that.' Brian appears on the track 'When Death Calls'.

All too soon the all-girl group Fuzzbox persuaded Brian to lend his experience to their single 'Self', just before former Frankie Goes to Hollywood vocalist Holly Johnson asked him to contribute some guitar work to the single 'Love Train'. And when his good friend ex-Genesis guitarist Steve Hackett wanted him to join their mutual friend Chris Thompson in singing backing vocals on his album track 'Slot Machine', he could hardly say no. But arguably it meant most to Brian when his hero Lonnie Donegan approached him to ask if he would write a song for inclusion on his forthcoming album. Brian didn't hesitate, and he and Lonnie share vocals on the jaunty 'Let Your Heart Rule Your Head', a number which would also turn up four years later on Brian's own solo album.

All this intentional flurry of activity carried Brian through to December, when he treated himself to a night out attending a gig by the heavy metal rock band Bon Jovi at London's Wembley Arena. Brian was a great fan of their music and was thrilled when their lead guitarist, Richie Sambora, invited him up on stage for the encore. Says Richie, 'Brian, Elton John and a whole bunch of guys came that night and so we just called them all up on stage to jam with us. We played the Beatles' "Get Back" and a couple of other numbers. It was great.' Brian had not expected this and wasn't armed with his guitar, which at first put him off, but when he tried to opt out Richie thrust one of his own guitars at him. That was the only time Brian can ever recall guesting with another band minus his precious Red Special.

For Sambora that night lit an important friendship between himself and Brian. He reveals, 'It was one helluva jam and I'll always remember it. But what was really cool was something which happened after the gig. Brian gave Jon [Jon Bon Jovi] and me some really sound advice. This was right when our career was about to take off in a huge way, and Brian's advice to us was never to work our asses off to the point of burning ourselves out. You know – not taking time to smell the roses along the way, that kind of thing. That's what he felt he and Queen had often done, and he couldn't get it over strongly enough to us how important it is always to try to be there – to live the moment and savour it, because all too soon it'll be over and you'll have missed clean out on enjoying it.'

It was advice that both Richie and Jon took seriously to heart, made all the more special, says Sambora, because it came from Brian. He explains, 'That night at the Wembley Arena was the first time I'd met Brian in person, but I'd watched and admired him since the three nights out of five I went to see Queen open for Mott the Hoople at the Uris Theater on Broadway back in 1974. I was knocked out. Queen were absolutely fantastic and Brian made a big impression on me. I was just a teenager at the time, but I never forgot it.'

Brian's last guest appearance of the year was once more with Bad News, this time at the Marquee Club. Hiding behind the speakers with him that night, besides Jimmy Page, was the legendary Jeff Beck. Beck refers to Brian as, 'The guv'nor – the best pop-oriented guitarist there is', maintaining that all aspiring guitar players now desperately want to play Brian's licks as once they used to want to play his. 'That Marquee gig was very special for us,' admits Nigel Planer. 'You don't often get the chance to play on the one stage with three musicians like May, Beck and Page.'

All through that year Queen had been writing and recording material for a new album, and by the beginning of 1989 that work was complete. There had been some changes to their way of working this time – all the words and music were credited collectively to Queen, as opposed to individual band members. This meant that all four worked on each song regardless of whose idea it had been. It also meant a four-way royalty split on each number which, bearing in mind Brian's feelings of past injustices in this department, made life happier all round; indeed, the arrangement suited everyone so well that they wished they'd adopted it years before. The release date hadn't yet been set but was expected to be late spring.

It was quite early in 1989 that Brian first got involved with the British Bone Marrow Donor Appeal. The charity's aim at that time was to set up a proper register of potential donors – people who had their blood tissue-typed and were ready and willing to donate some of their bone marrow to a patient whose type matched theirs. It had been brought to his attention that a very brave young leukaemia sufferer, Denise Morse, had asked to have his tender ballad 'Who Wants to Live Forever' played at her funeral. This touched Brian very much.

One of the charity's co-founders is Malcolm Thomas, who had lost his own little daughter some years before to aplastic anaemia, and it was he who contacted Brian. He explains, 'Denise was a remarkable woman. She had come out of remission and decided she would bring Christmas forward for her family because she knew she wouldn't be around for the real thing. It was in a lot of newspapers at the time and she appeared on the *Wogan* show on TV. Although she was dreadfully ill she worked really hard on the campaign. Denise died in March 1989, and of course I went to her funeral. It was the first time in my life that I'd heard a record being played at a funeral, and it was a song called 'Who Wants to Live Forever' by Queen. Denise had been a huge fan of theirs. Afterwards the song kept playing over and over in my head, so I decided there and then to send a letter telling them how this record had become the heart of the BBMDA. I didn't know then, but because it had been mentioned in the newspapers, at exactly the same time Brian's mother had been talking to him about the funeral and our charity.'

Malcolm was asked to come to Pinewood Studios where Queen were making a video, and during the lunch break he and Brian talked in the privacy of the dressing room. Says Malcolm, 'I told Brian the whole involved story that went back to my initial search to find a donor for my daughter, and all that had happened along the way. It was also important for me to get across to him that the BBMDA wasn't one of those charities run by out-and-out businessmen, but rather that it consisted mainly of ordinary families who had either lost loved ones or – against the clock – were desperately trying to find a way not to. To my astonishment Brian simply looked at me and said, "OK, what can I do?"'

Brian eventually suggested that they should re-record 'Who Wants to Live Forever' in a way that would generate maximum publicity. 'Because of Brian we suddenly found ourselves doing a series of high-profile television interviews, starting with the BBC's *Daytime Live*,' says Malcolm. 'On that programme Brian and I asked for children to come forward to be auditioned to record the number, asking them to send in a tape of themselves singing. You would not believe the response we got! It was incredible – something close to ten thousand tapes, including videos and everything, poured in. People had gone to extraordinary lengths.'

Neither Brian nor Malcolm had banked on this sort of reaction; but, nothing daunted, they split the tapes between them and set about listening to each one. 'It was a herculean task,' admits Malcolm, 'and the talent out there is truly amazing. But eventually we shortlisted it to sixty – half boys, half girls. Brian put together an arrangement of the song which was straightforward enough for the auditioning kids to sing, and they were all invited to the Abbey Road Studios.'

It was debatable who were the more nervous – the children gawping at the inside of a recording studio, or their parents busy staring around the Studio Two itself, the famous Beatles sanctuary. The children, however, acquitted themselves very well. Says Malcolm, 'Brian and I listened to all of them. They were also being taped so that we could listen to them again afterwards.' Eventually the numbers were whittled down to two, Ian Meeson and Belinda Gillett, who were invited to Olympic Studios in Barnes for the actual recording. Again Brian organized the session, arranging this time for an orchestra backing track and cajoling Roger and John to come and play on it too.

The re-recorded version of 'Who Wants to Live Forever' raised over £130,000 for the British Bone Marrow Donor Appeal, and Malcolm is adamant that Brian's help has been, and still is, essential. 'He did an enormous amount for us in terms of getting us publicity, launching laboratories and raising public consciousness about what we do. He's been marvellous, and because of that we have already saved many children's lives. He is extremely passionately involved. Without Brian quite simply we would not have the organization that we have today. His intervention at that point in time was crucial.' He adds, 'I was absolutely delighted when he agreed to become the Patron.'

Brian's nature is such that, having once embraced a cause in which he firmly believes, his commitment is absolute. It seems invidious to single out any one person or family, since all involved in the charity are as important and committed as the next, but one sick little girl in particular occupied a special place in Brian's heart. Katherine Jones from Benson in Oxfordshire had been invited to Olympic Studios for those recording sessions, and from that first meeting Brian ended up spending quite a bit of time with her, growing close to her and visiting her regularly in hospital as her condition helplessly deteriorated in the race to find her a donor. Tragically, time ran out for little Katherine and she died.

Music at this time was more important for Brian than ever. His best outlet when he was emotionally troubled was to write songs. He could, and did, confide in Tony Iommi about the problems in his personal relationships, but he is at heart an intensely private man and it may have been easier to invest his emotions in his very personal lyrics than to talk about them to anyone.

The first studio-recorded Queen album for almost three years was due for release towards the end of May, but before that came the first single from it – 'I Want It All', a thumping hard rocking number. Its video, directed by David Mallett, was the one shot in Pinewood Studios without an audience, and it was the first public display of how much Freddie had changed. His ill health was clearly taking its toll: although he still managed to look good he was dressed unusually conventionally; it was obvious that he had lost weight; and his face, despite its designer stubble, betrayed a gaunt, almost haunted look. His voice, though, remained as strong and powerful as ever, convincingly conveying the uncompromising defiance of the song. It charted instantly at number three, Queen's highest entry yet.

On 22 May *The Miracle* album was released and went platinum in its first week. Queen record covers had always involved a great deal of thought, time and effort, but the sleeve for this stylish album was perhaps the most unique of all. Artist Richard Gray had used technologically advanced computer graphics to create the effect of all four heads merging into one, each face blending into its neighbour to striking effect.

A week later, for the first time in close to a decade, Queen agreed to be interviewed as a band. It was their friend Radio 1 DJ Mike Read who pulled off the coup and managed to corral all four for a rare one-hour question-and-answer session. The subject of why the band were no longer touring inevitably came up; Freddie replied that it was something which no longer held any challenge or attraction for him. The real reason would emerge in time, but right then no one was admitting that Freddie was just too sick to undertake strenuous tours, not to mention subjecting himself to that kind of intense public scrutiny.

Like the others, Brian hadn't been told anything by Freddie, but he was no fool and knew in his heart what was really wrong. They had all been friends for twenty years and, despite ups and downs, were very close. It upset him greatly to think of Freddie being so ill, and he understood perfectly well why they couldn't tour. But at the same time the fact that he couldn't get out on the road and expend his pent-up emotions and energies through gigging handicapped his ability to handle pressure, which in turn added to his acute sense of nervous tension. He was very restless and candidly confessed, 'Taking the touring side of things away messed up my life – really, without exaggeration. I feel it's taken the whole balance out of my life. I badly want to play live with or without Queen. If we can't come to some kind of arrangement within the band I'll get my own project together – but I can't stand it much longer.'

The second single to be released off *The Miracle* album was to be 'Breakthru'. For the video they decided they wanted to be filmed performing the number on board a speeding train, and so set about looking for a private railway to hire. They chose the Nene Valley Railway, which ran on a line near Peterborough. An old steam engine was renamed *The Miracle Express* for the occasion, and Brian White, press officer with the Nene Valley, remembers, 'The filming itself took place over the full length of the line, which is chiefly set in water meadows.' He goes on, 'At the beginning of the video you see the train bursting through an apparently solid bridge arch – in fact it had been filled with realistic-looking polystyrene bricks. I think the effect is brilliant, and it was filmed only the once. It took about three days in all, but Queen were there for just one. I'm afraid to say that the staff are used to film crews working on the railway and anyway they are more interested in the noise of a steam engine than who arrives to shoot, but I do know that everyone in the band seemed to enjoy the whole thing enormously.'

The raising of money for charity was again in Brian's thoughts a few weeks later when he was approached to do his bit to help the survivors of a devastating earthquake in Armenia. Live Aid had initiated the habit of rock stars banding together to record charity singles, and on this occasion Brian along with Roger, Tony Iommi, Pink Floyd's Dave Gilmour and Paul Rodgers, among others, gathered to record a cover version of Deep Purple's 1977 hit 'Smoke on the Water' under the band name Rock Aid Armenia. The single entered the charts in December and stayed there for five weeks, peaking at number thirty-nine.

For Brian most of that autumn was spent touring the world, principally doing PR for Queen but also promoting various charity projects like Rock Aid Armenia and the British Bone Marrow Donor Appeal. In between he snatched time for a brief holiday with Anita in Los Angeles, determined to try and relax and fool around. Unfortunately one sunny morning Brian's idea of fooling around was to try out his son's skateboard – after all, how hard could it be to roll along a pavement standing upright on a bit of flat board on wheels? He soon found out when he ignominiously fell off and managed to break his arm. Not being able to play the guitar for a while, combined with a lot of physiotherapy, taught him to leave this skilled activity to Jimmy in future. Brian flew back to Britain to work with a friend of Anita's, Gareth Marks, who had been playing the lead role in the London stage musical *Buddy*, based on the life of Buddy Holly. Recently he had decided to branch out and make an album, and Brian had agreed to guest on the track 'Lady of Leisure'.

In November Brian again did a guest spot, this time with the legendary Jerry Lee Lewis on stage at the Hammersmith Odeon, playing guitar on the number 'High School Confidential'. Like many musicians, Brian had always greatly admired Lewis, so it was a big thrill for him to perform live with the man himself.

Back in August a third single had emerged from *The Miracle* album, 'The Invisible Man', which had been followed up in October by 'Scandal' – a clever poke at the world's press. In November a fifth single was released, the title track itself – 'The Miracle'. The video for it was again highly unusual, this time featuring four lookalike child actors who made a first-rate job not only of resembling each band member but also of performing exactly like them. The miniature May had practised to perfection all Brian's idiosyncrasies and, with a Red Special replica hung around his neck, threw himself completely into his role. Freddie's young double absorbed his appointed character so well that it's said Freddie found himself imitating the boy when the band joined the children on stage towards the end of the video!

The Miracle album was a huge success and, inspired by this, Queen decided to get straight back into the studio to record a new one. In late November Brian flew to Montreux to join the others at Mountain Studios, although his broken arm, still in the process of mending, restricted him somewhat.

For Brian the end of the eighties couldn't come fast enough. The last three years had been a personal nightmare, witnessing the disintegration of his marriage and the death of the father he adored, coupled with the continuing and gruelling strain of Freddie's developing illness. In the past Brian had looked to the arrival of a new decade with at least a degree of optimism. Right then the nineties only looked set to hold yet more heartache for him.

IT'S LATE

Brian spent New Year's Day 1990 in a recording studio, along with several other artists calling themselves Rock Against Repatriation. They were working on the by now almost obligatory charity single – this time a cover version of Rod Stewart's hit 'Sailing' in aid of the Vietnamese boat people who were about to be forcibly repatriated to Vietnam from Hong Kong. Then he rejoined Queen as they threw themselves into work on a new album; once again all the words and music were to be credited collectively. Relations during work on *The Miracle* album had been unusually harmonious because the new arrangement had cut out the inevitable arguments and territorial infighting which had previously erupted over individually written numbers. Though still no one voiced it, it seemed highly likely that this would be the last album they would record as a band; strife of any kind was therefore to be avoided at all costs.

The following month Brian flew back to London in time to team up with his old Mott the Hoople mates, Ian Hunter and Mick Ronson. They were appearing at the Hammersmith Odeon and had persuaded Brian to join them on stage to play on 'All the Way from Memphis', one of their best-known hits. He had needed little cajoling and it was a real blast from the past for him, bringing back vivid memories of the time when

Queen supported Hoople on those early seventies' tours. In reflective mood, he couldn't help indulging in thoughts of the rough-and-ready but excitingly uncertain days back then, comparing them to their current controlled superstar status which for such a long time had been marred by sadness in his personal life. That concert might only have lasted a few hours but it meant a lot to Brian, if only because it served as a bridge to happier times.

Queen's enormous popularity, as it happens, was the reason that all four members of the band had currently congregated in London. The British Phonographic Industry had decided to honour them for their outstanding contribution to British music and they were to be presented with an award at the annual ceremony at the Dominion Theatre in February, hosted by Jonathan King. Queen, formally dressed in dinner jackets, received their award from BPI chairman Terry Ellis. That night was the first time Freddie had appeared in public for several months, and there was no hiding his hollowed features. Not surprisingly this sparked off a rash of new rumours, compounded by the fact that, unusually, it was Brian and not Freddie who took the mike to make the acceptance speech.

Paying little heed to the stir, Queen gave the dinner laid on for the celebrities after the ceremony a clean bodyswerve and headed instead for a Soho club they had hired to host their own special party. Although previously they had chosen to appoint 1981 their tenth anniversary year, for their own reasons they unofficially made 1990 their twentieth anniversary, at least for the purposes of that night's bash, and they had invited every employee, former employee and Queen connection they could trace. Over four hundred turned up, their numbers gradually swelling as defectors from the BPI dinner gatecrashed the much livelier Soho do.

Many of the guests there that night were privately shocked to see Freddie looking so drawn, but when he was photographed by a lurking journalist as he was leaving the club in the early hours of the following morning, looking downright haggard, it became a matter for wider public concern. Fred's picture was splashed over the front page of a national daily newspaper, distilling rumour into real fear for his health, especially among his already jittery fans. Freddie tried to scotch these fears by maintaining publicly that he felt fine and denying that he had the dreaded AIDS virus. Many Queen fans desperately wanted to believe him even though he had added that he would not be touring in the foreseeable future and would be returning with the band to the studio to carry on with the album.

About now Brian was approached by Jane L'Epine Smith with an unusual request. Jane had had twenty years' experience as a casting director and had just embarked on an ambitious project which was also to be her first theatre production as director. Says Jane, 'When I decided I was going to do *Macbeth* the main thing for me was to try to make it accessible to all sections of the public. Shakespeare tends to have a very stodgy image, and I wanted elements in my production which would be attractive to all walks of life so that they would come and see it and maybe move over to a new experience. I'd always admired Queen and thought that Brian would be ideal to compose the music for the play.'

Unacquainted with any of the band, Jane approached Brian through their office. 'I got a phone call from Jim Beach next day saying he had given my letter to Brian and he was interested, so could I come along to talk about it. Director Malcolm Ranson came with me, but I was extremely nervous,' she admits. Jane's nerves, however, were unwarranted. There was instant rapport between herself and Brian, and there and then he agreed to take on the project. 'He didn't want to think about it or anything,' says Jane. 'I was thrilled, of course, but had to explain that I still hadn't raised all the necessary finance. That wasn't a problem with Brian, though. It was a case of when you're ready, I'll do it.' Jane left Queen's offices elated. She adds, 'The fact that I could now tell potential investors that Brian May was doing the music was a huge plus.'

Brian promised to keep in regular touch with Jane over the coming months and began work. He had recently installed a home studio in his house and it was here that he experimented with various ideas. This way he could also keep his *Macbeth* music separate from the studio work under way for the new Queen album. He was both excited and apprehensive about the theatre project, worried that his interpretation of Shakespeare could be too radical and not what Jane had had in mind.

Writing music for *Macbeth* wasn't Brian's only diversion, however. Although he and Chrissy had split up, he naturally continued to maintain as much contact with his children as possible. Jimmy, now twelve, was mad on computer games and in particular loved the science fiction ones marketed by Games Workshop, Europe's largest manufacturer of these games. He would often drag his dad into one of their stores in the hope of getting Brian to buy him their latest offering, and eventually these visits came to the attention of the firm's Projects Manager, Andy Jones.

Says Andy, 'I was told that Brian and his son were in the habit of visiting one of our central London branches, so I left word at the shop that the next time they came in Brian and Jimmy would be very welcome to come and look around our design studio, to meet the artists and miniature makers.' He goes on, 'We have what's called Warhammer World, which includes Warhammer novels and magazines. Anyway, Jimmy arrived clutching his *White Dwarf* magazine. He was very excited at meeting the designers and went around claiming all the autographs he could. It was quite ironic, because the designers were all waiting with their Queen albums under their arms, hoping to get Brian to sign them!'

Brian pumped Jones with an endless stream of questions, and learned that Games Workshop were about to expand. Andy explains, 'I was telling Brian that we were just about to set up our own record label, Warhammer, and that we had signed our first band called D-Rok. Immediately he said he'd love to come along and play on a couple of tracks of D-Rok's album.' Andy couldn't believe his ears. 'He was serious, even though Queen were in the middle of recording an album in Switzerland. So we sent Brian a tape of the band's songs and within days he got back to me to say he'd come along quite soon.'

D-Rok's lead singer Simon Denbigh didn't believe it when Andy Jones told him that Brian May was coming to record with them. 'Well, you don't, do you?' he reasons. 'We got the shock of our lives when Brian walked in. He was brilliant – certainly the nicest megastar I've ever met.'

Exactly where Brian turned up was a recording studio converted from a slaughterhouse at Driffield, near Bridlington on the Yorkshire coast. Andy Jones recalls, 'What struck me as being particularly nice was that when Brian arrived he'd taken the trouble in a very short space of time not just to listen to the tape but to learn all the songs. So he was all genned up in a way none of us expected and said right off, "Let's get into 'Get Out of My Way'." It was great for the boys in the band.'

'We were all very nervous of meeting Brian,' admits Simon, 'but he was very understanding and really complimentary about our music. He liked our ideas and what we were trying to do, which was a great morale booster because we respected him so much. I also think he'd been quite surprised when he listened to the tape, because he'd agreed to come even before he'd heard us. I mean, we could have been useless.

He was such a straight, down-to-earth person to work with, and very good-humoured. In fact at one point I even forgot myself and told him to tune up, but he took it great.' He goes on, 'Our guitarist Chesley asked Brian if he could have a go on his famous Red Special, and he let him!'

The young band were aware of Brian's reputation for experimenting with new equipment and had been goggled-eyed at the device he had turned up with. Simon explains, 'It was a special kind of zoom, a little box you plug into and get all sorts of effects out of. It was a prototype, the only one, and did some fantastic things.' To their astonishment, when the time came for Brian to go he casually offered to leave it with them to try out, although he said he would need it back in Switzerland quite soon for his work there. 'We were delighted at him trusting us with it, especially Chesley. But,' Simon admits, 'we never touched it. We never seemed to have much luck with our equipment and had blown up a couple of amps. One even melted! So we were scared stiff we'd somehow break his zoom which, apart from anything else, must have cost a packet!' Brian appears on just one track, 'Get Out of My Way', of D-Rok's album *Oblivion* which was released later that year on the brand-new Warhammer label.

Keeping occupied was certainly the name of the game for Brian. By July work on the Queen album had shifted to Metropolis Studios in London. Unlike the situation with previous albums, however, this time there were plenty of breaks and Brian used these to work on the *Macbeth* music for Jane. Tony Iommi did manage to tear him away long enough to join Black Sabbath on stage one night again at the Hammersmith Odeon, but Brian was now dividing most of his time between the two recording projects. The Queen album now had a name – *Innuendo* – and was scheduled for release at Christmas 1990.

Macbeth was due to open in November, which meant that time was approaching for Brian to present his work to the theatre company. He had worked very hard on it and the music was highly ingenious, but his confidence was at a low ebb and he had doubts. Jane recalls, 'Right from the start we had wanted a dangerous production – something exciting and startling which pulled on all the senses,' She goes on: 'The first time Brian brought the music to us, he was extremely nervous in case we didn't like it. Also, the equipment he had didn't work and that got him all the more fidgety and uptight.' But if Brian was riddled with apprehension, Jane wasn't; patiently watching him get both himself and the tape recorder in order, she knew it would be worth the wait. 'When we heard it through,' she says, 'all of us quite individually stood up and applauded. It was absolutely wonderful.'

Relieved, Brian could at last let himself unwind. It had meant a lot to him to write this music, whose switches of mood from dramatic and compulsive to hopeful and buoyant show just how closely tuned to the play he was. 'He got very involved,' agrees Jane. 'In fact, he even came to the rehearsals and did the warm-up exercises with the cast. He took part in everything.'

His heavy involvement with the theatre company had another bonus, for it helped to sidetrack him from the business problems brewing around the band. Dissatisfaction had set in with Capitol Records and their handling of Queen in the American market, so the band's sights had turned some months ago to finding a new US label. The task of extricating them from their contract with Capitol devolved as usual on Jim Beach, but it has to be said that Capitol were very accommodating, to the extent of selling back the rights to the entire Queen back-catalogue – albeit on payment of a rather substantial sum of money. Nevertheless being in full possession of these rights gave Queen a powerful and valuable asset; one, moreover, which they could dangle before any record company interested in signing them. The queues formed overnight, but it was the new Walt Disney Corporation-owned Hollywood Records who landed the deal by coming in with a bid which wiped the floor with their competitors. Since no one wanted to hang around, contracts were signed at the beginning of November.

About now it became clear that the *Innuendo* album was not after all going to be ready for a Christmas release, much to EMI's understandable displeasure since the market at that time of year is massive. The delay, however, had been unavoidable: Freddie's health had been creating serious problems and at times caused lengthy lay-offs. It was also possibly their best album to date and they felt that for that reason, if for no other, they did not want to rush it.

The strain of Freddie's illness and of trying to keep it secret was becoming a heavy burden on them all. Although Brian understood and fully endorsed the need to try to protect Freddie from the prying eyes of the press, it was unquestionably becoming harder and harder to lie with any semblance of authority. Journalists persistently tried to corner him on why Queen's flamboyant singer had become a virtual recluse in his Kensington mansion.

It got so bad by the second week of November that Brian had to concede to the press that Freddie was suffering from strain and exhaustion, and that the years of hard work and high living were now catching up on him. He said no more than that, and even emphatically denied that there was any vestige of truth in the rumours that Freddie had AIDS. Yet next day the *Sun* screamed into print with the bold headline: 'IT'S OFFICIAL! FREDDIE IS SERIOUSLY ILL.' Brian's careful remarks hadn't confirmed anything of the kind, but it didn't stop the paper from highlighting the references to AIDS and running the story with a damning picture of a staring-eyed, drawn and very unfamiliar Freddie.

Brian managed to put this pressure behind him for a while when on 19 November *Macbeth* opened at London's Red and Gold Theatre with Roy Marsden in the leading role. 'It had a five-week run,' says Jane, 'and Brian came practically every night to give the production his visible support. I think the project had come at the right time for him, when he was needing something to take his mind off his problems. It was the right time, the right thing and the right chemistry. The Queen office was great, too – they let all their members know. Of course, a lot of those fans came purely because of Brian's involvement, but some of them came out afterwards saying, "Wow, I didn't know Shakespeare could be . . . ". Brian also did a lot of publicity for us – he was just wonderful all round, in fact.'

The music made a huge impact. According to Jane. 'The piece he wrote to be played when people were filing into the theatre was particularly startling. It starts quietly and builds up and up to a big bang, timed exactly for when the first scene bursts on stage with flashing lights for the fight sequence. The whole production had a very atmospheric, black and white cinema effect to it, and that's what came across vividly in the music.'

While Brian had been attending the theatre for those five weeks the press hounds were still stalking Freddie, capturing him on camera at the end of November discreetly leaving the Harley Street premises of a top AIDS specialist. But Brian tried his best to avoid being trapped into answering an unfeeling barrage of questions, and tried instead to concentrate on filming a video for their new single 'Headlong' from the *Innuendo* album, now rescheduled for release early in the New Year.

EMI had agreed to release the title track, 'Innuendo', as the UK single. An unusual number with its *Bolero*-type rhythm, it was released in January 1991 and went straight to number one in the British singles chart. But Hollywood Records were adamant that no American radio station would play a track six and a half minutes long – that's what they had said about 'Bohemian Rhapsody' – and wanted Queen to agree instead to the release of the raucously energetic 'Headlong'. So the band disappeared into Metropolis Studios for a couple of days to film a performance video to accompany it.

In early December Queen's video of the 1986 Magic Tour Wembley Stadium gig was released; then a few days later, at a party organized by the band's fan club at the Astoria Theatre in London, Roger played a gig with his band, the Cross. Brian was at the party and at one point joined the Cross and played a couple of numbers from his solo album *Starfleet Project*, as well as the old Queen rocker 'Tie Your Mother Down'. The latter was quite an experience for Brian. It had been many years since he had performed that number, and it was the first time he had shared vocals with Roger. The combination of rustiness, strangeness and the absence of Freddie's customary strong lead made it hardly surprising that Brian forgot the words to his own song.

THE DARK

Early in January 1991 Brian had again joined Freddie, Roger and John at Mountain Studios in Montreux, but this was a gathering with a difference. Over the New Year Freddie and Roger had met to talk, and the outcome was that Freddie wanted the band to get back into the studio without delay to do what recording they could. He had been in considerable pain throughout the recording of the *Innuendo* album and at times had only managed to come into the studios one day a week, sometimes less. It was now that Freddie told his three close friends what they had already guessed long ago – that he was dying of AIDS. He told them, 'I want to work till I fucking well drop. I'd like you to support me in this.'

All during the previous year while struggling to complete their new album it had been a poignant and painful experience to harbour, as they did, their unspoken fears. Now that the 'secret' was out in the open among themselves, as they set to work recording some B-sides for use on singles, suddenly every day became intensely precious. The already enormous respect that Brian had for Freddie only deepened as he watched his friend cope with uncomplaining and often black-humoured bravery. In some ways, too, Brian tried to draw some strength from Fred's attitude to shore up his own still very shaky grip on his problems which, in his grief at knowing he was soon to lose someone else to whom he was close, inevitably began to grow.

When Brian returned to London he once again committed himself to charity work – this time producing the theme song for the 1991 Comic Relief campaign. This year the song was to be performed by television comedians Gareth Hale and Norman Pace. Norman explains, 'Producer Richard Curtis had sent out a leaflet to everybody who'd been involved in Comic Relief asking if they had any suggestions. Gareth and I came up with the idea of calling the whole day The Stonker, thinking we could write a song called 'The Stonk' – you know, a silly thing that could perhaps become a dance as well. Richard liked the idea and asked if we would write it and sing it.' He goes on, 'Brian had apparently been in touch with Curtis some time before, saying that he liked what he was doing with Comic Relief and if there was anything he could do, he'd be delighted to help.'

Richard Curtis, co-writer with Ben Elton of the award-winning *Blackadder* comedy series which starred the rubber-faced actor Rowan Atkinson, at once asked Brian if he would produce Hale and Pace on the theme song. Says Norman, 'Gareth was on holiday and Richard asked me to come along to an Indian restaurant and meet Brian May, who was interested in producing 'The Stonk'. This was like a thunderbolt to me! I'd been a Queen fan for years and in particular a big admirer of Brian's talent, so of course I went like a bullet. Now this was the very day that 'Innuendo' crashed straight into the charts at number one, so Richard and I were sitting at this table in the restaurant, squinting every two minutes at our watches and saying things like, "Well, you know, Brian's bound to be celebrating and whatnot. Maybe he won't show – understandable when you think of it." But there was never a danger of Brian not turning up as promised, and suddenly he walked in and joined us.'

That evening Brian invited Richard and Norman back to his house to listen to a tape he'd made for them. 'I was amazed,' confesses Norman. 'We'd written it as this honky-tonk type thing, but Brian had gone and put in Queen-like chords and added all sorts of sounds to it. My first reaction, I admit, was that it sounded a bit peculiar – but only because I was used to it as we'd written it. But Brian was so enthusiastic. He heard possibilities in the song that we'd never had any intention of creating. It was marvellous. Anyway, we happily went along with the rewrite and within two weeks of that Indian meal Gareth was back from holiday and we were in the studios.

The actual recording of 'The Stonk' took place at the end of January at Metropolis Studios in London. 'It took five days in all,' recalls Norman, 'and was a total education. When Gareth and I do songs for our shows, a band comes in and plays the backing track and we sing – that's it. But working with Brian was an entirely different experience. As a producer he's very painstaking. It's all done layer upon layer. We had something like three drum layers – Brian had dragged in Roger Taylor as well as his friend Cozy Powell. He even roped in Rowan Atkinson, who was also in the video of course, to play drums too, and Tony Iommi played guitar with Brian. For two days Brian had been laying the bass line and piano and generally being in charge all round, and we just turned round and said, 'Look, Brian, get your guitar out and play yourself!' which he did. I was stunned at how long he took to get his guitar right – something like two whole hours! Talk about being a perfectionist!'

The entire experience, especially Brian's way of working, made a lasting impression on Norman. 'Two things I noticed,' he states. 'First, he has a brilliant musical ear. He hears things that no one else hears, but when he singles out the wrong note you say, "Oh, yeah! I hear it now!" The second thing is his incredible concentration over great long stretches of time – fourteen hours or so. His concentration never wavers for a second. It might sound a stupid thing to say, but Brian can even *eat* and still concentrate at exactly the same pitch. I was amazed at how much he put himself into it.'

It wasn't, however, a one-way street. Right then Brian was more than happy to absorb himself in something, and he resolved to relax and enjoy the company of the two lively comedians. Like everything else about Brian, his sense of humour is of a quiet and inward variety. Not for him the practical joker or the loud brash wit; he has his own way of appreciating the lighter side of life. For Gareth and Norman, used to robust banter, it took a day or two to figure out what that way was.

'Brian's got a real good sense of humour,' says Norman, 'and we all got on very well together, but for perhaps the first two days Gareth or I would toss some off-the-cuff remark at him and he'd look long at us and we'd think, "Aw, God! I hope he's not offended!" Then slowly a broad smile would cross his face and he'd thump us on the back once he'd worked out what we were getting at. Don't get me wrong – he's not slow on the uptake. It's just a combination of our brand of humour and the fact that he analyses things so much. He'd come in one day, for instance, and pick up on a throwaway line from two days earlier. It's funny,' Norman adds, 'sometimes when you get the opportunity to work with famous people you go into it with great respect for the guy and come out the other end feeling really let down. With Brian my respect only grew. I'll never forget it, and it's unlikely I'll ever top the experience either.' 'The Stonk' was released on 25 February and after a couple of weeks went to number one in the charts, eventually raising in excess of quarter of a million pounds for charity.

On 2 February Queen's *Greatest Hits* album re-entered the charts. Then two days later the new album, *Innuendo*, was released and, like the single, bolted straight in at the top. But any pleasure at this success was seriously undermined by the sight of Freddie's condition the day before, when the band had congregated at Limehouse Studios in London. Directed by Hannes Rossacher and Rudi Dolezal, they were to film a video for what was planned to be the next single released from *Innuendo*, 'I'm Going Slightly Mad'. The sequences they filmed all portrayed various exaggerated forms of madness, and included daft scenes with Roger riding a tiny tricycle in circles while being chased by an insane-looking Freddie in long winkle-picker shoes, both arms arched threateningly above his head. Brian at one point was made up to resemble a gigantic penguin for his race with three of the real birds. But the reality behind the nonsense could hardly have contrasted more.

On film there is no concealing Freddie's drastic weight loss, despite the fact that he wore an extra layer of clothes under his suit to pad himself out. His face, supposed to be *à la* Byron, was heavily covered with white make-up in an attempt to hide his sunken features, and any revealing hair loss was buried beneath an obvious wig. But it was his weakness which permeated the entire three freezing winter days. A bed had been made up behind the sets so that he could lie down in an attempt to regain his strength between takes. The scene where he crawls on all fours in front of John, Roger and Brian lounging carelessly on a settee was particularly painful for him, although in the final cut he hid it so well that no one could tell. But for those in the know it was very distressing.

Journalists, meanwhile, were continually skulking about outside the studios hoping to catch an unguarded snippet of conversation, to trip someone up – anything that might give them the low-down on Freddie. They got no joy from any of the Queen officials: the word still was that Freddie was fine and continuing to enjoy himself. 'I'm Going Slightly

Mad' was released a month later, on 4 March.

Brian felt utterly helpless: it was purgatory to have to stand by and watch the wasting disease take its toll on his old friend. The previous year at times like these his answer had been to hole up in a studio and thrash out his feelings on gutsy rock numbers such as 'I Can't Live with You' and the powerful 'Headlong', which was released on 13 May as the third single from the new album. Now his solution was to try to alleviate some of his inner trauma by intense songwriting. He was still working on ideas for a solo album, storing them up for the future, and found in it a much-needed escape for his deeply troubled mind.

In late spring Brian undertook an extensive tour of the USA and Canada to promote *Innuendo*, in an effort to boost Queen's supposedly somewhat flagging popularity in America. He took with him his constant companion, the Red Special, and played impromptu for his listeners on live radio shows. The tour was a great success. Hundreds of people rang in to talk to him on air, and still more Queen fans mobbed each building he visited. The grass-roots devotion of the band's American fans proved to be as deep as ever and gave Brian the kind of comfort he so desperately needed.

As well as promoting Queen on this tour, Brian had occasionally taken advantage of the airplay to try out a few ideas for his solo album. He felt it was very important to test the water; now he felt reassured that he had an eager audience out there ready to snap up his album as soon as it became available. When the tour finished he headed at once for Montreux to get to work on it.

While Brian had been out of the country, the rest of Queen had set out filming what would be their last-ever video for a number written by Roger and called 'These Are the Days of Our Lives'. It was a touching, indeed highly poignant, ballad, again from the *Innuendo* album. Brian was filmed separately and integrated in the final cut in the editing room.

In early summer Brian had been approached by the advertising agency Ogilvy & Mather, who handled promotion for the Ford Motor Company. They were planning a new series of Ford ads on British television and wanted Brian to write a tune to accompany them. He had never written for a commercial before, but, always interested in a new challenge, agreed to do it. He came up with 'Driven by You', which Ford loved, and the ad campaign began in early July.

For years now Brian seemed to have been under siege from one person or other hoping to involve him in their particular project, and

August 1991 was no exception. In two months' time a massive guitar festival was to take place in Seville in Spain as a precursor to the Expo '92 celebrations planned for the following year. The idea was to coax the best guitarists in the business to perform live on the same stage for an evening and the organizers, Tribute Productions, asked Brian if he would be musical director. Again he said yes.

Almost from the start, though, Brian worried about having taken on this responsibility. First, he had to form a backing band by selecting some of rock's elite to perform with him. Many phone calls later he had his shortlist – a who's who in rock which included drummers Cozy Powell and Steve Ferrone, bass players Nathan East and Whitesnake's Neil Murray, together with Mike Moran and Rick Wakeman on keyboards. The vocals were to be handled by Paul Rodgers, formerly of the bands Free and Bad Company, and Extreme's Gary Cherone. And among the guitarists joining him were ex-Eagles member Joe Walsh, Nuno Bettencourt, Steve Vai and Joe Satriani – often quoted in 1994 as being 'the greatest guitarist in the world'.

Joe himself makes no such claim, and when Brian approached him in 1991 he felt over-awed by the honour. He recalls, 'I discovered there was a shortlist with names on it like B. B. King and Paul Rodgers. I was very flattered to be included.' Joe continues, 'I flew to rehearsals in London and that's the first time I met Brian. His job as musical director was a very difficult one, but he put everyone at their ease at once. We rehearsed for two or three days and I can vividly remember feeling so thrilled that I was standing there with Brian May. My friend Steve Vai felt the same – in fact there was one particular moment when Steve and I were standing shoulder-to-shoulder watching Brian get all these brilliant Queen sounds out of his guitar right there in front of our eyes and neither of us could believe it was happening. We looked at each other just speechless with delight. After that we went to Spain and had just one day's rehearsal, and then it was the show.'

Brian took the stage with his illustrious assembly on 19 October 1991. Joe recalls, 'It was a real big thrill for me, although I was very tense inside. I couldn't help but be aware that on stage that night were musicians from very different backgrounds. Some were legends in the business that go way back, like Paul Rodgers and Joe Walsh. Then there were the new guys like me and Steve getting our feet wet.'

One of the undoubted highlights was when Paul Rodgers, in better voice than ever, led the others in a magnificent, nerve-tingling rendition of the Free classic 'All Right Now'. For many who remembered the original brilliant 1970 version, that night's rendition topped it by a mile. Joe agrees, '"All Right Now" was a song I'd grown up with, and here I was actually backing Paul Rodgers himself singing it. I keep saying it, but for me it was very, very special.'

The honour, however, according to Paul Rodgers, was all his. He had known Brian and Queen since the mid-seventies, their paths – as is the nature of their business – crossing at regular intervals over the intervening years. Says Paul, 'Then Brian called me one day and asked if I'd like to be part of this Guitar Legends night he was organizing. It was very nice to be asked and in fact I'm very grateful to Brian, because in a way it was that night which got me back in the public eye.' He goes on, 'Joe's right – it was an incredible night with an incredible on-stage atmosphere, and backstage too, as it happens. We were all rehearsing down in the dungeons below the venue and there was a great feeling about it. One minute you were literally practising away, then the next you were thrust up top, out on stage. I think everyone there will remember that event for a long time.'

A few days before that Seville gig Queen released their fortieth single, 'The Show Must Go On'. The haunting lyrics immediately alarmed fans, who read a hidden fatalistic meaning into every line. The video released to accompany the single premiered on *Top of the Pops*, which was a compilation of scenes from their heyday, looked uneasily like an obituary and did nothing to allay fears that the end of the road was near.

They were, of course, right. Freddie was now desperately ill. The AIDS virus infects brain cells and the central nervous system, creating a host of neurological disorders beyond the immune deficiency which makes the body unable to fight infection. By early November Fred had been bedridden for weeks, suffering blind spells and night sweats, tormented by strange and painful skin rashes, plagued with oral thrush and having to use breathing apparatus. At the end he would be unable even to speak.

He had recently been visited by Dr Brian Gizzard, head of the AIDS Unit at London's Westminster Hospital; that visit increased anxieties that he did not have long left. It must have been unimaginably heartbreaking for everyone close to him. Although his doctor, Gordon Atkinson, was in constant attendance there was little he could do for Fred now except try to alleviate his pain.

Brian, like the others, tried to keep his distress to himself but even at this terrible time he had another concern to deal with. Since Ford had started running their adverts in July, the music he had penned had created a stir. Loyal fans had had no trouble in recognizing Brian's unique guitar work and had immediately bombarded both Ford and the Queen office with cries that the band were being ripped off. Once they had discovered the truth, demand had quickly mushroomed for the music to be released as a single. After some careful consideration Brian had decided he would let 'Driven by You' go out as a solo single. PR wheels had been set in motion, and the release date was set for 25 November.

Now that seemed very bad timing. Clearly Freddie would not last very long now, and Brian felt terrible at the thought of his solo single coming out at such a time. He talked to Jim Beach about stopping it, and he in turn spoke to Freddie. Although his strength was seeping away by the day Freddie's answer bounced back to Brian in typical fashion: he must go ahead because, if nothing else, just think of the boost to sales if he did die! His flippancy, though shocking in the circumstances, was very Freddie. Seriously, Freddie was determined that his friend was not to worry – indeed he was adamant that Brian was to go ahead. Joe Satriani recalls, 'Brian told me that Freddie was very very insistent that he was to go ahead both with his single and his whole solo career. Freddie supported Brian literally right up to the end.'

The end, as it happens, came quicker than anyone expected. Another of Brian's friends, Joe Elliott, recalls, 'Brian was in a very bad way about this time. I rang him to ask how he was coping, and as usual he tried to hide it. He said, "Aw, well – OK, I guess." He said that Freddie hadn't got long left. Forty-eight hours later Fred died.'

For months Freddie's life had been made a misery by the press camping on his doorstep and hassling anyone entering and leaving the house. Their telephoto lens had been trained on the bedroom curtains, ready to snap him should he show his face for a split second. All this was to further the quest of heartlessly proving, even though it was being furiously denied, that he really did have AIDS.

On Saturday, 23 November they got their answer in the shape of an official statement read to the pack gathered outside Garden Lodge. Freddie had worked on it himself and decided the timing. He stated that he had been tested positive for HIV and that he had AIDS. It had come to the point where he felt he wanted to tell his friends and fans, and he hoped they would join him and his doctors in fighting the dreadful disease. What Fred wanted most was to say that he had AIDS and that there should be no shame or stigma attached to admitting it.

The statement made headline television news that night, and the following day front pages around the world carried the story. Later that Sunday, 24 November 1991, at exactly 7 p.m. Freddie, at the age of forty-five, passed away in his sleep. He had died of AIDS-related bronchial pneumonia.

Sunday itself had been more busy than normal, with selected visitors urgently coming and going. Dr Atkinson had been in attendance, and in fact had not long left to go and pack an overnight bag when he was hastily called back. Mary Austin, pregnant with her second child – Freddie was already godfather to her son Richard – had been one of those tending Freddie in his last few weeks. She had not long left his bedroom in tears, and it was his good friend Dave Clark, holding Fred's hand and softly sobbing, who was at his bedside when he finally gave up the fight.

No amount of warning can really ever cushion us from the trauma of a loved one dying, and everyone was distraught. In an effort to avoid being individually and personally pressed to comment to the media Brian, Roger and John issued a joint public statement which talked of their overwhelming grief at losing Freddie, and of what a privilege it had been to know him and to have shared in his life. But privately each had to try to handle his own particular grief as best he could.

Brian's closest friends knew how much strain he was already under and, whilst immensely sad for Freddie, they were seriously worried about how Brian would cope. Joe Elliott again rang him. 'When our drummer Rick Allen lost his arm in a car crash Brian was the first to phone,' he says. 'Again, when our guitarist Steve Clark died, he was first to call. I don't mean it was some kind of weird race, and I didn't want to intrude on his grief, but I was so concerned that I rang Brian as soon as I'd heard that Fred had died. I have to say he was a lot better than I'd expected, at least in one sense. Of course he was extremely upset, but he also felt a deep sense of relief. I could relate to that because of how I felt when Steve died. In Fred's case, in the last week he suffered so very much that it took a bigger love actually to wish him gone for his own sake. Of course there had been industry rumours about Fred having AIDS; they were rife. But it wasn't officially announced until the day before. Brian and the others, though, had lived with it for a long time – having to lie and deny had added enormously to the strain of their personal pain. And Brian was in a lot of pain anyway. He's a big guy, you know, but he has round shoulders. That's because he carries all the pressures for everyone else on those shoulders.'

Floral tributes started to pour in from all corners of the world, from mourners in all walks of life. The Hammersmith Odeon erected a billboard dedicated to Freddie and even the London cab drivers, it's said, driving along West Cromwell Road, which is close to Fred's home, dipped their lights and did not pick up fares as their way of paying tribute.

Three days later, at the West London Crematorium in Kensal Green, Freddie was cremated. It was a private funeral with only a handful of close friends joining his family. Freddie's parents, devout Parsees, followed the ancient Zoroastrian faith and the service was conducted in accordance with its rites. The clear, strong voice of his friend Montserrat Caballé filled the air, but for Brian it was a harrowing ordeal.

Several stars paid tribute in the press to Freddie, but perhaps his friend Wayne Eagling best sums the man up when he says, 'On stage Freddie was very flamboyant, of course, but in private he was very quiet unless he felt very comfortable with you. I think he was always extremely brave in everything he did. He was never afraid to face up to the world and what was perceived as normal and conventional. It was a great shame that he had to go. You feel so cheated. With Freddie, who knows what was still there to come out. He was a very smart man indeed, and no one with that brain and talent would have ever been satisfied to remain still. Still, we must be thankful for what he left us.'

One week later Brian and Roger appeared on breakfast TV talking about the loss of Freddie and how much they missed him. At the end of the official press release there had been mention of the remaining band members hoping to stage some celebration of Freddie. When pressed by the presenter to elaborate, Brian talked of perhaps staging a concert, although the details were still vague.

In the ensuing days, weeks and months it began to dawn on people how long Freddie must have known of his illness and how carefully he had concealed the fact. The AIDS incubation period is currently thought to be some five and a half years. Freddie's anxieties had come to a head back in 1986 when a former lover, Tony Bastin, had died of AIDS at thirty-five. Tony had been Fred's constant companion for two years from 1980, and his occasional lover after their split. Frighteningly, AIDS then also claimed the life of another former partner, Russian Nicolai Grishanovich who had previously been Kenny Everett's lover. Fears that he himself would fall victim had driven him into retreat at Garden Lodge in what had turned out to be a vain attempt to avoid the terrible disease.

Brian, Roger, John and Jim had agreed to release on 9 December, in tribute to Fred, the classic 'Bohemian Rhapsody' – this time as a double A-side with the as yet unreleased 'These Are the Days of Our Lives'. It could now become known that making the video for the latter number had been a deeply painful experience for everyone mentally, and in Freddie's case physically too. Even standing upright had been an enormous ordeal for his pain-racked body and had taken great courage. The single stormed to number one, where it lodged for the second time over a Christmas period; all royalties went to the AIDS charity, the Terrence Higgins Trust.

Amid all this emotional upheaval Christmas for Brian was little more than a blur. As had been agreed, his single 'Driven by You' had been released on schedule – as it turned out, the day after Freddie's death. It was a huge success. 'Bohemian Rhapsody' reigned at number one, earning a great deal of money for the charity, and it seemed that every music chart boasted Queen albums. Yet none of it meant anything to Brian. By the end of 1991 he had come through five years of what he felt was absolute hell. His marriage had foundered, he had lost his father, and now Freddie had gone. He had tried so hard to keep himself together for the sake of those who depended on him, but his ability to cope had been fragmenting at an alarming rate and now it had come dangerously close to breaking point.

He was trapped in a weird limbo where outwardly he could see himself carrying on apparently as normal, meeting people, talking, signing autographs – but all the while he felt he was breaking up into tiny pieces, haemorrhaging confidence, shattering irrevocably. And no one could see this, no one could help. He felt he didn't exist as a person any more, and on his own admission he nearly drove off a bridge in a bid to escape his desolation and despair.

It's very hard to say just what it was that pulled Brian back from the brink. It's doubtful if Brian himself even knows, but somewhere he found the strength. He knew he desperately needed peace, needed to rest and needed to get away from Britain. Before the year was out he flew out to his home in Los Angeles where he metaphorically pulled up the drawbridge and gave himself a chance to get well, to regain control of his emotions and to mend his broken life.

BACK TO THE LIGHT

To strengthen the emotional healing process, during 1992 Brian continued his own proven form of therapy – writing and recording more solo material. Queen's music, meanwhile continued to dominate the charts. Hollywood Records decided to release 'Bohemian Rhapsody'/'The Show Must Go On' as a double A-side on 6 February, donating all royalties to the Magic Johnson Aids Foundation; on the 12th, at the annual British Phonographic Industry Awards at the Hammersmith Odeon, 'These Are the Days of Our Lives' ran clean away with the award for the Best British Single of 1991. Brian, Roger and John also received a special award made posthumously to Freddie. In accepting it Brian, brimful of emotion, confessed, 'If Freddie were here he would go and tell me to put this on the mantelpiece. He would say, "Look, mum, dad – that's what I did, and I'm proud." We're•terribly proud of everything Freddie stood for. We feel his spirit is with us.'

It was at this ceremony that their previous hints of a plan to honour Freddie in style crystallized into an announcement that the band were to stage an enormous concert in his memory on Easter Monday, 20 April, at Wembley Stadium. All monies raised were to be donated to various charities and the gig was to double as an AIDS Awareness Day. Within six hours of going on sale the following day, all tickets had sold out for what was already seen as likely to be the biggest gig since Live Aid. No one yet knew who else would be appearing, but no one cared. They just wanted to be part of what they were sure was going to be an exceptional day.

Gerry Stickells undertook the task of masterminding the organization, and he and his team of experienced helpers quickly set up their base at Queen's Bayswater offices. There was an enormous amount to deal with, but he had years of experience in handling mammoth Queen tours and set about his task with military precision.

The job of inviting the artistes to take part devolved on Brian, John and Roger. It was good for Brian because it kept him on his toes and gave him little time to dwell on anything else. Freddie had been enormously popular within the music business and they were inundated with requests from bands and stars, all desperate to take part. As Roger later confessed, 'In the end, we chose folk who had some links with Freddie and who were very famous, because this show was going to be seen all over the globe.'

One of the first groups Brian contacted was Def Leppard. Joe Elliott remembers, 'Brian rang me and said they were organizing this gig. They didn't have a British band, you see, and so we were real honoured. It was a proud moment for us, to be specifically asked by Queen. I couldn't believe Brian was actually asking *if* we'd appear. Blimey – I'd have swum over for it!' The list of accepting artistes grew daily.

Near the end of March the band left Gerry and his team to carry on with the organization whilst they took up working residence at a studio in Shepherd's Bush to rehearse for the gig. Now the stark reality of performing without Freddie really hit home. It was bad enough not having Freddie there to belt out their old familiar hits at rehearsal, but they all shuddered to think what it was going to feel like when they took the stage at Wembley without him.

The plan was to split the evening in two, with half a dozen bands playing between 6 p.m. and 8 p.m., at which point the 'celeb section' would begin. For the rest of the evening various stars would take lead vocal on a Queen hit with backing from Brian, Roger and John. This meant rehearsing with the artistes and so, after two weeks at Shepherd's Bush, rehearsals moved to Bray Studios in Berkshire.

The stars who turned up to work on their number with the band included Ian Hunter, Mick Ronson, George Michael, Roger Daltrey, Lisa Stansfield, Liza Minnelli, Elton John, Robert Plant, Gary Cherone, Annie

Lennox and Paul Young. Some of them had never sung a Queen number before, and in most cases the key had to be altered, as trying to emulate Freddie proved too difficult. There was an excellent feeling of togetherness, however, and those who were prone to displaying a certain degree of temperament left their egos at the studio door and rehearsed hard to make it the best tribute possible.

With over a dozen artistes to work with, it would have been impractical as well as unnecessary to have all the stars there at the same time. Paul Young explains, 'Brian, Roger and John were obviously there all the time, but we had our rehearsal times arranged in advance and just went along and got to work. In my case it was a couple of hours on a couple of days.' Paul had been invited by Roger to join the line-up. 'They showed me a list of the songs left for selection and I chose 'Radio Ga Ga'. The first day I turned up at rehearsals we started up the song with the drums – then Brian started playing, and suddenly it was Queen! Freddie was fabulous: there's no doubt about that. But for me Brian is the real embodiment of Queen – the distinctive Queen sound, I mean.'

On a personal front, particularly in relation to just how different he feels Brian is from most of his contemporaries, Paul has this to say, 'You know, once you become a celebrity it's very easy to find yourself distracted every ten seconds because there are always so many people trying to talk to you, to catch your attention in some way. I know that's the nature of the business, but you end up not being able to hold a conversation with anyone for more than a couple of minutes. Or if you do, you're suddenly edgy, itching to move on as if something's wrong. You can't help it. Your whole life's run that way. Brian, though, is different. He *takes* the time to talk, to communicate with people, and equally *gives* the time to listen – always. In this business that's unique.'

Meanwhile accolades of another kind were still being bestowed on Queen. Five days before the gig Brian and Roger attended the annual Ivor Novello Award Ceremony at the Grosvenor House Hotel in Park Lane to receive the Best Selling British A Side award, again for 'These Are the Days of Our Lives'. Brian in his own right was also presented with the award for Best Theme from a TV/Radio Commercial for 'Driven by You'. At this ceremony Brian and Roger in turn handed over a cheque to the Terrence Higgins Trust for more than one million pounds, which represented the proceeds from sales of the single 'Bohemian Rhapsody'/'These Are the Days of Our Lives'.

Easter Monday, 20 April, was a bright, dry day for the seventy-two

thousand crowd crammed into Wembley Stadium. The event was officially billed as 'The Freddie Mercury Tribute. Concert for AIDS
Awareness', and for many the journey had begun days before. Then
they had bunked down on the Sunday night in sleeping bags on the cold
hard pavements outside the stadium, determined to be first in when the
gates opened at 4 p.m. the following day. On entry each person was
handed a red ribbon to wear, to symbolize their support in the fight
against AIDS.

As the crowds flooded into the Wembley ground, backstage the
artistes had been gathering all day. A bar had been specially set up so
that the stars and their guests could meet, have a drink and try to relax.
The atmosphere was a strange mix. Says Joe Elliott, 'In one sense it was
light-hearted and up, very positive. People popped in and out of each
other's trailers and dressing rooms all the time. The good thing was that
no hangers-on were allowed in this area, which is unusual – only the
necessary people were there, and it was a great feeling. But on the other
hand there was definitely a real sadness, and it was obviously different
in Queen's trailer. Just as it got to be a bit emotional later on stage – but
that was understandable.'

It also meant a lot to Spike Edney to feel that everyone performing
there that night was doing it for the right reasons. He explains, 'Live Aid
was great, but over the years I'd become very sceptical of events like
this. It just seemed that anybody who didn't get on the Live Aid bill
made bloody sure they appeared at any charity gig that came along
afterwards, cynically seeing the exposure as a big boost to their careers.
But it wasn't going to be like that this time.'

At 6 p.m. Brian, Roger and John opened the show to deafening
applause and a sea of red banners proclaiming 'FREDDIE MERCURY –
AIDS AWARENESS'. Brian addressed the crowd: 'Good evening,
Wembley and the world. We're here tonight to celebrate the life and
work of one Freddie Mercury. We're going to give him the biggest send-
off in history!' Roger promptly took over. 'OK. Today's for Freddie, it's
for you, it's to tell everybody round the world that AIDS affects us all.
That's what these red ribbons are all about, and you can cry as much as
you like.' Then John spoke up, thanking all the artistes who had given
their time and energy to pay tribute to Freddie, ending with the
poignant pun, 'First of all the show must go on.'

Metallica was the opening band on stage, followed some twenty
minutes later by Extreme. Then Def Leppard appeared. 'Roger gave us

a nice introduction,' says Joe. 'We had some technical problems with Rick's drums, but it didn't matter. It was a brilliant experience playing to seventy-two thousand people in brilliant sunshine. The nice thing, too, although it probably escaped a lot of people, is that there were a lot of internal tie-ups at work that night. For instance, Liza Minnelli led the finale because Freddie admired her so much, and of course Ian Hunter and Mick Ronson were there because Queen had played support to Hoople just before making it big themselves.'

Spinal Tap, U2 by satellite, then Guns 'n' Roses kept up the increasingly emotional momentum until about 8 p.m. when, as planned, the second half of the evening got under way. Brian, Roger and John returned to the stage and with a sudden and familiar explosion of smoke bombs plunged straight into the hard rocking 'Tie Your Mother Down', with Brian singing lead. A moment later Joe Elliott joined him at the mike, taking over lead vocal and turning in a highly creditable performance.

As Joe hurtled off Brian announced, 'I'd like to introduce you to an old friend of mine, Mr Tony Iommi.' Out into the glare of lights strolled Tony, in time to play the distinctive intro to the Who's 'Pinball Wizard', which in turn heralded the arrival of Roger Daltrey to lead the band in 'I Want It All'. Says Tony, 'I was really proud to play that night – it was a very raw experience. It had been building that way for weeks in rehearsals for the whole thing. It was all friends there that night, and I think it showed just what Queen have achieved over the years.'

A dozen top artistes and more then streamed on, one after the other, to perform their chosen Queen hit. Elizabeth Taylor, now National Chairperson for the American Foundation for AIDS Research (AmFAR), made a guest appearance to deliver an emotive speech about AIDS and Freddie. David Bowie performed 'Under Pressure', dueting with a stunning Annie Lennox, and for many one of the night's highlights was when Ian Hunter swung into Mott the Hoople's classic 'All the Young Dudes' with a line-up which included as well as Queen, Mick Ronson, Joe Elliott and, on sax, Bowie, who had originally written the number.

The most touching moment, however, undoubtedly came when, after Robert Plant had felt his way through 'Innuendo' and 'Crazy Little Thing Called Love', Brian surrendered his guitar to sit at the keyboards. He wanted to sing a very special personal tribute to Freddie, and it wasn't a Queen number but rather one of his own compositions, never aired till now. He said, 'My only excuse for playing it is, it's the best thing I have to offer.' Slowly, almost achingly, he sang 'Too Much Love Will Kill You'. He has said of the number, 'We worked on that song for a couple of days and I never went near an instrument. I never touched a piano to the point where we were going to put down a demo. By that time the song was totally finished. It was obvious in my mind how it should go. The piano was immaterial really. The only thing that mattered was getting the feeling across. I wasn't concerned about anything else.' The heartfelt lyrics are ambiguous enough to have been written specially about Freddie if you choose to read them that way, and that night they reduced the Wembley crowd to a deafening hush.

Tony Iommi was amazed when he discovered his friend's intention to perform the solo piece. 'It was one day at rehearsals. I'd just turned up and heard someone playing a piano and singing a number called "Too Much Love Will Kill You", and I thought it sounded good. In all the years we've been mates we've jammed together a lot, sometimes playing non-stop while all the gear's being stripped down and packed away around us. But I never saw Brian as lead vocal, I must admit. You don't, when someone is as good as he is on guitar and has only ever sung harmonies before, which is a different thing altogether. But I stood there in the doorway behind Brian watching and listening to him and thinking: Bloody hell! He can sing after all!'

As the evening progressed it was becoming clear that Brian was finding it hard to keep his emotions in check. When he announced Liza Minnelli on stage before the finale he was visibly close to tears, his voice strained to breaking point. All the artistes joined Liza in a throaty, bluesy rendition of 'We Are the Champions', which ended with the singer/actress looking heavenwards to holler, 'Thanks, Freddie. We just wanted to let you know we'll be thinking of you!'

At the dawn of the eighties AIDS, if it had been heard of at all, was for the most part dismissed ostrich-like by the general public as an affliction visited upon an unsavoury fringe of society. Then in October 1985 the clean-cut all-American film star Rock Hudson died of the disease, and suddenly the media were full of hysterical reports so that for a time it acquired the ignorant label 'the gay plague'. Today AIDS has become an all too real and frightening part of culture the world over. Immediately after that gig Queen set up a special charity, the Mercury Phoenix Trust, specifically to oversee the allocation of all monies raised by the Easter event.

Publicly they had said their goodbyes and done it proudly. Privately the fall-out was much harder to bear. Tony explains, 'Immediately after the show was over, in private, it hit Brian hard, very hard – hit them all. It was so, so sad. John was just in bits. It was a case of: right, that's it, over, final. I'd be as well opening up a shop or something. They'd been very brave and it was highly emotional. There was this dreadful feeling of no more, it's finished. I felt it myself, strongly, had seen it lurking and building up all the preceding weeks and months. They'd been so close, we'd all been close – all there together for Freddie. Then suddenly that was it – nothing but a terrible vacuum.' Spike adds, 'At the meal afterwards a lot of people were going around patting each other on the back and everything, but the four of us just sat at the table staring silently into space, completely drained.'

There was no escaping it, though. It was now time to let go, not only of Freddie but also of the band itself. Brian once described Queen as the most stable family he had had, but never for a second did he or the others consider trying to carry on as Queen. Brian has stated categorically, 'It would be wrong of us to go out with another singer, pretending to be Queen. Queen stopped at that point. I don't feel it in my bones that we should keep Queen alive. I don't think it would be right for Freddie.' The announcement that Queen was disbanding came soon after the Easter tribute, and ended an extraordinary era spanning two decades.

But for Brian the dignified demise of Queen was not to spell the end of his own musical career. Difficult though it was for him to see it in this light right then, he had to believe that it marked a new beginning with new challenges to be faced. That meant disciplining himself to concentrate on nurturing this bridge to a fresh future. He also needed to relax and circulate again; fortunately May brought him a welcome diversion. Hank Marvin, one of Brian's early guitar heroes, invited him to guest on his forthcoming album.

Says Hank, 'I've admired Brian's guitar playing since "Killer Queen". I remember the first time I heard it: I was driving along when it came on the radio, and I was immediately struck with the expertness of its musical construction. Queen were so very different from what else was happening at that time – bluesy stuff and glam rock. But then, they have been consistently different. I've always thought, too, that Brian was the perfect foil for Freddie's operatic vibrato. Lots of Queen stuff is very grand and showy, and Brian's guitar sound with these big power chords as well as the melodic solos balanced everything perfectly. It had to be big to match Freddie's delivery.'

He goes on, 'You know, there are a lot of really good guitarists around in the nineties, but very few have developed a sound and style that are truly recognizable. A lot of them tend to be clones of Joe Satriani or someone, but then a few manage to create their very own sound, like Joe and like Brian.'

Speaking of his approach to Brian, Hank says, 'Basically how it developed was that in the time immediately after Freddie's death there was a lot of Queen music being played everywhere and it reminded me of how good they were. I thought it would be a nice tribute to their excellence to record some of their music, but then I sat on the idea for a while because I felt it might be cashing in on Freddie's death and I wouldn't have wanted that at all. But then one day my manager came up with the idea of doing a duet with Brian May.' He continues, 'From there I thought I could combine that with my original idea, in that we could choose one of Freddie's compositions and donate the royalties to one of the charities – as it turned out, the Terrence Higgins Trust.' The number they decided on was 'We Are the Champions'.

For both men it was a pleasure and a privilege to make music together. Hank could tell that Brian was still in a very raw state: it was clear that losing Freddie had reminded him of the death of his father – a gnawing ache never far from the surface. 'Yes, there was a lot of hurt there,' agrees Hank. 'Brian had been very close indeed to his dad. I picked up on that almost immediately because he talked of him a lot when we were together.'

There was, of course, a happier connection with Harold May – the Red Special – and Hank was as guilty as any budding young guitarist of being super-curious about the famous instrument. 'I found Brian's guitar incredibly difficult to play, though,' he admits. 'He uses very light gauge strings and also it's constructed in a highly unusual way. With a Fender, for instance, the length of the string from nut to bridge is 25½ inches, and a Gibson is 24¾ inches. The shorter the strings, the less tension in them, which makes them easier to bend. Now Brian's guitar has a 24-inch measurement, which makes it easier still to bend the strings. I'm used to having to push hard to produce various effects, and when I tried Brian's guitar I couldn't control the thing. It was like playing on fuse wire – it just went away from me. To some extent, of course, it's always difficult playing someone else's guitar – but his is highly individual. It's an absolutely fascinating instrument. Imagine playing a guitar you made with your dad that actually works! It's got woodworm holes in it and everything. Plus it's never been refretted, but it has a good tone and when you crash into it, it gives you a very hot sound.'

For Brian it was a dream come true to work with his teenage idol. In an interview on Australian radio he later confessed that his reaction on walking into the studio to meet Hank had been, 'I can't believe this – if someone had told me twenty years ago that I'd be dueting with Hank Marvin I just wouldn't have believed them!' While enjoying their time together, Hank was also carefully weighing up the younger man. He reveals, 'Brian's a great guy, a deep thinker and very sensitive. At that time it seemed to me, too, that he wasn't over-confident and seemed genuinely in need of a lot of reassurance.' Hank's album, which includes their duet, was titled *Into the Light* and was released later in the year.

While Brian was working with Hank he was contacted by Charles Leary, then chairman of Imperial College Jazz & Rock, a players' society which had formerly been the Jazz Club. Because of Brian's past association with Imperial College, Leary asked if he would become the club's Honorary President. Brian wrote back that he would be delighted to accept, adding, 'The building [the Beit Building which had housed the Jazz Club room in his day] was of course the centre of my life for a considerable time. I lived and loved and suffered and painfully grew there. Now I am of course living and loving and suffering in a different place. Ha Ha.'

But his gentle attempt at levity was less than convincing, and in fact Hank was not far off the mark about Brian's sense of apprehension. Brian spent the first half of June beavering away in his home recording studio as he put the final touches to his album. Recording solo after all those years of working as part of Queen had been a strain in itself. At times the mosaic of musical ideas made all the sense in the world. Then again he would often find himself sitting back at the end of a day feeling lost, wondering if he had anything worthwhile on tape and finding it impossible to judge objectively. The thought of going solo was an extremely daunting one, but he had invested so much of himself in each of the songs and to deviate from his intended path was unthinkable.

Joe Elliott had been keeping in touch with Brian around this time and he concurs with Hank. 'Brian had invited me round to his house earlier in March when he was working on the album. Cozy was there, laying down the drum track for 'Resurrection', and Brian was definitely tentative about the strength of his voice. I don't mean he wasn't confident as such, but he was playing me a fistful of tapes and kept saying he wasn't sure if he could nail it. He wasn't looking for an emotional crutch or anything. He was simply worried that his voice would come over as weak, when it's not weak at all.'

It didn't surprise Tony that Brian should ask Joe. 'He was very worried about his singing and he asked Joe because Joe's a singer Brian respects. OK, so no one is going to turn round and say, "Hey, Brian, you're a crappy singer." But he needs genuine opinions and he knows where he'll get them.' Tony goes on, 'But it wasn't all about whether he could make it as a lead singer. Brian was very nervous about going solo at all, because it's a huge step to go from being in a major band to going out on your own. And after headlining all those years you're back to playing support, and that comes into it as well. But he had to do it. After Freddie's death, on top of everything else he very much wanted to do something of his own. He was so upset and it had been so very hard on him. They'd had their ups and downs like anyone else, but it was still a terrible shock. Brian had been left with this frightening feeling: what do I do now? He had to get out there and throw himself into it.'

As far as the material was concerned, Joe Elliott picks up. 'He'd sunk such a lot of emotions in that album, but it would be a mistake to analyse every lyric and take them as an exact reflection of what was going on in his life. Whether it's clever or not I don't know, but you can listen to some tracks and, while there is certainly a troubled cry for help in there, it doesn't have to be aimed specifically at his broken marriage – it can just as easily be attributed to losing Freddie. It's aimed, too, at any listener who can relate it to their own life and what's going wrong in it. It was undoubtedly an enormous and terrible blow for him to lose someone he was so close to – personally I know it ripped the heart out of Brian. But, having said that, he was in great spirits after the album was finished. I remember us being in a car together around that time – Brian played "Nothin' but Blue" on the tape deck and I couldn't get it out of my head for days afterwards. It was great.'

As if to endorse Joe's caution against taking his lyrics too literally, in the sleeve notes which accompany his solo album *Back to the Light* Brian himself speaks of it not being the story of his life, and advises listeners to 'take it with a small pinch of salt'. Yet he makes no attempt to hide the fact that the events of the last five years have irrevocably changed his life, describing himself at the time of writing those notes as 'someone quite small and insecure' and going on to confess, 'In my mind, this album was always called *Back to the Light*. At its beginning

I felt no real hope of finding the light; now it glimmers dimly, encouragingly, but always intermittently in the hall of mirrors around me.'

Those notes were dated 20 July 1992. 'Too Much Love Will Kill You', the first single to be released from *Back to the Light*, entered the charts on 5 September and climbed to number five. DJ Bob Harris, who twenty years before was one of the first in the music industry to recognize and support Queen's talent, watched this rebirth with interest. He says, 'I think it was very brave of Brian. After being part of something as enormous as Queen it would have been very easy to hide away.'

Immediately, all Brian's friends ranged loyally behind him to support his break into a solo career. Joe Satriani says, 'After the death of Mr Mercury – as most people who have experienced the tragic break-up of a band know – it feels impossible for you to continue. But I'm really glad Brian did decide to launch his solo career. He has such a lot of music in him and a great deal more to give.'

Among the many people he thanks on his album notes, Brian singles out Satriani for special appreciation over a 'magnificent guitar' which made its debut on the track that Joe Elliott, himself also credited, couldn't forget – 'Nothin' but Blue'. Satriani explains, 'During rehearsals for the Expo '92 gig Brian asked to play my chrome guitar. I took it off immediately and gave it to him. God, it sounded like Brian May coming out of my guitar! He seemed really to like it. After the Seville thing I wanted to give Brian a present as a way to say thank you. I just felt he had given me so much and I'd given him nothing. Now there are very few of these chrome guitars around, and so I had one made with a special neck and just sent it to Brian one day. I didn't expect to see it mentioned on his album, though. That was real nice.'

September sparked off a hectic round of interviews for Brian in the press and on TV and radio. Asked whether he would back up the album with a tour, he told one breakfast TV interviewer, 'Me, Cozy Powell, Neil Murray and some of the friends who guested on the album are going out to South America to rehearse and do a few gigs. If we feel we have a good vehicle then we'll come back here and tour. I don't want to do it unless it's right. I don't want to go out unless people have value for money.'

When pressed on the challenge of making that mental leap from the side of the stage to the centre he was equally candid. 'Strangely enough, I'm up for it. I wouldn't have been a few years ago, but I've changed a lot over the last five years. I was working through all kinds of personal crises, a lot of which you'll find on the album in a way. It's very much a journey from someone who is locked in a very dark place to someone who feels he can see a little bit of the light.'

Before he could leave for South America, however, Brian managed to find a moment to rendezvous a second time with Hank Marvin. 'When I was in the UK in October to promote my album,' says Hank, 'I met up with Brian again. He was busy auditioning for a guitarist in a west London rehearsal room and so I went along to say hello. Brian said bring your guitar and we'll try out this new device he was working with – an Eventide Ultra Harmonizer, which is a very good and intelligent process indeed. We had a bit of a session, then played some Shads stuff etc. Brian was playing rhythm.' He adds, 'The funny thing was, as Brian was playing I looked round and saw him with this pained, suffering look on his face and he muttered, "Um. I don't think I'm such a good rhythm guitarist as I thought!" and he was dead worried about it. We played some very melodic tunes, stuff from *Back to the Light*. I think 'Last Horizon' was one of them. Then we played twelve-bar blues for about half an hour non-stop at seriously loud volume – I jokingly accused Brian of concealing ear plugs under all that hair!'

As enjoyable as this interlude with Hank was, though, Brian's thoughts could never stray far from the serious business of embarking on his first major outing as a solo performer. October saw the birth of his new group, the Brian May Band; the line-up was himself on lead guitar and lead vocal, Cozy Powell on drums, bass player Neil Murray, rhythm guitarist Jamie Moses and Spike Edney on keyboards, as well as backing singers Shelley Preston and Cathy Porter.

It was, in a way, a second version of the band, as Spike explains, 'The first version evolved when Brian put the Guitar Legends night together at Seville. That one included Rick Wakeman and Mike Moran plus three backing singers, but Brian didn't like the feel of it. It was a very stressful time for him, of course, and he wasn't even sure at that point that he wanted anything to do with forming a new band full stop. Then when he did decide he wanted to tour, and had the opportunity of going to South America, he put together a scaled down version of the band.' He continues, 'We didn't have much chance to rehearse – something like three days – and then we were thrown right into performing, doing several shows supporting Joe Cocker and also the B52s in Argentina, Chile and Uruguay.'

Unprepared or not, the tour begun, and the fears Brian had

expressed that he might not give value for money in his gigs proved unfounded. He spent a hectic October and November stamping his authority on thrilled audiences night after night, and it was something which he had needed badly. He openly refers to himself as 'a person who needs to be on a stage', and in the last six years he had sorely missed touring with Queen. But forcing himself into being the focal point of the band was, he admits, a tough wall to breach, and for all his years as a seasoned performer the first few gigs frankly terrified him. 'I was nervous. The first three were quite awkward. I didn't know when I was supposed to be singing or playing at any one time, and combining the two was quite difficult. And also, making this connection with the audience . . . . But for number four we were in Velez Sarsfield, in the same stadium Queen used to play. I was supporting Joe Cocker and something happened. The audience were incredibly up and pleased to see us. They also seemed to know the words to the new stuff as well.'

Spike categorically confirms those initial nerves. 'No, for a start Brian didn't enjoy it at all. It was pretty much a shock to him, being out front and all that and it took a while for him to find his feet, but the South American audiences were great and, having loved Queen so much, they were supportive of Brian. As I've said, we were playing support for most of the tour. But then we played our first headlining gig in a club in Rio and the response he got was terrific, which was a great boost to his morale.'

It was a newly confident Brian who returned home to take close stock of the progress of the title track 'Back to the Light', when in mid-November it became the second single to be released from his solo album. It was around this time, too, that Brian spent a relaxing evening as a guest of a special friend of his, the veteran guitarist Bert Weedon.

As a youngster Brian, like millions of others, had watched Bert give guitar tuition on TV, marvelling at his skill and versatility. Bert for his part had closely followed Brian's career with Queen, but the two had never met until 1990 when both attended the annual ball of the Grand Order of Water Rats – the biggest showbiz charity in the world – held at London's Grosvenor House Hotel. Says Bert, 'There were well over a thousand guests there that night. Suddenly out of the blue a waiter appeared at my table with a note from Brian, saying he'd like very much to meet me. I was delighted, because I'd admired Brian for years, so I went straight over and joined him and we got chatting.'

An immediate friendship sprang from that night. Bert goes on, 'In

1992 I was voted King Rat and at the celebration ball I particularly wanted Brian with Anita to be my special guests at the top table. During the cabaret Brian suddenly announced that there was going to be a special tribute to me, because it was me who taught the world to play the guitar. I don't know about that, but it was a really nice thing for him to say.'

A string of performers promptly queued up to take the stage; they included George Harrison, Lonnie Donegan, Bruce Welch, the Bachelors, Joe Brown, Phil Collins and the DJ Mike Read, followed by Brian. 'When each of them stepped up the crowd gave them a big cheer,' recalls Bert. 'But when Brian was announced, there was an enormous cheer.' They played Bert's very first 1959 hit, 'Guitar Boogie Shuffle', and it was a very emotional moment for the writer of the world's best-selling guitar tutor, *Play in a Day*, reputed not only to have launched over four million guitarists but also, by their own admission, to have been a formative influence on such future stars as Sting, Mark Knopfler and Mike Oldfield.

For Brian it was a special pleasure to honour his friend. In fact it was his second opportunity to do so, for a few weeks earlier Bert had been the subject of the television programme *This Is Your Life*. In a recorded message – he was still on tour – he had said, 'Folks, this guy is a legend and an incredibly nice guy. There's about a thousand and one of us so-called guitar heroes out here, who, whether we like to admit it or not, first saw live TV guitar playing by Bert Weedon . . . thank you for spreading the guitar and spreading your enthusiasm, and also for spreading a lot of warmth to all of us out here who are very happy to know you.'

Soon Brian was off on his travels again, this time making an extensive and exhaustive PR tour of Europe. Yet, hectic though life was, he still found time to guest on a track for his friend, singer Paul Rodgers. Paul was busy recording an album entitled *Muddy Water Blues* as a tribute to the late blues great. He wanted to include guitarists whom he personally admired and respected, and moreover who each played in a different style. Dave Gilmour, Jeff Beck, Brian Setzer, Richie Sambora and Trevor Rabin were just a handful of those on his 'wish list', and during discussions Brian's name too had come up. Paul explains, 'I did backing tracks of certain numbers together with vocals, then wanted to invite particular guitarists to play on particular tracks – sort of matching track to guitarist. One day there were a few of us in a room considering the song "I'm Ready" when someone said he thought its walking bass line was reminiscent of the one on Queen's "Crazy Little Thing Called Love". I'd been hoping Brian would be able to play on my album anyway and this track seemed just right for him, so I immediately went for it and rang him.'

Brian wasted no time in meeting up with Paul at the Power House recording studios in early 1993. 'It took us about four hours,' recalls Paul, 'which is quick, but Brian was right into it. He just arrived, had all his gear set up and said, "Right, what do you want me to play?" To be honest I didn't really feel qualified to tell him, so I said, "Do what you feel."' He goes on, 'Brian's not known as a blues guitarist and it was an unusual and challenging step for him, but he proved up to it of course – and somehow he still managed to sound like himself!'

Brian next involved himself briefly with Frank Zappa's son Dweezil on his latest album, under the watchful eye of producer Gary Langhan who had worked on Queen albums from the days of *Sheer Heart Attack*. Then it was back to support duty, this time with the American band Guns 'n' Roses. Their first date was in Austin, Texas in February before a fifteen thousand capacity crowd.

That night it was hammered home hard to Brian just how much things had changed. Describing the experience as being 'a bit like jumping off a cliff and being fed to the lions simultaneously', he was all too aware that he had to do more than stroll on stage and be greeted with ready-made adulation. He had in fact to relearn the art of winning a crowd over. But this, of course, was just the kind of challenge on which he always thrived, and he succeeded in style. It was just as well, because not long into the tour an unforeseen spanner was thrown unceremoniously into the works.

Spike explains, 'Axl [Rose] suddenly had a few problems and promptly cancelled some shows, which of course left us high and dry. We had to hastily arrange dates for ourselves to play as headliners. We did already have some headlining gigs planned in New York and LA, but now we had to quickly fix ourselves up in Cleveland, Philadelphia and Baltimore as well. It didn't quite feel it at the time, but with hindsight it was great experience for us.' He adds, 'Brian's confidence this trip was very much up and down, depending really on how tired he was, but he was always convinced that he could make it work.'

In late April, with hardly a check in his step, Brian once again paid a short visit to South America. Not long after his return he was saddened to learn of the death of former Mott the Hoople lead guitarist Mick Ronson from liver cancer; he was just forty-six. Brian had happy memories of Mick stretching back some twenty years, and he looked tired and pensive when photographed hurrying through Heathrow Airport on 4 May with Anita to catch Concorde to New York.

The break, however, was all too brief before he embarked on a solo assault on the UK, kicking off at Edinburgh Playhouse in early June. He loved what he was doing, but by this time he was definitely feeling the strain of being on the road; he was also aware that he had taken on a totally different kind of responsibility. Although backed by trusted musicians, playing solo was a whole new ball game. In the past with Queen he could roll into town, go shopping and arrive at the venue with just enough time to change his clothes and go on stage. Now he realized that, as both frontman and lead guitarist, he hadn't a single moment to call his own.

Yet although he found it taxing, he still felt that every night he went out there he could do a little bit more – that each night was new and exciting, with hidden reserves just waiting to be mined. His one concern was his voice and whether it would hold out. Hours before taking the stage for that first Edinburgh gig he confessed, 'It's every singer's worry, and I've joined that band of people who get up in the morning and think, "Do I have a voice today?"' Before embarking on his solo career Brian had worried about whether he was a strong enough singer, yet the question of enlisting a vocalist for his new band was a definite non-starter. He is adamant, 'I wasn't going to let anyone else sing for me now. After Freddie, I'm sorry, there just isn't anyone.'

In the official programme to accompany his British tour Brian had included a piece on the British Bone Marrow Donor Appeal, of which he is Patron, and Malcolm Thomas had been put in charge of fund-raising activities at these gigs. Says Malcolm, 'Brian's fans were very generous indeed to the BBMDA, which was excellent and much appreciated. But what I was perhaps even more delighted at was the fans' response to Brian. One particular night, at the end of a gig at Cardiff, the reaction of the crowd streaming out afterwards was really strong. There was this universal feeling that they were fully aware that they'd just seen Brian May that night, as opposed to Brian from Queen, and I know that that was very important to him. He'd been terrific – had really got it together and turned in a powerful performance.'

Bert Weedon shared Malcolm's feelings when he went to see Brian at the Hammersmith Apollo (formerly the Odeon). Says Bert, 'What struck me most watching him that night was how much charisma he exudes on stage. His rapport with his audience was very real, very strong.' He adds, 'It's become popular lately for people previously known only as guitarists to have suddenly taken up singing, and in some cases not particularly successfully. But that's not the case with Brian – he's a very good singer. I couldn't help thinking that night that he's set to be an enormous star in his own right.'

Mid-June saw the release of Brian's third single, 'Resurrection', which dropped into the UK charts at number thirty-two. The video, featuring Brian and Cozy Powell playing amid scenes of a volcanic eruption, was exciting and tense. In July his band rejoined Guns 'n' Roses for some European dates. 'Our last gig,' says Spike, 'was supporting Guns in Paris. That gig was something else, but I think the highlight for everyone was when both bands where on stage at the same time playing "Knocking on Heaven's Door"!'

The tour wound up just in time for Brian to keep a promise to do some guest work for yet another friend, guitarist Gordon Giltrap. They had first met back in 1990 at London's LBC radio station. Says Gordon, 'Brian was there to talk about the music he'd written for *Macbeth*, then running at the Red and Gold Theatre, and I was at that point appearing at the Shaw Theatre, which was a major concert for me.' According to Giltrap both men were well aware of the other's reputation as a guitarist. 'It felt as if I'd known Brian for years. Anyway, we got chatting. I'd actually taken a couple of guitars along with me to play, and Brian ended up having a jam session with me on air that day.'

In spring 1993, when Gordon decided to re-record a twenty-fifth anniversary CD single of his hit 'Heartsong', on which he hoped to include a clutch of guest artistes, Brian was top of his list. 'I was very lucky in that several good musician friends agreed to guest,' he says, 'including Steve Howe, Midge Ure, Neil Murray and Rick Wakeman. But Brian was the first one I thought of, the first one I rang and the first to say yes.'

Brian had scarcely finished his tour when he turned up as arranged on 29 July at Workshop Studios in Redditch, Worcestershire – a tiny basement twenty-four-track recording studio and, as Gordon puts it, not at all state-of-the-art. The first equipment to be wheeled in by Brian's guitar tech Jeff Banks, comprised two of the now famous VOX AC30 amps as well as a recent model of the new Guild BHM1 guitar built in

Brian's name. But the focus of attention, as ever, was the Red Special – 'the old girl', as Jeff affectionately calls it. 'I couldn't help staring at it,' says Gordon. 'It has to be one of the most famous, if not *the* most famous, guitar in the world.' He goes on, 'It was a great day, a great experience. He cut several tracks and at one point did a four-part harmony section absolutely live, which was out of this world.' It had already been agreed that the proceeds of the CD were to be split equally between the Mercury Phoenix Trust and Elton John's AIDS Foundation.

To commemorate his *Back to the Light* album Brian had come up with an ingenious idea. For years he had been renowned for using a predecimal sixpence coin in place of the conventional plectrum; recently he had commissioned from the Royal Mint a commemorative limited edition sixpence. One side shows Brian's head in profile along with the words 'Back to the Light', while the reverse displays the initials 'BM' in the centre flanked by the words 'First Pick' and 'Official 1993'. Before he left the studios that day Brian presented two of these special coins in their presentation cases to Gordon and his wife, as a memento of their afternoon recording together. Then at last he could devote some time to himself and his family. Two days later he took off on holiday with his three children, each accompanied by a friend – just himself and six kids getting away from the madding crowd.

Since September 1992 Brian had kept up a demanding round of engagements and, having at last allowed himself to run out of steam, he very much needed to relax and unwind. Queen as an entity is something very precious to him – a huge part of his life from which he would never wish to be divorced. Coming to terms with its demise had been hard on him: vulnerable and exposed, unsure about taking his first uncertain steps alone. But he had come through, and could now look back on a massively successful launch into his new career.

Tony Iommi agrees, 'In 1992, when Brian was channelling all his energies into going solo, I knew he was nervous and scared. But he went storming off and I'm convinced he'll be bigger than ever and a major star in his own right. I'm really proud of him – proud that he's proved it to himself. He's kept up a non-stop schedule, I know, but that's always Brian's way of keeping on top of things because at the back of his mind there'd been this feeling – can I do it? Well, he's more than shown that he can.'

Within a matter of weeks Brian was living up to Tony's assessment and refusing to slow down, for no sooner had he seen August out than arrangements were confirmed for an autumn tour to take the Brian May Band to Canada, the USA, Japan, Britain and Europe. It began on 12 September in Winterthur, Switzerland, and, according to Spike, everything went well that night. 'What was really special, though,' he says, 'was the moment when Brian sang "Love of My Life" and stopped just like Freddie used to, and the audience sang the song right back to him – just like they used to, to Fred. That meant a lot to Brian.'

By the time they hit the Albert Hall on 3 December, Brian had now grown accustomed to this kind of response. His confidence too had strengthened with each performance, and his personal interaction with the sell-out crowd, some of whom brandished giant inflatable hammers during the number 'Hammer to Fall', was both genuine and natural – although later, backstage, he confessed to some fear as to how long his voice would hold out. 'Last Horizon' from the album *Back to the Light* had been released in December, just as the tour finished up in Portugal on 18 December.

Able now to reflect on Brian and his approach to handling his own band, Spike reveals, 'It's very important to him to be one of the guys. For instance, on some of our European dates Brian would be offered a limo while the rest of us were bunged on to a bus. Brian would promptly shun the car and get on the bus with us, saying he wasn't about to sit all alone when he'd rather be where the fun is.' He goes on, 'A lot of people talk about Brian's great sensitivity and gentleness and so on. They're right, but you must never overlook the fact that he also has a will of iron. He does have very definite ideas of what he's doing and where he's going with his band. He's very ambitious, wants to make music and works extremely hard to the point of sometimes making himself ill. But that's just the way he is, and right now he's going all out to establish himself firmly in his own right.'

Towards that end, early February 1994 saw the release of the first live recording of the Brian May Band when *Live at the Brixton Academy* entered the UK album charts at number thirty-one, rising steadily to nestle comfortably in the top twenty. Pleased with its performance, Brian ploughed his energies into planning his musical future. Anticipating life after Queen, Roger Taylor had once spoken for them all when he vowed, 'We don't want to become old, rich and useless.' Brian has followed this through by being the first of them to carry on round that blind corner.

With his options wide open he commenced work on material for a new album, tentatively with a view to launching it in spring 1995, backed by a world tour, but these plans ran aground when he found himself getting involved in various solo projects. He guested with singer Jennifer Rush on her 1994 album *Out of my Hands*, their duet being Brian's haunting ballad 'Who Wants to Live Forever'. On its German release, the album charted in the top ten. Then months later radio producer Dirk Maggs approached Brian with an interesting proposition.

A Radio 1 FM series entitled *The Amazing Spiderman* was scheduled to run from January to March 1995, and Maggs asked Brian to write its theme music. In collaboration with dance producer Justin Shirley-Smith he co-wrote *The Amazing Spiderman Mastermix,* which by half way through the programme's run became so popular with listeners that it was rush-released by EMI. By the time his work with the BBC was over at the end of 1994, Brian had every reason to be well satisfied. He now ranked as the ninth highest wage earner for that year in UK rock, grossing approximately £4.5 million.

In the meantime he, Roger, John and Jim Beach had come to the decision that, despite the dissolution of the band after the 1992 Freddie Mercury Easter Tribute, there was unfinished business as far as Queen recordings were concerned. In spring 1994 they rereleased four Queen albums as well as making plans to bring out for Christmas 1995 what Brian confirms is to be the final Queen album, containing previously unreleased tracks, on which Freddie also worked while still capable of doing so in the early months of 1991. Over a period of weeks he joined Roger and John in Metropolis Studios to put the finishing touches to it. He also worked at arranging Freddie's lyrics in the privacy of his home studio at Surrey, where he has since confessed he often felt that the ghost of his late friend was watching over his efforts.

The final Queen album is sure to find an historic place in rock history, allowing Brian, like the other two, to go his own way again, picking up where he left off in developing the full scope and potential of the Brian May Band. Whatever path Brian May's musical future takes one thing is clear – his undeniable talent and influence will continue to play a valauble role in rock for years to come.

DISCOGRAPHY

QUEEN
SINGLES (UK)

'Keep Yourself Alive'/'Son and Daughter'
Cat. no. 2036   Released 6.7.73
Highest chart position (–)

'Seven Seas of Rhye'/'See What a Fool I've Been'
Cat. no. 2121   Released 23.2.74
Highest chart position 10

'Killer Queen'/'Flick of the Wrist' (double-A)
Cat. no. 2229   Released 11.10.74
Highest chart position 2

'Now I'm Here'/'Lily of the Valley'
Cat. no. 2256   Released 17.1.75
Highest chart position 11

'Bohemian Rhapsody'/'I'm in Love with My Car'
Cat. no. 2375   Released 31.10.75
Highest chart position 1

'You're My Best Friend'/'39'
Cat. no. 2494   Released 18.6.76
Highest chart position 7

'Somebody to Love'/'White Man'
Cat. no. 2565   Released 12.11.76
Highest chart position 2

'Tie Your Mother Down'/'You & I'
Cat. no. 2593   Released 4.3.77
Highest chart position 31

The First EP:
'Good Old Fashioned Lover Boy'/'Death on Two Legs (Dedicated to)'
Tenement Funster'/'White Queen (As It Began)'
Cat. no. 2623   Released 20.5.77
Highest chart position 17

'We Are the Champions'/'We Will Rock You'
Cat. no. 2708   Released 7.10.77
Highest chart position 2

'Spread Your Wings'/'Sheer Heart Attack'
Cat. no. 2757   Released 10.2.78
Highest chart position 34

'Fat Bottomed Girls'/'Bicycle Race' (double-A)
Cat. no. 2870   Released 13.10.78
Highest chart position 11

'Don't Stop Me Now'/'In Only Seven Days'
Cat. no. 2910   Released 26.1.79
Highest chart position 9

'Love of My Life' (live)/'Now I'm Here' (live)
Cat. no. 2959   Released 29.6.79
Highest chart position 63

'Crazy Little Thing Called Love'/'We Will Rock You' (live)
Cat. no. 5001   Released 5.10.79
Highest chart position 2

'Save Me'/'Let Me Entertain You' (live)
Cat. no. 5022   Released 25.1.80
Highest chart position 11

'Play the Game'/'A Human Body'
Cat. no. 5076   Released 30.5.80
Highest chart position 14

'Another One Bites the Dust'/'Dragon Attack'
Cat. no. 5102   Released 22.8.80
Highest chart position 7

'Flash'/'Football Fight'
Cat. no. 5126   Released 24.11.80
Highest chart position 10

'Under Pressure'/'Soul Brother'
Cat. no. 5250   Released 26.10.81
Highest chart position 1

'Body Language'/'Life Is Real (Song for Lennon)'
Cat. no. 5293   Released 19.4.82
Highest chart position 25

'Las Palabras de Amor (The Words of Love)'/'Cool Cat'
Cat. no. 5316   Released 1.6.82
Highest chart position 17

'Back Chat' remix/'Staying Power'
Cat. no. 5325   Released 9.8.82
Highest chart position 40

'Radio Ga Ga'/'I Go Crazy'
Cat. no. QUEEN 1   Released 23.1.84
Highest chart position 2

'I Want to Break Free' remix/'Machines (or Back to Humans)'
Cat. no. QUEEN 2   Released 2.4.84
Highest chart position 3

'It's a Hard Life'/'Is This the World We Created'
Cat. no. QUEEN 3   Released 16.7.84
Highest chart position 6

'Hammer to Fall'/'Tear It Up'
Cat. no. QUEEN 4   Released 10.9.84
Highest chart position 13

'Thank God It's Christmas'/'Man On the Prowl/Keep Passing the Open Windows'
Cat. no. QUEEN 5   Released 26.11.84
Highest chart position 21

'One Vision'/'Blurred Vision'
Cat. no. QUEEN 6   Released 4.11.85
Highest chart position 7

'A Kind of Magic'/'A Dozen Red Roses for My Darling'
Cat. no. QUEEN 7   Released 17.3.86
Highest chart position 3

'Friends Will Be Friends'/'Seven Seas of Rhye'
Cat. no. QUEEN 8   Released 9.6.86
Highest chart position 14

'Who Wants to Live Forever'/'Killer Queen'
Cat. no. QUEEN 9   Released 15.9.86
Highest chart position 24

'I Want It All'/'Hang On in There'
Cat. no. QUEEN 10   Released 2.5.89
Highest chart position 3

'Breakthru'/'Stealin''
Cat. no. QUEEN 11   Released 19.6.89
Highest chart position 7

'The Invisible Man'/'Hijack My Heart'
Cat. no. QUEEN 12   Released 7.8.89
Highest chart position 12

'Scandal'/'My Life Has Been Saved'
Cat. no. QUEEN 14   Released 9.10.89
Highest chart position 25

'The Miracle'/'Stone Cold Crazy (live)
Cat. no. QUEEN 15   Released 27.11.89
Highest chart position 21

'Innuendo'/'Bijou'
Cat no. QUEEN 16   Released 14.1.91
Highest chart position 1

'I'm Going Slightly Mad'/'The Hitman'
Cat. no. QUEEN 17   Released 4.3.91
Highest chart position 22

'Headlong'/'All God's People'
Cat. no. QUEEN 18   Released 13.5.91
Highest chart position 14

'The Show Must Go On'/'Keep Yourself Alive'
Cat. no. QUEEN 19   Released 14.10.91
Highest chart position 16

'Bohemian Rhapsody'/'These Are the Days of Our Lives'
Cat. no. QUEEN 20   Released 9.12.91
Highest chart position 1

ALBUMS

Queen
Cat. no. EMC 3006/CDP7 46204 2 (UK), HR 61064 (USA)
Released 13.7.73 (UK), 4.9.73 (USA)
Highest chart position 24 (UK), 83 (USA)
Award status Gold (UK and USA)

Queen II
Cat. no. EMA 767/CDP7 46205 2 (UK),
HR 61232 (USA)
Released 8.3.74 (UK), 9.4.74 (USA)
Highest chart position 5 (UK), 49 (USA)
Award status Gold (UK and USA)

Sheer Heart Attack
Cat. no. EMC 3061/CDP7 46206 2 (UK),
HR 61036 (USA)
Released 8.11.74 (UK), 12.11.74 (USA)
Highest chart position 2 (UK), 12 (USA)
Award status Gold (UK and USA)

A Night at the Opera
Cat. no. EMTC 103/CDP7 46207 2 (UK),
HR 61065 (USA)
Released 21.11.75 (UK), 2.12.75 (USA)
Highest chart position 1 (UK), 4 (USA)
Award status Platinum (UK), Gold (USA)

A Day at the Races
Cat. no. EMTC 104/CDP7 46208 2 (UK),
HR 61035 (USA)
Released 10.12.76 (UK), 18.12.76 (USA)
Highest chart position 1 (UK), 5 (USA)
Award status Gold (UK and USA)

News of the World
Cat. no. EMA 784/CDP7 46209 2 (UK),
HR 61037 (USA)
Released 28.10.77 (UK), 1.11.77 (USA)
Highest chart position 4 (UK), 3 (USA)
Award status Gold (UK), Platinum (USA)

Jazz
Cat. no. EMA 788/CDP7 46210 2 (UK),
HR 61062 (USA)
Released 10.11.78 (UK), 14.11.78 (USA)
Highest chart position 2 (UK), 6 (USA)
Award status Gold (UK), Platinum (USA)

Live Killers
Cat. no. EMSP 330/CDP7 46211 8 (UK),
HR 61066 (USA)
Released 22.6.79 (UK), 26.6.79 (USA)
Highest chart position 3 (UK), 16 (USA)
Award status Gold (UK and USA)

The Game
Cat. no. EMA 795/CDP7 46213 2 (UK),
HR 61063 (USA)
Released 30.6.80 (UK), 30.6.80 (USA)
Highest chart position 1 (UK), 1 (USA)
Award status Gold (UK), Platinum (USA)

Flash Gordon (Original Soundtrack)
Cat. no. EMC 3351/CDP7 46214 2 (UK),
HR 61203 (USA)
Released 8.12.80 (UK), 27.1.81 (USA)
Highest chart position 10 (UK), 23 (USA)
Award status Gold (UK and USA)

Greatest Hits
Cat. no. EMTV 30/CDP7 46033 2 (UK)
Released 2.11.81 (UK), 3.11.81 (USA)
Highest chart position 1 (UK), 14 (USA)
Award status eleven times Platinum (UK),
Platinum (USA)

Hot Space
Cat. no. EMA 797/CDP7 46215 2 (UK),
HR 61038 (USA)
Released 21.5.82 (UK), 25.5.82 (USA)
Highest chart position 4 (UK), 22 (USA)
Award status Gold (UK and USA)

The Works
Cat. no. EMC 2400141/CDP7 46016 2 (UK),
HR 61233 (USA)
Released 27.2.84 (UK), 28.2.84 (USA)
Highest chart position 2 (UK), 23 (USA)
Award status Platinum (UK), Gold (USA)

The Complete Works
Cat. no. QB1
Released 2.12.85 (UK), not released in USA

A Kind of Magic
Cat. no. EU 3509/CDP7 46267 2 (UK),
HR 61152 (USA)
Released 2.6.86 (UK), 3.6.86 (USA)
Highest chart position 1 (UK), 46 (USA)
Award status Double Platinum (UK)

Live Magic
Cat. no. EMC 3519/CDP7 46413 2 (UK),
not released in USA
Released 1.12.86
Highest chart position 3 (UK)
Award status Platinum (UK)

The Miracle
Cat. no. PCSD 107/CDP 792357 2 (UK),
HR 61234 (USA)
Released 22.5.89 (UK), 6.6.89 (USA)
Highest chart position 1 (UK), 24 (USA)
Award status Platinum (UK), Gold (USA)

Queen at the Beeb
Label/Cat. no. Band of Joy/BOJ 001
BOJCD 001 (UK)
Released 4.12.89 (UK), not released in USA
Highest chart position 67 (UK)
Award status None

Innuendo
Cat. no. PCSD 115/CDP7 95887 2 (UK),
HR 61020 2 (USA)
Released 4.2.91 (UK), 5.2.91 (USA)
Highest chart position 1 (UK), 30 (USA)
Award status Platinum (UK), Gold (USA)

Greatest Hits II
Cat. no. PMTV 2/CDP7 97971 2
Released 28.10.91 (UK), not released in USA
Highest chart position 1 (UK)
Award status four times Platinum (UK)

Classic Queen
Cat. no. HR 61311 2 (USA only)
Released 3.3.92
Highest chart position 4 (USA)
Award status Platinum (USA)

Live at Wembley
Cat. no. 7 99594 2 (UK), HR 61104-2 (USA)
Released 26.5.92 (UK and USA)
Highest chart position 2 (UK)
Award status Gold (UK)

The 12" Collection
Cat. no. HR 61265-2 (USA only)
Released 15.9.92
Highest chart position 11 (USA)

BRIAN MAY SOLO RECORDINGS

SINGLES

'Star Fleet'/'Son of Starfleet'
Cat. no. EMI 5436 (UK), B5278 (USA)
Released 24.10.83 (UK), 1.11.83 (USA)
Highest chart position 65 (UK)

'Driven by You'/'Just One Life'
Cat. no. 6304
Released 25.11.91
Highest chart position 6

'Too Much Love Will Kill You'/'I'm Scared'
Cat. no. 6320
Released 24.8.92
Highest chart position 5

'Back to the Light'/'Nothin' but Blue'
Released 9.11.92
Highest chart position 19

'Resurrection'/'Love Token'
Released 1.6.93

'Last Horizon'
Released 12.93

ALBUMS

Starfleet Project
Cat. no. EMI/SFLT 1078061 (UK),
Capitol/MLP 15014 (USA)
Released 31.10.83 (UK), 1.11.83 (USA)
Highest chart position 35 (UK), 125 (USA)

Back to the Light
Cat. no. EMI/Parlophone PCSD 123 (UK),
HR 614042 (USA)
Released 21.9.92 (UK), 23.2.93 (USA)
Highest chart position 6 (UK)
Award status Gold

Live at Brixton Academy
Released 2.94

INDEX

Brian May is the Patron of the British Bone Marrow
Donor Appeal, a charity that is saving the lives of leukaemia victims
by finding them bone marrow donors. Donations are desperately
needed to help continue the life-saving work. Collections are taking
place at each venue, Please help if you can.

For further information or donations contact the BBMDA,
18 Warwick Street, Rugby CV21 3DD